'This is a remarkably well written, sophisticated novel ... people and places ... all come alive on the page...' *Literary Review*

'The quality of Hardisty's writing and the underlying truth of his plots sets this above many other thrillers' *West Australian*

'Searing ... at times achieves the level of genuine poetry' *Publishers Weekly*

'Beautifully written' Tim Marshall

'Vividly written, utterly tropical, totally gripping' Peter James

'Beautifully written, blisteringly authentic, heart-stoppingly tense and unusually moving' Paul Johnston

'The writing is sublime – the beautiful, vivid descriptions of flora and fauna and exotic locations have lyrical rhythm ... *Turbulent Wake* really showcases the author's writing talent ... I could read this book forever and it's likely to become one of my all-time Orenda favourites' Off-the-Shelf Books

'A taut, explosive thriller with intelligence that tears along at whip-crack pace and delivers in spades' Mumbling about...

'Takes the reader on a fast-paced explosive journey' Swirl & Thread

'Hardisty's prose is taut and thrilling, his plot is compelling and the complex strands of the book are all pulled together in a way I did not see ... A first-class read' Live & Deadly

'A hard-hitting thriller with a compelling plot' Books, Life and Everything

'Be prepared for an addictive read, where reality and fiction collide in an astonishing story' Varietats

'Hardisty is without a doubt honing his skills as a writer and a storyteller … Hardisty can take his place up there with the best of them … an exceptional read' Cheryl M-M's Book Reviews

'A very gripping story with a high cost of human life. This is a hard-fact story where nothing is held back, the emotional impact is very personal' Books from Dusk till Dawn

'Together with the stunning imagery to describe the most barren of landscapes, and his brilliant character structuring, a Hardisty novel does not disappoint' Segnalibro

'This book was really enjoyable. I loved the plot and the pace was spot on! The characters are great and I thought it was a thriller that was really gripping in all the right places' Donna's Book Blog

'The language used in this novel is quite beautiful, the imagery as evocative as it is stark and shocking and used to brilliant effect throughout. It manages to convey a powerful message without appearing overly preaching in its execution' Jen Med's Book Reviews

'This is the most detailed, intelligent and captivating series out there with a heck of a lot of heart added for good measure!' Damppebbles

'This novel has so much atmospheric detail … There is so much action-packed delight in this book!' Vanessa Turns Pages

'Paul E. Hardisty has brought these places to life with his writing. The descriptions are vivid, stunning and beautifully written … Paul E. Hardisty has a very skilful pen … full of emotion and heart, jammed packed with thrills and exhilarating to read' Emma's Bookish Corner

TURBULENT WAKE

Canadian Paul Hardisty has spent twenty-five years working all over the world as an engineer, hydrologist and environmental scientist. He has roughnecked on oil rigs in Texas, explored for gold in the Arctic, mapped geology in eastern Turkey (where he was befriended by PKK rebels), and rehabilitated water wells in the wilds of Africa. He was in Ethiopia in 1991 as the Mengistu regime fell, and was bumped from one of the last flights out of Addis Ababa by bureaucrats and their families fleeing the rebels. In 1993 he survived a bomb blast in a café in Sana'a, and was one of the last Westerners out of Yemen before the outbreak of the 1994 civil war. Paul is a university professor and CEO of the Australian Institute of Marine Science (AIMS). The first four novels in his Claymore Straker series, *The Abrupt Physics of Dying*, *The Evolution of Fear*, *Reconciliation for the Dead* and *Absolution*, all received great critical acclaim and *The Abrupt Physics of Dying* was shortlisted for the CWA John Creasey (New Blood) Dagger. Paul is a sailor, a private pilot, keen outdoorsman, conservation volunteer, and lives in Western Australia. Follow him on Twitter *@Hardisty_Paul*.

Turbulent Wake

PAUL E. HARDISTY

**ORENDA
BOOKS**

Orenda Books
16 Carson Road
West Dulwich
London SE21 8HU
www.orendabooks.co.uk

First published in the United Kingdom by Orenda Books 2019

The story 'Blue Nile' was originally published in the
anthology *Sunshine Noir* (White Sun Books, 2016).

A catalogue record for this book is available from the British Library.

ISBN 978-1-912374-71-7
eISBN 978-1-912374-72-4

Typeset in Garamond by MacGuru Ltd
Printed and bound by CPI Group (UK) Ltd, Croydon CR0 4YY

For sales and distribution, please contact *info@orendabooks.co.uk*

For my mum

TURBULENT WAKE

First Snow

The world was different then.

Looking back, the old man was no longer sure if this realisation was new, had come upon him slowly over years, or if perhaps, somehow, he'd known it back then, as a child. This lack of certainty did not change the truth of it, however. The world was entirely different now. In tone and texture, in scale and colour and voice, in the abundance of animals and birds, in the everyday behaviour of people, in the places that were once covered in trees and bushes and meadows and later transformed into houses and roads and shopping centres. Even the weather was different, back then.

It was the year before the men came and cut down all the big elms on their street. Summer had been hot, had seemed to last forever. The first frost came as a profound surprise, as if the neighbourhood had been suddenly shifted north, closer to the Arctic Circle. The boy's father piled the brown and gold elm leaves into mountains on the front lawn. The boy loved to jump into them and roll inside the piles until he was covered, the sweet smell of the new-dead leaves strong inside him, so that the old man could smell it now, so much closer to the end than the beginning.

The boy knew it was close. Days were shorter. Three mornings in a row now he'd awoken to see frost crusting the grass, icing the naked branches of the trees. Porridge for breakfast, mittens and hats to school, steam in your breath, Christmas coming. Hockey season imminent, perhaps a new pair of skates, if he was lucky. Time thick and heavy and viscous, unwilling to be rushed, infinite. Completely trustworthy. And the boy, who had not yet learned of relativity, had no conception of time's variant properties, its fluidity or its ultimate dependency on the observer.

And every night the boy would lie in his bed and stare at the window and the glow from the streetlight through the curtains. He would watch the slow progress of a car's passing headlights thrown as a wedge of light angling left to right across the ceiling, and he'd hope that tomorrow would be the day.

Sometimes, lying in the darkness, unable to sleep, he'd think about his father's gun. He'd found it in the closet in his bedroom, hidden inside a shoe box in the back, among a pile of other boxes. It was a short thing, with a barrel that spun like the ones he'd seen cops carrying on TV, and spaces for six bullets. Smith & Wesson it said on the handle. He found the bullets, too. He wasn't sure how to work it, how to open the barrel up so you could put the bullets in. He'd tried putting them in from the front, but they didn't fit. He knew he wasn't supposed to play with it, that it was dangerous. He didn't tell anyone about it, put it all back the way he found it. Except for three bullets. Those he kept. There was a whole box. No one would miss them. He'd put them into his treasure tin, hidden it away in his desk drawer.

In his head he knew how it would be. He'd wake and it would still be dark. The first thing he'd notice would be the quiet. As if someone had thrown a blanket over the city, muffling its groans, its cries and complaints. He'd jump down from his bed and run to the window, duck under the heavy curtains. His little brother would be there beside him. He'd help him up on to the ledge, so he could see out. And there it would be. A new world. Everything transformed, softened somehow, all the hard edges rounded out, corniced and bevelled, houses and cars and trees, the street and the kerbs and gutters made pure. And in the yellow cones of lamplight, thick heavy flakes streaming down and down.

The boy lay listening to his brother's breathing, the slow, whispered rhythm drifting up from the lower bunk, and the occasional rattle of the radiator, the gurgle as the hot water flowed through the pipes. The wind in the trees outside the window. He was warm and safe and excited. Tomorrow might be the day.

March 5th. On the plane, flying to London

You never really know anyone. Especially the ones you love.

I push the stack of papers into the seatback pocket and take a deep breath of pressurised air. Seven miles below, the checkerboard prairie stretches away like a looping dream, one where you're stuck in a place and you can't get out, even though you know it's a dream and if you could just wake up it would be over. Except, of course, it's not. It's my life, laid out before me in endless miles of iced-over prairie, a recurring pattern of abandoned hope and gutted wilderness that unspools at the terminal edge of a horizon that once held so much promise. The brother I didn't get a chance to know. The mother who disappeared. The father who pushed me away. The wife who got sick of me and found someone else. And now, apparently, the uncle I never even knew I had.

If family defines you, then I am perilously fucking close to indeterminate.

And this is how he decides to tell me.

I went my whole life thinking that I had my old man pegged. Sure, he'd travelled some, even taken me with him a few times when I was younger, when my mother was still around. But my strongest memories are of him arriving and leaving, going away for hours at a time, returning red-faced and covered in sweat, and then for days and weeks for work, always on his way to the airport or coming back from it. Occasionally, he'd bring me something home: a stuffed baby alligator the time he went to Louisiana; a tiny woven prayer mat from Jordan (for a six-year old?); a Calgary Flames hockey jersey from Canada (now, that was cool). Most of the time, though, he was just absent, even when he was home. Usually, it was me and Mum and my brother, and then later just me and Mum, in whatever place he'd dragged us all to at the time. Now, it's just me.

Everything about my old man was from another time. The clothes he wore. The way he spoke and acted around other people. The stories he told. I mean, what kid who has grown up with access to the internet wants to hear stories about steam trains and writing love letters (the old-fashioned kind with paper and pen and envelopes and stamps) and getting places by ship, making calls from phone boxes and using fax machines and typewriters and all that old museum stuff. I can remember now, looking back, just tuning out when he started one of his stories. Not that he did it that often; just every once in a while. Usually when he'd had a couple of whiskies after dinner – when we still sat down, the four of us, and ate dinner as a family – he'd start into one. And then, well, I'd just sit there watching his mouth move and the way his neck would tense up as he spoke and that stupid way he'd furl his brow for emphasis, and I never heard a word. Now, I wish I'd listened.

No wonder he left all this shit behind.

The funeral was a pretty lame affair. Not many people showed up. A couple of his old friends came, guys with old names like Robert and Paul and Tobias, looking like they were planning to follow him in the not-too-distant future, with their thinning grey hair and grey beards and those watery, faraway eyes that weep regret. Makes you wonder. A whole life lived, and I bet not even those old guys with their burst-blood-vessel faces and dodgy, shuffling gaits had the slightest idea who he really was, what was really going on inside that head. I mean, I as sure as shit never did. And I know my mother never did either.

The funeral home did a crap job. I regret doing it that way, now. The pastor or whatever he was started out calling him Walter. Did it three times, Walter this and Walter survived by such and such. The prick didn't see me waving at him till he'd blown it three times, me sitting there in the front row, mouthing Warren. Warren, *for fuck's sake. It wasn't how he would have wanted it, I know. Mostly because he wouldn't have wanted anything. 'Just throw me over the side so the sharks can get me', I remember him saying once, somewhere – was it on that last sailing trip we all took together, me, my brother Rhys, Mum and Dad, in the Greek Islands? I must have been eight, seven maybe. I still have vivid memories of some of it: the dolphins riding our bow wave that time, the way they looked up at me with those dark, knowing eyes; the view from the highest point on one of the islands – I can't remember the name of the place now – looking out across the sea and all those pretty white buildings along the shore; rowing back to the boat one night in the dinghy, Dad at the oars, Mum in the bow laughing at something he'd said, the lights from the village dancing on the dark water all around us like stars.*

She was beautiful, my mother. Everyone said so. I don't have many photographs of her, or of him for that matter. In one of the few that have somehow survived, they are sitting under an old stone archway. The sea is faded blue behind them. Mum is in a short skirt. Her long legs are folded elegantly to one side, her honey and rosewood hair blows around her face. She is smiling. She had great teeth, a big mouth, high cheekbones, a ski-jump nose that was a little too big for anyone to call her looks perfect, but she was beautiful in a strong-looking kind of way – robust and healthy and symmetrical with lovely blue eyes. In contrast, he looks flawed. A nose broken one too many times. An inverted arch of teeth that left dark gaps on each flank of his rarely seen smile (other than his two front slabs and molars, his top adult teeth never came in, so the small baby teeth were still there). He is unshaven, his hair longish, sea-and-sun waved, unruly. Dad is holding Mum's hand. In that moment, they look happy. He was never in her league, and I know for a fact that he knew it, too. He told me once, I can't remember when or where. 'Son,' he said, 'always marry up in the gene pool. I sure did.'

He would have hated it, today, the funeral. I don't know why I did it. Seemed right at the time – to mark his passing somehow. I've always hated that use of the word: passing. Just call it what it is. Death. The End. And we never talked about it, of course, at the end. Not like we didn't have the time. I went to see him, of course – more than once – but he didn't want me there, made that very plain. 'Don't you have something better to do?' he said to me. I mean, what does a guy say to that? Fact was, I did have better things to do. So in the end you get what you get, Dad. Not like it makes any difference. Not one bit.

And I suppose it makes finding all this stuff that much more of a mystery. I hadn't been inside the place for ages, not since the year I moved to London, the year I met Maria and everything was so great – before it all started to go to shit. But that's another story. From the outside, my dad's place looked much the same, the caragana hedge out front that much taller, the paint on the shiplap siding peeling, the blue spruce we planted that spring when I was a kid, huge now, towering. I'd only gone to have a quick look, figure out what it would take to have someone come in and clean the place out, so I could put it on the market. I was only in town for a couple of days. I had to organise the funeral, sort out stuff with the lawyers, and then get back to London for an important work meeting. I knew the place would be a mess, but I was totally unprepared for what I found.

The first thing I noticed was the smell. How can I describe it? Not unpleasant, exactly. There wasn't food rotting in the sink or a dead cat in the bathtub or anything. It was complex. Old books. Smoke from his wood-burning stove. The varnish he used on his pine floors. Tobacco and whisky and stale sweat from the dozens of old pairs of running shoes piled in the front entranceway. Him. Hints of what had killed him.

The place was a museum. That's what it was. His own museum. Stacks of books everywhere, old furniture, junk from his travels – carved stuff from Africa and the Middle East, ceremonial masks on the walls, carpets on the floors, pictures his grandfather had painted, a few bad watercolours he'd done himself. The basement was full of old junk – old-style skis and boots, hiking gear, ice axes and pitons, three or four old bicycles, a bench full of tools, everything covered in rust and dust. There were traces of Mum there, too: some of her old clothes in the laundry-room closet that he'd never bothered to clean out, a half-used bottle of her perfume under the downstairs sink, an old cookbook layered in dust. Relics. Hints. Archaeology.

He never told me what he wanted done with all of it. The will left me the house. I guess that meant everything inside it, too.

I was about to leave when I decided to check upstairs. An unmade bed, his tatty, ancient clothes in the closet. The room he used as a study was up there, too. And that's where I found them, in the back of the room, on the lower shelves, almost lost in a lifetime of dust-covered books and ledgers and files: thirty-seven black bound journals. No markings, nothing to indicate what they contained. And set on top of the journals, a stack of unbound papers held together with a single elastic band. I grabbed the papers – I'm not sure why, perhaps because they were the only things in the room not buried under half an inch of fine grey powder – and stuffed them in my bag along with a few old photos I found of my mother and my brother. There were even a couple of me there, propped up in old frames on the desk, a forgotten past staring out at me like a reminder of who I might have been, of who he wanted me to be.

And now I'm sitting on the plane on the way home. Home? Back to London, anyway – and I'm going through that stack of papers. And who would ever have believed it? My old man – the crusty old engineer with the arthritic knees and the dodgy shoulder, whose bookshelves were always filled with awesome stuff like Geomorphology *and* Sedimentary Geology *and* Finite Element Analysis for Structures *(all of it headed for the bin – no one wants that old crap), whose favourite activities until his joints gave out were long-distance running and swimming – was a wannabe author. Yep. A goddamned writer.*

I mean, I'm laughing here. If you'd come up to me and told me my old man had been a make-up artist, or a closet thespian or even a politician, I couldn't have been more surprised. He was the least artistic person I ever knew. The least expressive. The least, well, sensitive. All that stuff. I mean, after Mum died and he decided to send me off to boarding school in England, he drove me to the airport. He got me checked in and we walked to the security screening together, me with my carry-on bag and all my fears, standing there in that big echo chamber. And when they called my flight, he just shook my hand and said, 'Good luck, son'. And that was it. No hug, no last words of advice. Nothing a normal person might expect a father to say to his twelve-year-old son who is about to travel to a new school in a new country. Sure, I'd travelled. I was an international kid – third-culture kid they call us – but this was something different. There was no one I knew waiting for me at the other end. Just the lady from the school who was supposed to meet me at Heathrow. She would be holding up a sign for me when I exited Terminal 4.

So, I went. After security, I found a place where I could look back and see him standing there. I waved and tried to smile, as much for him as for me – I knew the strain he'd been under. I swear he was looking right at me, staring with that stupid, sag-faced expression of his. I waited, thinking that maybe he hadn't seen me, after all. I waved again, but you know, he never waved back. And so yeah, I'm laughing. Because now I'm imagining him sitting somewhere in front of his typewriter, or just long-handing it in one of those dozens of journals that fill the lower shelves of his study, cranking out all of these stories, and yet that one thing, just waving to me that day at the airport, he couldn't do.

I leaf through the papers. The first story, the one I just read, is hand-written on yellow lined foolscap, dated the day before he died. You can see the tremors that were shaking his body apart in every fractured vowel, each mutilated consonant. I thumb the corner of the next one. He has scrawled the title, 'COLLAPSING INFINITY', in capital letters across the top of the page so that the curved spine of the C inks the left-hand edge of the foolscap, and the face, chest and feet of the terminal Y perch on the cliffside and stare out into the abyss. He must have written them both in hospital, but I have no idea how they got into the manuscript. They are at the top of the pile, a stack of unbound A4 papers about the thickness of a Petit Larousse *dictionary. I flip through the whole thing, count twenty-five stories in all. The earliest is dated May 1990. It's called 'Chub Cay'. I was ten months old when he wrote it. We were living in Calgary at the time. It looks as if it was typed out on one of those old manual typewriters where you fed the paper into a roller and the key stroke would send a hammer on to a carbon ribbon set against the paper. Slow and noisy. I can remember the sound coming from his office when I was small. Always just figured he was working. I would never have dreamed that he was writing this stuff.*

I've only read the one so far, but they seem to cover his whole life. And as far as I can tell, he never told anyone. If I hadn't changed my mind and looked around his study, it would have all been chucked out. It would have all disappeared into a landfill somewhere, or been recycled into newsprint pulp, or incinerated, who knows.

It pisses me off that he didn't tell me about it. The last time I saw him he was lucid enough. He even said that it would be the last time. Said it with a smile. The bastard knew he was going to die. And you know, standing there, looking down at him, knowing it was going to be the last time, I felt ashamed for him. Ashamed for his weakness, ashamed that he was so frail, so powerless. When I was a boy, I used to think he was the biggest, strongest man in the world. There was nothing he couldn't do. Even in his fifties he was still fit and active. He ran a marathon at fifty-four – did it in just over three hours. And then in the last couple of years he went downhill really fast. Just kind of got old one day. It must have killed him being there in that place, that way, the tubes in his nose and that stupid hospital gown they made him wear – the kind that opens in the back – and the way his skin looked so winter shut-in pale. Christ, when it's my time, put a gun to my head. I'm still surprised he didn't ask me to end it for him, just pull me close and whisper into my ear, 'Just shut the door and put a pillow over my face, son. You owe me at least that.'

But I don't owe you a thing, Dad. Not a goddamned thing.

What I don't understand is this: why spend all those hours and days and years pouring out all this stuff, and then when you're down to your last chance to connect, the one person on the planet who still gives even a partial shit, who you might think still holds a shred of love for you, you just send him packing out into the sleet, without telling him about it? He wasn't stupid, my old man. Not by a long shot. Fucking smart, actually. With numbers and engineering and the like. Not so smart about people, though. And yet he took the time, over a forty-year period, to write all of this. He must have known that I had so many questions. About my mother, about what happened between them, about why he sent me away after she was gone. About my brother. And that last time, knowing it was all here in this stack of papers, in all those journals (I will call the contractor as soon as I land and make sure he saves the journals, and a couple of the masks and paintings) – that was his opportunity to make it, somehow, better. Not good. But better. An explanation. And yet he chose to look at me with those eyes, those still-piercing, desert-landscape eyes of his, and tell me to get out. Better things to do. Surely.

And so, yeah, you never really know anyone. I mean, they can sit there and look you in the eye and tell you how they feel, about what moves them, about what they hate. They might even, if you're lucky, tell you that they love you. But it's nothing. A breath, is all. Just a breath. Hell, most people don't even know themselves, couldn't describe what they were really about if they wanted to. And besides, even if you could, who wants ever to be that vulnerable, that naked? Everyone hedges. Maybe that's what he was after. Maybe he was just trying to figure himself out, understand why he did some of the things he did, why some of what happened in his life went the way it did. I hope he got what he wanted from it. I really do. Although I never really knew him, I would like to think that at the end he came a little closer to knowing himself. We should all be so lucky.

Collapsing Infinity

He opens his eyes and looks out at the snow-covered parkway and across the steaming white rooftops, towards the dim memory of the mountains. A breakfast – cold porridge, a plastic bowl of gaily coloured fruit salad, slightly burned toast – sits on the bed tray before him, ignored. Overnight, snow had drifted up and swallowed the cars that had been abandoned the night before. He'd lain awake and watched their owners, one after the other, stall on the hill, trying for a while to free themselves as the snow piled higher around them, and then finally giving up, trudging towards the lights of the hospital. Now, a lone plough, its orange light flashing in the pre-dawn grey, fights against the burial, its big V-blade sending twin streams of road snow curling away, like surf breaking on a West African beach long ago.

'How are we this morning, Mister Scofield?' It's the nurse, the pretty one with the freckles and the face of a ten-year-old, open and innocent, the skin so smooth and supple, her bottom lip in a pout. He notices that she has applied some balm or gloss that makes her lips look wet. Something stirs deep inside of him, shivers like an echo for a moment, retreats. She reaches under him and plumps his pillow, then winds up his bed a bit, so he can look outside without straining. She knows that's what he likes to do, does all day, every day: stares out of the window across the winter city and the foothills that he can sometimes see in the distance if the day is cold and the cloud has moved off. Never the television. They must think he is crazy, all of them, with their drapes closed against the day and screens flickering the remaining hours away in front of their faces.

'Did you sleep well?' she asks.

He nods, doesn't smile. He has never been big on smiling. Perhaps it was because he'd never had his teeth fixed to make them look straight and white. They were good teeth, had outlasted other parts of the machinery – no decay, strong, did their job. It hadn't been until later in life, after he'd married again and divorced, that he'd even realised they were an issue for others. He'd never smiled much before, anyway. He'd always wanted to be taken seriously, to be serious. Smiling wasn't serious.

'No breakfast again?' says the nurse, checking his IV.

He shakes his head. 'No, thank you.'

'The doctor says you must eat.'

He pushes the tray away. This was not how he'd imagined it would be, not how he'd ever wanted it. How did it happen? Your life unfolded, you made decisions or didn't, things happened and didn't, and what you thought was an ocean stretched out before you turned out to be only a teardrop.

'I want you to help me,' he says to the nurse.

She smiles at him. Her teeth are even and white, lovely. For a moment he imagines that she was the girl who'd married his son, had borne his grandsons.

'Of course, what can I do?' she says.

He pointed to the IV line. 'Morphine.'

She checks the line again, his chart. 'You can dose yourself, as you like.'

'No,' he says. 'I want more.' He is conscious of his own voice, cracked and dry and old. 'A lot more.' He looks straight into her clear, pale eyes. What beautiful children she would have made. He wonders if she knows yet that nothing else matters.

She stands a moment looking down at him. 'You know I can't do that, Mister Scofield.'

'Why not? I'll never tell.' He curls the corner of his lip.

She doesn't flinch. 'If you are in pain, I will speak to the doctor about changing your dosage.'

He shakes his head. 'I like the pain.'

She doesn't understand, he knows. How can she? She still sees time as an ocean, can't fathom this most cruel of illusions. Maybe that's not so bad either, he thinks. Regardless, we're looking back at each other from different shores of this same ocean. The only difference is that I can see you, but you can't see me. Time has accelerated for me, and passes still so slowly for you. Relativity applies. My only language now is the handful of events that I can recall, that stand out among the thousands of hours and days passed undifferentiated in offices and schoolrooms and bedrooms. Necessary, perhaps, but now I regret each of those wasted days.

But these two dozen or so times of my life, he thinks, these might be worth telling, remembering. The problem is I have no one to tell them to. No one left. Perhaps that, in itself, is one of the stories: how I came to be alone. And he wonders if these few moments are not shared, not somehow transcribed, will it be as if they had never occurred at all, and would it matter? He wonders if she would want to listen to his stories, those that might provide her with some glimpse of how to navigate the collapsing infinity between them.

The nurse is standing there, looking at him while he is thinking this. 'Do you want me to get the doctor?' she asks.

He shakes his head slowly. 'The doctor can't help me,' he says. 'But you can.'

March 5th. Thirty-two thousand feet

It's my second trip back to London from Calgary in as many weeks. Last week, he was still alive. Now he isn't.

Both times, it was Dad's lawyer, an old friend of his, who contacted me. You better come out here, he said, if you want to see him. He doesn't have long. And then: there is the matter of the will, the house. You should be here in person.

Robertson isn't happy about all the extra time off I've had to take. It's busy right now at work, some big deals we are working on. Rachel, my daughter, isn't happy either. She makes that very clear now, every time I see her. Last month on our weekend together I took her to the Imperial War Museum. She hated it. Complained every step of the way. Finally, I gave up. We walked out into the rain and took the Tube back to my flat, where she spent the rest of the day messaging her friends until it was time for me to take her back to her mother's.

Maria is never happy. I've reconciled myself to that now. It started years ago, and just deepened. Looking back, I knew it was happening, and for a long time, I tried to make her happy, to conform to her expectations. It took years, but when I finally realised what she actually wanted, I gave up. It's been worse since we split, somehow. Angrier, more specific.

Does someone always have to lose?

I try to stretch my back, push my legs out, but the aluminium frame of the seat in front digs into my shins. Twisting on to one side helps a bit, but the pain in my lower back won't abate. I've gotten soft. I would never admit it to anyone, but I know it's the truth. My core is weak. Fat has settled around my waist. All this time in aeroplanes and cars and offices has made me soft. Everything now seems an exercise in control — hold back my emotions, rein in my temper, restrain the physical side of myself, that part of me that always felt the most natural, the most real. Working with my hands. Fighting. Riding fast. Really fast.

I try to get to the dojo or out for a run whenever I can, but there always seems to be a reason not to go now. Weakness breeds weakness. I am a shadow. Unsexed.

And though I know there are no answers there, I keep reading.

Chub Cay

The plane banked low over the water. The boy could see the white arc of the beach and the green of the palms and, further out, the many different colours and patterns of the sea. It was his first time in a small plane and he clutched the arm of his seat hard, his face pressed up against the window. The plane righted and he could hear the sound of the engines change, see the flap along the back edge of the wing starting to come down and feel the hole in his stomach as the plane started to lose altitude. They were coming in to land.

The boy looked through to the cockpit and watched the pilots. He liked the way they reached up to the overhead panel to work the switches, the way they flew the plane with small movements of the wheel and the throttle levers. He liked the light-green headphones they wore, the way they spoke calmly into their headset microphones as they guided the plane down. Outside, the island was gone and there was only the deep-blue colour of the sea and the puffy white clouds in the distance and the line where the sky met the sea. Soon they were low enough that he could make out individual waves on the surface of the sea, the little white crests where they curled over and the dark furrows between them. And then the sky-coloured shallow water appeared beneath them, and it was so clear the boy could see down through to the sandy bottom and the darker patches scattered there, the brown of rocks or perhaps the corals that he had read about and looked at pictures of, but never seen. And then quickly the shallows were gone and there was a white beach and a flash of green and then the rocky grey of the centre of the island rushing up towards them.

The plane landed with a thump and rolled to a stop.

The boy looked over at his mother. Her hair was up in a colourful scarf, her eyes hidden behind a pair of oversized sunglasses. She was wearing a short dress made of some light material that left her arms and her legs bare. He thought she looked cold. But he could tell that she was happy and excited. They had arrived. They were in what she called one of their 'times of feast'. To him, these times meant presents at Christmas and on birthdays, parties, holidays in warm places. But he knew they meant other things to his mother.

The chief pilot, the one with four yellow stripes on his epaulettes, unclipped his seat belt, got out of his seat and walked back into the cabin. He wore a white short-sleeved shirt with a pair of wings sewn above the left pocket and green-tinted sunglasses. He looked very young for a pilot, the boy thought, much younger than the ones he'd seen flying the jets that took off and landed at the big airports.

'Welcome to Chub Cay,' said the young pilot. He pronounced it *key*, like the thing you put in a lock. He had fair hair and the hair on his forearms looked almost white against his tanned skin. 'We'll be back here in a month to take you out,' he said, smiling at the boy's mother. 'Have a great Christmas.'

'Say thank you to the captain, boys,' his mother said. She was smiling at the young pilot, and the pilot was looking back at her through his sunglasses.

The boy and his brother chimed up with overlapping *thank you sirs*, and the young pilot reached out and tousled their hair, all the while looking at their mother.

'Where is your dad, young fella?' said the pilot to the younger boy, who was only nine and a half.

'He has important business to do,' the boy said, before his brother could answer.

'I'm sure he does,' said the pilot.

'His company owns this island,' said the boy.

'Well, that's what I've heard,' said the pilot. 'And that's why we're taking very good care of you and your pretty mama here.' The young pilot smiled and reached out to tousle the boy's hair as he had done with his brother's, but the boy pulled away. He didn't like this young pilot anymore.

'My father will be here for Christmas,' said the boy.

'Then I'll see you all then. I'll be flying him in.' The young pilot started towards the back of the plane, then threw open the rear door and let down the stairs. 'Ladies and gentlemen, if you will please disembark by the rear stairs,' he said with a bow.

The boy's mother laughed and stood and smoothed her dress. She was tall for a lady and had to stoop to avoid hitting her head on the cabin roof. 'Come on, boys,' she said. 'You heard the nice captain.'

The boy unbuckled his seat belt and followed his mother and brother down the stairs. The pilot started to unload their suitcases and line them up on the crushed coral. A strange-looking car was waiting at the edge of the runway. It was open and low to the ground and had very small wheels. A man in a big white hat was in the driver's seat. He waved to them and the car started out towards them.

'That'll be the colonel,' said the young pilot as he unloaded the last of the bags. 'Better watch out for that one,' he said, smiling and wiping his forehead with the back of his hand. 'If you know what I mean.'

'Thanks for the warning,' said the boy's mother. She was smiling as she said it.

'You bet,' said the young pilot, handing her a card. 'Well if you need us, just call. No job too small, no ask too tall.'

The boy's mother laughed, and taking the young pilot's hand in hers, she leaned her head towards his and said something that the boy could not make out. The young pilot looked back at her for a moment with his mouth slightly open, and then he smiled at her, clambered back into the plane and pulled the door closed. The boy decided that he did not want to be a pilot, after all.

The strange car pulled to a stop and the man in the white hat – the one the young pilot had called the colonel – jumped out. He was a big man, with square shoulders and thick legs. 'Mrs Clifton,' he said, taking her hand in his big bear's paw. 'I'm Colonel Rafferty. Everyone calls me Raff. Welcome. Welcome to the island. We're so glad you could make it.' He kissed the boy's mother on the cheek and, as he did it, he put his big hand on the small of her back.

'Boys,' she said, pushing herself away from the colonel with one hand and holding her scarf in place against the breeze with the other, 'say hello to the colonel. He works for your father's company. He runs the island. Isn't that right, Colonel?'

'I certainly do,' he said.

The boys shook hands with the man. They all got into the car and drove to the far end of the runway. The colonel stopped the car and they sat with the sea breeze flowing over them, the smell of the sea strong now, as they watched the twin-engine plane taxi to the far end of the gravel strip and turn to face them. Then the engines roared and the plane started down the runway. As it gained speed, the boy saw the front wheel come off the ground and the rudder on the tail moving. Then one wing dipped slightly towards where the wind was coming from and it was up and crabbing sideways as it climbed. When the plane flashed over them with a roar the boy heard his mother let out a little 'oh' as her headscarf flew away.

After the colonel had retrieved the scarf, he drove them along a rocky shore where the waves sent towers of white spray foaming into the sky. 'We call this the blowholes,' he said, looking back over his shoulder at the boys as he drove. 'We can come and explore here later, if you like. But don't come here without an adult, OK? It's very dangerous. It's an old coral reef. There are miles of tunnels and caves under this rock, and the currents are strong. Years ago, they say a boy, the son of a local fisherman, got lost in here. They never found him. The old timers say his body was swept out to sea and the sharks got him.'

'Do you hear that, boys? This is a dangerous place.' The boy's mother had unpinned her hair and as she looked back at them it streamed across her face.

'Can we go tomorrow, Mum?' said the boy.

'It's up to the colonel, darling. Let's get settled in and we'll see.'

'And you might like to know that there is another family staying with us at the moment,' said the colonel. 'They have a boy and a girl, about the same ages as you two.' The colonel looked over his shoulder again. 'What do you think, lads?'

The boy frowned. His father had told them that they would have the island to themselves. He decided that he would not be friends with the other children. He and his brother would play their own games, do their own exploring. His father had told them that they would have their own house by the beach. He hoped they wouldn't have to share a house with the other family.

'They don't say much, do they?' said the colonel.

The boy's mother laughed.

They were on a narrow crushed coral track now, winding through a grove of leaning palms. Their trunks were smooth and the fronds rustled in the warm breeze. The sea was close. Through the trees he could see the shallow, pale yellow-blue water he had seen from the plane, and beyond, a line of churning white and further out, the deep blue of the deep ocean. And it seemed to the boy that this was the most beautiful place he had ever seen. He couldn't wait to explore the island. He would go to the blowholes. He would explore the caves the colonel had spoken of, and he would swim in the yellow-blue sea and look for fish and shells and the other creatures he'd read about and seen pictures of – conches and barracuda fish and corals and turtles. He was eleven and three-quarters. He would do it alone.

They did get their own house. It was right on the beach, with palm trees all around. There was a big veranda out front with some chairs and two hammocks and big windows that were really doors and opened up all along the front, so that during the daytime the breeze flowed through the house and it was cool. The floors were of polished wood, perfect for racing the Hot Wheels he'd brought with him, and when he lay on his back on the floor, he could see the wooden beams of the roof and the crinkled sloped metal that kept the rain and sun out. He and his brother had their own room, with a bed each and a big wooden armoire for their stuff. And right out the front door was the sea.

His mother stood on the polished floor and twirled like a dancer. 'Aren't we lucky, boys?' she said. 'It's paradise.'

The colonel returned later in the evening when it was almost dark and the boy and his brother were in their pyjamas and ready for bed. He walked in and put a bottle of something on the table. Then he showed the boy's mother how to light the hurricane lamps and helped her open out the mosquito nets and secure the louvered shutters all around the house, so that the breeze would flow through at night. The boys went to bed and their mother came with one of the lanterns to kiss them goodnight.

'When is Dad coming, Mum?' the boy said.

'Tomorrow, around lunchtime.'

'Is tomorrow Christmas?' said the boy's brother.

'No, sweetheart. Tomorrow is Christmas Eve.' She kissed them both again and then stood and dimmed the lantern. 'Now go to sleep. We have a big day tomorrow.'

The boy was very tired, but he was too excited to sleep. He lay and listened to the swish of the waves on the beach and the sound of the breeze though the palms.

When he woke much later it was very quiet. He could hear his brother breathing nearby. He pulled away the light sheet, got out of bed and walked to the window. He peered through the louvers. The beach was very white and dark palm shadows striped the sand. Silver lights sparkled across the water. And there, on the veranda, barely visible in the half-darkness, the colonel and the boy's mother. From where he stood he could only see the back of the colonel's head, but he knew it was him. She was facing him. Her hair was down and she was holding a glass. The boy stood very still and watched and listened. After a time, the colonel reached for a bottle and refilled her glass. The boy could hear the clink of the bottle against the edge of the glass, then the deep rumbling of the colonel's voice and his mother laughing for a moment, then her familiar shush and more giggling. The boy didn't know how long he watched them, but they were still there, together on the veranda, when he finally crept back into bed. Much later, he heard the colonel's car drive away.

The next morning, Christmas Eve, the colonel came in the car and drove them down to the harbour for breakfast. The boy didn't say anything about what he'd seen that night, and neither the colonel nor the boy's mother mentioned it. The harbour was a new project, the colonel said. He called it a keyhole harbour, and it had been cut into the grey rock of the island to make a small marina. They'd only finished the work a few months ago. There was a little restaurant on the quay with a bar for the adults and a place that looked like a living room with a piano and couches and a TV. They were just sitting down at one of the tables in the restaurant when the other family came in. The father was wearing shorts and a straw hat. He was much shorter that the boy's father, and fatter. The mother was also short and fat. The little boy looked like his mother. But the girl was tall. She was wearing a yellow-and-white dress that tied at the back and black Keds running shoes, and her hair was tied up in a ribbon the same colour as her dress. There was a big scab on her knee. As the family approached, the boy's mother told them to stand up and she introduced them in that classroom way grown-ups did. The girl was called Georgina. She was thirteen and had freckles. They were from Ohio, the father said. When the boy's mother told the other family they were from Canada, Georgina laughed.

After they'd finished breakfast, the adults ordered more coffee and the kids were allowed to leave the table. The boy's mother told them not to go far. Their father was arriving soon, and they would go to the airstrip to meet him.

The two younger boys ran outside with a soccer ball.

Georgina hung back, walked beside him. 'You're short,' she said.

'My mum says boys grow late.'

'You say mum funny. It's *mom*.'

The boy, who knew nothing of girls, did not reply.

'I'm going to explore,' said Georgina. 'Want to come?'

'Where?' said the boy.

'The beach,' she said. 'It's close.

The boy, who wanted to go but was unsure, glanced back at his mother, who was talking to the girl's parents. 'Are we allowed?'

The girl crumpled her nose. 'Of course, silly. We've been here for two weeks. I know the whole island by heart.' And before he could answer she was out the door. 'Come on,' she called to him.

The boy ran after her. She led him along a narrow rocky trail through thick green bushes. They came to a gap in the rock. The sides were steep, and far below they could hear the water rushing through. It was a long way down.

'Come on,' she said. And before he could answer, she'd stepped back and jumped across the gap to the other side. As she jumped, the hem of her dress flew up and the boy could see her tanned thighs and a flash of white underpants. She turned and put her hands on her hips and smiled at him. 'Well? Are you scared?'

The boy stepped back as she had and jumped. It wasn't far, and he cleared it easily. They walked on through the bushes and came to a small cove with two rocky points and a white sand beach between. They were completely alone. The girl took off her Keds and tied the laces together. 'Come on,' she said, swinging her shoes like a handbag. 'Let's wade.'

The boy took off his shoes too and they waded through the shallow water. Fish of every colour and shape darted around their feet.

'You're lucky,' she said. 'We're leaving the day after Christmas.'

This did not seem to need an answer, so the boy said nothing. They waded to the far point and then the girl took his hand and led him up the beach to a flat rock. 'You want to try something?' she said.

'Sure,' the boy said.

She reached into her pocket and pulled out a cigarette and a book of matches with the blue Pan Am logo on the front. 'Have you ever tried one?'

The boy shook his head. His father smoked cigars, but his mother always said smoking was bad.

'It's one of my mom's. Want to?'

'Did you steal it?'

'What if I did?'

'Nothing.'

She put the cigarette between her lips. 'So, you want to?'

'I don't know.'

She opened the match book and pulled out a match. 'Promise not to tell?' she mumbled around the cigarette.

The boy nodded. She struck the match, held the flame to the end of the cigarette and drew in a deep breath. After a while, she let the smoke pour back out through her nose. She seemed very experienced.

'You try,' she said, holding the burning cigarette out for him.

The boy shook his head.

'You're scared.'

'No, I'm not.'

'Scaredy cat.'

'I'm not scared. I don't care what you think.' The boy reached into his pocket and pulled out a bullet and showed her. 'You know what that is?'

The girl shook her head.

'It's a thirty-eight-calibre bullet.'

The girl's eyes widened. 'Where did you get it?'

'I have a gun, back home. It's a Smith and Wesson revolver.'

'You do not.'

'I sure do. If you come to my house, I'll show you.'

'Kids don't have guns.'

'It's my dad's, but he gave it to me. I'm going to be in the army.'

The girl thought about this as she smoked.

'You stole it, didn't you?'

'What if I did?'

The girl took a last puff, stubbed the cigarette out on the rock. 'Come on,' she said. 'We should get back, gun boy. Your daddy will be here soon.'

'Don't tell anyone.'

'I won't if you don't,' she said.

∧∧

They met the plane at the airstrip. His father was not on it. His mother cried as they drove back to the harbour. In the restaurant, the colonel helped her telephone the office in Canada. She spoke for a while on the phone and when she finished she was crying again. The colonel offered her his arm and she took it. He walked her to the bar and poured her a drink.

Christmas came the next morning and the boy's father was not there as he had promised he would be. There were stockings at the foot of their beds when they woke. Inside, the boy found a new Polaroid camera, the kind that gave you a developed picture right after taking it. You only had to wait a minute and then peel the cover off and let it dry. There was also a small album to keep photos in, and a book called *The Old Man and the Sea*, with a picture of a small boat drifting on a big lonely sea on its front cover. His brother got three new Hot Wheels cars and a cool loop-the-loop track. The boy was pleased that his present was so much more grown up than his brother's. He would be a photographer when he grew up and travel to beautiful places and take pictures.

They took their presents to their mother's room and climbed up on to her big bed to show her what they'd got. She sat up in bed and smiled and listened to them but the boy knew from her face and the streaks of make-up that she'd been crying again. He kneeled beside her, put his arms around her and kissed her. Suddenly she threw her arms around him and squeezed him very tight. She held him like that for a long time.

It was still too early for breakfast, so the boy took his camera and album and went to the beach. The breeze was gentle and warm and smelled of the sea, and the light seemed very fragile and new. The sand, which was made of pieces of coral that had been smashed up by the waves, was very white and the pieces stuck to the skin of his feet and legs. When he was far enough from the house, he took his first photograph. It was of the beach and the palm trees and the blue water and there was nothing man-made in it. After it had dried, he slipped it into the album and kept walking. As he walked, he thought about his father and why he hadn't come. He thought about his mother's tears and the way she'd held him for so long, rocking him back and forth until he'd asked her to please let him go.

After a while he stopped and let the waves wash up over his feet. The water here was shallow and very clear and the white sandy bottom shone back out in the morning sun so that the water glowed. Suddenly, a dark shape emerged from the deeper water and drifted towards the shore. At first, he thought it might be a shark, but as he watched it come closer, he saw that it was flat and very broad with a long, thin tail. It was very close now and the boy could see the black eyes and the big pumping gills and the delicate curling wings. It was a stingray. He'd seen pictures of one in the Jacques Cousteau marine biology book he'd got for his birthday. The boy stood at the edge of the shallow water and watched the creature hovering there. It was so close. What did it want, he wondered? Could it sense him there, see out from the water? Was it waiting for him to feed it? He stood for a long time, watching its gills pumping slowly, the wings curling and sending little puffs of sand up from the bottom. And then he remembered his camera. He swung the Polaroid from its strap, aimed through the little glass window and clicked. The machine whirred and a photo appeared from the slot.

He was peeling the cover from the picture when suddenly the ray thrashed its tail. A spout of water broke the surface and the boy jumped back, dropping the photo into the water. His heart was racing. He reached for the picture, but the ray thrashed again and the boy stumbled backwards and fell to the sand. He sat for a moment watching the ray, then he got up and ran back to the house.

'Mum,' he shouted. He leaped up on to the veranda and ran inside. 'Come quick. I've found something.' His mother was in the kitchen in her dressing gown, sipping from a mug of coffee. He told her what he'd seen, and she grabbed her hat and sunglasses and followed him out to the beach. The ray was still there, in the same place, quiet now. There were patches of sand on its wings. It seemed to be waiting for something.

'It's beautiful,' his mother said.

The boy reached down and picked up the photograph he'd taken. The water had ruined it. He raised the camera and centred the ray in the window. Something was different. He lowered the camera. The ray had grown a second tail.

'Look,' he whispered.

'The tail,' his mother whispered.

'It's getting bigger.'

'Does that happen?' said his mother. 'It seems very strange.'

The second tail was big now, growing fast.

'Look,' the boy said. 'It's wriggling.'

'Oh, my God,' said his mother. 'It's beautiful.'

'What is it, Mum?'

'Quickly. Take a picture.'

The boy took a picture. The tail was broadening now. The big ray hovered there at their feet, changing. He took another.

His mother reached down and squeezed his hand. 'It's a baby, sweetheart. The mother ray is having a baby. I didn't know they did it this way.'

And then, very quickly, there it was. A perfect little miniature ray, hovering beside its mother in the shallow water. The boy took a photo of the mother and the baby. And then, very slowly, the two rays turned and glided away towards the darker water. When the boy looked up, he saw that his mother was crying.

Later that day, they went to the restaurant and had a Christmas lunch with the colonel and the other family. There was Christmas music and decorations, and the colonel dressed as Santa and gave out presents to everyone. Even the grown-ups got presents. After lunch, they played games and then everyone went for a swim. The grown-ups got very excited and loud and laughed a lot, and someone put on a Beatles record and the boy's mother danced with the colonel and then the other parents joined in.

When it got dark, the colonel drove them back to the house. The boy's mother got them ready for bed, tucked them in and kissed them goodnight. Before she had even closed the door, the boy was asleep.

In his dream, his mother was crying. She was standing with a phone to her ear and the tears were streaming from her eyes and down her cheeks. He could hear a voice, a man's voice, coming from the phone but the words were scattered, swirling like leaves in the wind, and he wondered how she could understand what the man was saying to her. Oh, she said into the phone. And again, oh, almost breathless. He reached out to her. Mum, he said, who is it, Mum? But it wasn't a dream. He was awake. He could hear her. Oh, she said again. He lay in the darkness and listened. Sounds filled the room, loud to bursting. His brother breathing in the bunk below. The slow creak of the ceiling fan. Palm fronds sawing outside the louvers, brushing against the side of the house. The hush and sigh of waves caressing the beach. And again, that breathless question. Her.

He got up, grabbed his camera and crept to his bedroom door. He put his ear to the gap between the door and the wall and he could hear all of it, the water and the wind and the things moving inside the house, living and not. He opened the door and walked across the living room towards his mother's room. The moon was up and very bright and silver light shone through the shutters, so that the inside of the house was banded with strips of light and dark. When he reached his mother's bedroom, he stopped and put his ear to the door. It was very quiet. He waited a long time, standing there in the striped silver half-dark, but all he could hear was the rise and fall of the sea and the wind moving like breath through the house.

He was about to go back to bed when he heard it again, that earliest voice, that same soft vowel, and then, to his surprise, another deeper sound, like a dog growling. And then, his mother's voice again, louder this time, different. A cry of pain? Of fear? His heart started beating faster. Was she in danger? He reached for the door knob and slowly turned it. He eased the door open, just enough so that he could see inside.

His mother was sitting up in the bed, facing away from the door. The boy had never seen her naked before. Her back was pale in the moonlight, her head was thrown back and her breasts swung as she moved herself slowly back and forth. Underneath her, looking up at her, was the colonel. The boy watched as his mother leaned forwards and kissed the colonel on the mouth. Without thinking, the boy raised his camera and pressed the button. Before the machine started whirring, he pulled the door closed and very carefully walked to his own room and went back to bed.

The next morning, the colonel arrived as usual and drove them to the harbour. The boy's mother and the colonel were very quiet. The boy ate his breakfast and didn't say anything to anyone. After, he went to the beach with Georgina. They waded and held hands for a time and then went to the flat rock and Georgina smoked a cigarette.

'We're leaving today,' she said, exhaling blue smoke.

'I wish we were leaving today.'

'You're crazy,' she said. 'I love it here. I wish I could live here.'

'My mother doesn't like it here.'

'Not from what I can see.'

The boy turned to look at her. 'What do you mean?'

'She seems to be having fun. The colonel likes her.'

'I hate him. If I had my gun here, I'd kill him.'

Georgina stubbed out her cigarette. 'He is a little, you know, creepy.'

'I saw them kissing.' The boy showed her the photo he'd taken the night before.

She took it in her fingers and looked at it. 'That's not kissing, silly.' She leaned over and put her lips on his cheek. 'That's a kiss.' She pointed to the photo. 'This is called screwing.'

'Don't say that. It's rude.'

'That's what it's called. *Screwing*.' She seemed to enjoy saying it. 'They could have a baby, you know.'

The boy, who knew that men and women had babies together but did not know how it worked, felt suddenly very hot and light-headed.

'I wouldn't show this to your father, if I were you,' said Georgina. 'He might want to kill the colonel.'

The boy thought of the gun in the closet at home.

'If your mother does have a baby, he would know. From the timing.'

The boy had no idea what the girl was talking about. But he did know that when his father got angry he was very scary. The boy had seen him smash things in the house and threaten his mother. If his father went and looked for the gun, he would see that three bullets were missing. And if he did kill the colonel, he might go to prison. The boy decided that when he got home, he would hide the gun and the bullets so that his father couldn't find them and would think he'd lost them.

Georgina looked at the photo for a long time. 'I never knew you could do it this way,' she said.

'Do what?'

'Screw.'

The boy snatched the photograph from her hand. 'Don't say that.'

She took a puff on the cigarette, looked him in the eyes. 'We should burn it,' she said.

The boy nodded. She lit a match and they cupped their hands around the photograph to protect it from the wind. It burned fast, with a blue flame.

'You have to keep this a secret,' she said. 'You can never tell anyone.'

'I won't if you don't.'

March 5th. Somewhere over Greenland

I stuff the manuscript back into the seatback pocket and stare out of the window. Ten kilometres below, the cut and grid of the tamed prairie has given way to a wasteland of ruptured ice. My hands are shaking. I take a deep breath, hold it. Outside, the sky is clear and blue and the glaciers curve over the earth for as far as I can see. Sometimes I forget what a big place this planet actually is. Eight hours Calgary to London – it sounds so mundane. Imagine walking it.

After a time, I stop shaking, get up and walk to the front to ask the stewardess for a whisky and Coke. We chat for a while. She is pretty enough: long dark hair, brown eyes, a voice that warbles when she speaks. She is Vancouver-based, has a three-day layover in London. She smiles at me. Asks me whether I am going home. Not really sure where home is, I answer, immediately wishing I hadn't. A man my age, saying something like that. I trudge back to my seat, the fury returning.

No one left. No one left. I slump into my seat, stare out at the ice. I can't believe he wrote that. The self-pity – I would never have imagined that from him. I was right there with him just a few hours before he wrote that. He could have said it to me then, all of it. Did he think I wouldn't have listened, that it was all too far gone between us? And if he did want me to find these stories and read them, how did he think it would make me feel, to read those words? Did he even consider it?

Well, all I can say, Dad, is if you felt like you were alone, it was your own goddamned fault.

I reread the third story, the one about the Caribbean island. He never told me he had a brother, that I had an uncle. Never mentioned it once. Neither did Mum. I wonder if he ever even told her. When I get home, I'll do some checking, see if I can track him down.

It's hard to think of my grandmother that way, how he describes her. I only saw her a few times. We were overseas, and she was back in Canada in some small, mist-shrouded hamlet on the coast of British Columbia. I remember she lived alone in a tiny log cabin on the edge of the forest. I got a handwritten letter from Dad a month after she'd died. One line. Your grandmother died last week. Thought you should know. *That was it. Inside the envelope was an old black-and-white photograph, cracked and faded. A young man in a dark suit and tie, clean-shaven, dark hair, neatly parted to one side, emerging from the front door of a DC-3. He stands on the stairs and looks out, past the camera, out to his future. A lovely young woman stands behind him, one hand on his shoulder, the other on the handrail. She is dressed in an elegant white dress, white shoes and gloves, and a white pillbox hat. She is smiling, excited. At the bottom of the photograph someone has written,* Havana, Cuba. 1959. *I still have it.*

I get back up, get another whisky and Coke, talk to the stewardess again. I upgrade my estimation of her looks. Nice body. She asks me about London, about how I like living there. She smiles as she talks. Her eyes are dark. I like it fine, I tell her, still thinking about that island, about the uncle I never knew I had, my grandparents in Cuba. She starts telling me about her layover, what she has planned, but I'm not really listening. It's all backdrop. I'm spinning.

Are you alright? she asks, reaching out and touching the cuff of my jacket.

I realise I probably look like shit, tired, unshaven, dressed in this old jacket, these faded jeans. I mumble something, turn back to my seat, realise that I've let an opportunity slide. A chance to be happy, perhaps. How can you ever know?

Rape

The summer after that Christmas at the Cay, the summer of the killing, a new family moved into the neighbourhood.

The boy and his brother hid in the bushes across the street and watched the moving van arrive and the men unloading the furniture. A few days later, the boy's mother trooped them both down the street to welcome the newcomers.

They were dressed, at her insistence, in clean shorts and matching button-up shirts. She was carrying a basket containing a freshly baked loaf of bread and a jar of her homemade plum jam. As they walked, his mother told them that the woman who had just moved into the house on the corner was a divorcee, with two children. The boy could hear the stain of scandal in his mother's voice. He knew what divorce was. One of the kids in his class had parents who'd divorced. Not long after, the kid – a small, quiet boy named Michael – stopped coming to school. They never saw him again.

The boy's mother pushed open the rusted steel gate and made to step through the opening in the hedge into the garden. The boy stopped, pulled back on her hand.

'No, Mum,' he heard himself say. 'Don't go in there.'

The boy's brother smirked.

'What's wrong, sweetheart?' As she turned to face him, he saw her there in her light summer dress, her still-blonde hair done up in a thick blue ribbon, her face lit by the late-afternoon sun, silhouetted against the darkness.

'Yeah, what's wrong, War?' said his brother. 'Scared?'

The boy could feel his face burning. He'd always hated this house, with its dark shingled turret and cramped dormers, and the way the slate roof seemed to hang over the street like a rockslide waiting to crush a valley town. But what he hated most was the garden. Surrounded by thick hedges and ancient, near-dead elms, it reminded him of an old church graveyard, the headstone engravings weathered away, dates and names obliterated forever. Every day on the way to school, he'd cross to the other side of the street as he walked by. And each time, that same shiver would spider its way from his shoulders to the tips of his fingers as he hurried to put the house as far behind him as he could. Even when old Mrs Simpkins – who'd lived there since long before the war – had finally died, and her spinster daughter, Maude, was taken to a special hospital, and the house had sat empty for more than a year, he'd still avoided it.

'Stop being ridiculous,' said his mother, clamping down on his hand and pulling him into the garden.

'Scaredy cat,' said his brother.

His mother led him by the hand along the overgrown garden path and up on to the veranda, the constriction of trespass rising in his chest. Glass crunched under their soles as they approached the big, arched front door.

His mother tutted, reached for the heavy brass knocker. 'Old Mrs Simpkins really let this place go,' she said. 'People say she was never the same after her husband died.'

She let the knocker fall. It was a museum sound, metal doors and echoing marble.

The boy glanced at the places where cardboard had been fitted into the smashed window panes, and quickly looked away. 'No one's home,' he said. 'Let's go.'

'Nonsense,' said his mother. 'The new family moved in two days ago.'

'Part of a family,' he said.

His mother glanced at him, her mouth set hard. They waited.

The boy swallowed. Just a few days ago, not long before the new people had moved in, his friend William had come up with a plan to sneak through the hedge and into the garden with a bag of stones he'd collected at the ravine. Darkness had come, and they had stood hidden in the night shadows near the big hedge that ran from the street, back past the crumbling garage and into the gloomy depths of the property.

'I don't want to do it,' the boy had said to his friend. 'I don't like this place.'

'All the more reason,' Will had replied. 'It's only a house. It's empty. It can't hurt you.'

'We could get into trouble.'

'Don't be such a pussy.'

The boy had heard people say 'pussy' before, in this way. Adults. William always used adult words like fuck and spliff and fag. The boy wasn't sure what pussy meant, like this, just that it was vaguely derogatory, subtly effeminate and did not mean cat. He didn't want to tell his friend the truth, that he didn't know what these words meant, or that the reason he didn't want to go near the house, then, and now with his mother, was that it was haunted.

Two years before, playing soldier in the neighbourhood, he'd chanced cutting through Mrs Simpkins' back garden in an attempt to outflank the opposing army. The old woman's view on children entering her yard was well known, her wrath legendary, but he was determined to overcome his fear. He'd just clambered over the fence and emerged from the hedge into the garden when the garage door opened. Maude had stopped dead, staring at him with those Muskoka summer eyes and her mouth open in a little 'o' of surprise. Her hair was tied up in a scarf, he remembered. She held a scrub brush in one hand and a pail in the other. Her patched and greying nightdress was wet at the knees. He was about to turn and run when she smiled. It was not at all what he had expected.

He smiled back.

She pointed to the house. 'Mother made cookies this morning,' she said. Her voice was oddly childlike, a helium whisper. 'Do you want some?'

Remembering what his mother had always told him about being

polite, and her kind disposition towards the old widow and her spinster daughter, the boy had agreed. Perhaps this way Maude wouldn't tell the old lady that he'd been trespassing, and the report wouldn't reach his mother. The boy followed her inside and sat at the kitchen table as his eyes adjusted to the gloom. The old woman was standing at the counter. She turned as he entered, faced him. She was dressed all in black. Her silver hair was pulled back tight. Heavy eyebrows and thin, downcast lips seemed to tug open deep shadows under her eyes. It was the first time he'd seen her up close.

She pointed to a place at the table. He sat. The cookies were hard and tasted vaguely of mothballs, or cough syrup maybe, the milk warm and slightly sour. The boy ate, downed the milk as quickly as he could, shuddering through the aftertaste. Then the two women – Maude with her stringy, unwashed ash hair and nightdress and slippers, the old woman in her old-fashioned black dress buttoned to the neck – took him by the hand and started leading him up the stairs.

'Where are we going?' said the boy, pulling back.

'To see Father,' whispered Maude.

'Father? Whose father?'

'Mine, silly.'

'I thought he…'

'Come along, silly.'

They were at the top of the stairs, on the landing, the two women almost pulling him along now, leading him further into the darkness. As they reached the next flight, the boy dropped his weight and pushed his feet against the step. The women compensated. He could feel the strength of them, supporting almost his full weight now.

The old woman turned and stared at him. 'What is the matter, young man?'

'Please, I…' he hesitated, unsure what to say. 'I have to go.'

'Nonsense,' said the old woman.

'Please,' he said, squirrels running wild in his stomach. 'I don't want to.'

'Are you afraid of seeing Father?'

He imagined an invalid, an old man everyone had thought was dead, locked away for years, perhaps hideously wounded still, propped up in bed, his beard long and grey, a side table covered in medicine bottles and empty plates, stacks of books, and perhaps, because he was a soldier, a loaded revolver on the bedcovers. The boy nodded, holding back tears. 'I want to go home, please,' he said. 'I'm sorry for coming into your yard.'

Mrs Simpkins frowned, glanced at her daughter. Then she pushed back the brim of the plastic army helmet the boy was wearing. 'You want to be a soldier, don't you?'

The boy nodded. Every night he watched the war on TV and dreamed that one day, he too, might do those things.

'Then you must be brave.' She tightened her grip on his wrist. 'How can you be a soldier if you are not brave? Now come along. Father wants to meet you.'

The boy shook his head, wiped away his tears. 'Please,' he said. 'You're hurting me.'

'Father was a soldier,' said Maude. Her voice was barely audible, a whisper. 'He can teach you how to be brave.'

The place was dark, smelled like a museum – old carpets and dust and polish and all manners of things long since dead. Wooden floors creaked under thick-weave carpets as they walked. Heavy felt curtains held back the day. As they penetrated deeper into the upper reaches of the house, he became aware of a depth to the darkness. Faces stared out at him from dark, gilt-framed portraits. Pale silhouettes drifted past, severed heads in pale stone, wreathed bust-works on marble plinths. And the deeper they went, the quieter the women became, so that by the time they reached the big oak door at the far end of the corridor, they spoke only in whispers.

'Please,' said the boy. 'I want to go home. My mother is expecting me.' His heart was beating so hard he thought this might be what a heart attack felt like. He tried to think of a lie. 'I have swimming lessons.'

He turned to go, but Maude held him fast.

'This is Father's room,' she whispered in his ear. 'I've told him about you.'

The old lady opened the door and Maude led him inside. The darkness was complete.

'I'm scared,' said the boy. 'I want to go home.'

'Don't worry, young man,' whispered the old lady. It sounded like the blade of a shovel scraping ice.

He heard the rasp of a match being struck, the flare of a flame, the woman's face lit red for an instant, and then the hiss of a kerosene lamp. As the mantle took, the room materialised. A glass case covered the length of one wall. Inside were photographs, some framed, others spread over the dark wood shelving, a uniform jacket, brass button and cap badges, a handwritten letter, what looked like a bible, a revolver. Beyond, on the adjacent wall, a door half ajar, darkness beyond.

The two women faced an empty fireplace with a huge stone mantelpiece and looked up. A full-sized portrait of a man in uniform looked down at them. It was an old-fashioned uniform, khaki with a brown belt and boots and red lapel tabs. The man was handsome and had a big moustache narrowed off into fine points. His eyes burned with a strange darkness, like black stars. He held a stick in one hand, his officer's cap tucked under the other arm.

'Father,' said the old lady in her scraping wheeze, 'this young man wanted to meet you. He, too, wants to be a soldier.'

After a moment, the woman nodded. 'Yes, that is a good idea,' she said. 'Maude, show him Father's decorations.'

The daughter pulled the boy to the far end of the room, let go of his wrist, unlocked a chest of drawers and pulled open the top one. A rack of medals shone against a black velvet background, a dozen at least, tiled one upon the other, their ribbons in every shade of the rainbow, the obverses polished silver coins, stars and crosses in brass and gold.

The boy reached out to touch. Maude slapped his hand away with a loud hiss.

'You can't do that,' she whispered, clutching the sides of her night-dress. She turned towards the portrait. 'Sorry, Father,' she whispered. 'Yes, I will tell him.'

She faced the boy. 'You cannot touch them,' she said. 'If you do he will be very angry.'

The old woman was still in front of the fireplace, gazing up at the portrait, speaking in the hushed tones of half a conversation. The boy stood a moment looking at the daughter, this woman who seemed so much like a child. And then he ran.

He ran as fast as he could. Out of the room, along the darkened corridor, past the dead eyes and faces. Halfway along, his foot caught a fold in the carpet and he tumbled to the floor. His helmet bounced away towards the dark peripheries of a curtained bay. One of the women screamed. He scrambled back to his feet, didn't look back. His heart was beating harder than he had ever imagined possible, as if it would jump out of his chest. He gasped for breath, launched himself down the stairs, taking them three at a time. Was this what drowning felt like? Footsteps behind him now, Maude's voice calling. He sprinted through the kitchen, the half-finished cookies still there on the table. When he burst out on to the back step it was as if he'd risen to the lightened surface of a gentle ocean. He gasped in deep breaths of summer air. The door slammed shut on its spring behind him. In seconds he was away, over the fence and out on to the street.

The boy never went back to the house, never saw the old woman or her daughter again. For weeks after, he lived in fear that they would tell his mother of his behaviour. But as the days passed, and nothing happened, he began to think that perhaps he had escaped punishment. And then, one day after school, his mother came to his room. She was holding his army helmet in her hand. She set it on his desk and sat down on his bed.

'Maude brought this over today,' she said.

'Oh. Thanks,' he mumbled, waiting for the inevitable.

'Is there anything you want to tell me, Warren?'

He shook his head.

'You know that Maude is not well, don't you?'

'She was talking to her father. I saw her.'

His mother closed her eyes. She left them that way for a long time, as if she was sleeping. Then she opened them again. 'Maude's father was killed in 1942 at Dieppe,' she said. 'He was awarded a posthumous Victoria Cross.'

The boy had read about the VC, knew what it signified. 'What is posthumous?' he said.

'After you die.'

And that was when he knew. And it struck him as strange – that they would give a medal to a dead person, a ghost.

He'd never told William, or anyone else, about what had happened that day.

And so, not wanting to appear to be a pussy, he had followed William through the hedge and the two of them threw stones at the house until a neighbour shouted out in the darkness and they ran away, hearts racing through the hot, humid Toronto night.

Now, he stood with the results of his good aim crunching under his shoes and looked back over his shoulder towards the street.

The door opened.

The family seemed nice, normal. The divorcee was pretty, in a sad, damaged way. She smiled as she took the basket from the boy's mother.

'Sorry about the glass,' she said. Her voice was like the sound the wind made in the tree outside the boy's window in winter. 'The panes were broken before we moved in. I simply haven't had a moment.'

The boy could feel the colour rise in his face. He turned away, looked at the floor. When he looked back up, the daughter stuck her tongue out at him. She looked to be about his age.

'This is Todd,' said the divorcee, putting her hand behind her son's back. He was tall and lanky, with a brush cut and bad skin. He smiled at them.

'I'm in the army,' Todd said, standing tall.

'The reserves,' said his mother.

'For now,' said Todd. He turned his summer-lake blue gaze on the boy.

'The man who used to live in the house won the VC,' the boy said. 'He died at Dieppe.'

'I'm going to win a medal,' Todd said.

'He won it posthumously,' said the boy. 'That means—'

'I know what it means,' said Todd.

'Boys, please,' said Todd's mother, the divorcee.

Todd stared at the boy, held his gaze for a long time. 'You can come over sometime,' said Todd, 'if you want. I can show you the equipment the army gives us.'

The boy did not stay that day, despite the invitation. But over the next few days, the last days of summer, he did visit the older boy. He never went inside the house though. Todd had set up the old garage as his own place. There was an old sofa, a radio, a bench where he kept his army stuff. There was even a bed. The boy marvelled at Todd's steel and Kevlar helmet, felt the glory of its weight on his own head, down through his spine. The camouflage helmet cover was the same as the ones the US Marines in Vietnam used. Todd told him that as soon as he could get away, he was going to take a bus down to Detroit and enlist in the US Marines and go to Vietnam to fight. He let the boy try on his fatigues, sizes too big, put on the webbing, the ammunition pouches and the sling satchel, hold the bayonet. The boy decided that he, too, would go to Detroit and enlist in the US Marines when he was old enough. He'd go and fight. He hoped the war would last long enough. And then one day, he, too, would come home with a medal, be a man.

On the last Saturday before the new school year, the boy took his father's revolver from the place he'd hidden it, put it into his army-surplus carry bag and went to Todd's house.

'I've got something to show you,' he said when Todd opened the front door. 'It's a secret.'

They went to the garage. Todd turned on the light, locked the door. 'My mom is away,' he said. 'What's the secret?'

The boy pulled out the Smith and Wesson.

Todd held the gun in his hands, spun the barrel.

'Nice,' he said. 'Thirty-eight. Good at short range.'

'I've got bullets,' said the boy.

Todd put out his hand. The boy reached into his pocket and poured a handful of the .38 calibre slugs into Todd's palm. He liked the sound they made, the softness of the lead slugs against the hard-edged copper casings. Todd stood a moment weighing the ammunition in his hand. Then he loaded the chamber. His fingers were long and slender, the knuckles skinned.

He spun the barrel, levelled the pistol, aimed at the garage wall. 'I know a place we can shoot it,' he said, closing one eye and bracing his gun arm with his free hand. Then he put the pistol on the bench near the door. 'I'm going to Vietnam,' said Todd, after a moment.

The boy was very impressed.

'I could die,' he said.

The boy said nothing. He knew that soldiers sometimes died. He'd seen it on TV, in movies and in the news. He'd read about it in books. Two of his great-uncles had died fighting the Japanese in World War Two. One had been captured at Singapore, and later was being transported with other prisoners back to Japan when their ship was torpedoed by an American submarine. The Japanese locked the prisoners in the hold before the ship went down. He had nightmares about it sometimes.

'I'm leaving tomorrow,' said Todd.

'What did your mum say?'

'She doesn't know. I'm old enough. I'm not going to tell her. It's a secret.'

Todd took a step towards him, reached up and put his finger under the boy's chin. 'How old are you, War?'

'Thirteen next year.'

Todd glanced back at the gun. 'Does your father know that you have that?'

The boy shook his head.

'You wouldn't want him to find out, would you?'

'No.' Dread rose in the boy's stomach, gripped his chest.

Todd put his hands on the boy's shoulders. 'I need someone to say goodbye to,' he said, 'before I go to the war.'

'I can do that,' said the boy. 'I can say goodbye to you.'

Todd smiled. He had strong, even teeth, a nice smile. 'We can pretend,' he said.

'Pretend?' The boy could feel Todd's grip tighten on his shoulders.

'You know,' said Todd. 'Like in the movies. The soldier says goodbye to his wife before he goes to the war. She cries and tells him she loves him.'

'Your wife?'

'Like in the movies. We can pretend you are a girl.'

The boy shook his head. 'No. I'm not a girl.'

Todd pushed the boy back towards the bed. 'We can pretend,' he said, his voice suddenly deeper.

The boy's ankles hit the bedframe and he fell back on to the mattress, the older boy falling on to him, crushing the air from his lungs.

'Come on, War,' he breathed. 'I could die.'

The boy struggled, but the teenager pinned his arms. He reached with his free hand and pulled down the boy's shorts, ripped off his underwear, tore off his T-shirt.

'What are you doing?' cried the boy, ashamed now of his nakedness.

'Saying goodbye,' said Todd. 'Wives are supposed to be naked.'

'Stop, or I'll scream,' cried the boy.

'Go ahead. I'll tell your dad about the gun.'

The boy was aware of Todd's forearm pressed down across his upraised arms, the weight of the older boy's knee pushed down across his torso. And now, Todd's free hand moving across his chest, down towards his nakedness.

The boy thrashed his head, tried to flail his legs, but Todd was stronger and heavier. And then a hand over his mouth and nose, his airways blocked, his attacker's face above him, very close, pushing down on him. 'Fight me, and I'll kill you,' the older boy hissed. And then, when he thought he would pass out from lack of air, the hand was gone and he was flipped over on to his stomach. Something drove hard into the back of his neck, crushing his face into the mattress, and then a hand was opening him up, and something pushing into him hard, the pain rushing through him in pulses with the pounding, on and on until he was burning and crying out in agony, the shameful tears soaking the bedsheet and the breathing faster, everything covered in sweat until the shivering, grunting, crying out.

And then it was over. Todd rolled off him, lay open-armed on the bed. The boy scrambled from the bed, reached for his clothes. He stumbled to the bench and grabbed the gun. He turned, faced the older boy, raised the gun.

Todd's eyes widened.

The boy pulled back the hammer on the gun, pointed it at the teenager.

'What are you doing?' said Todd, sitting up on the bed. 'Are you crazy?'

Tears stung his eyes. Pain shot up his spine, hot and wet. The gun shook in his hands.

'War, don't, please.' Todd's voice was high now, like a girl's, his eyes wide with fear. 'I'm sorry,' he whispered.

The boy took a deep breath and eased the hammer back down. 'I hope you die,' he said. And then he turned and ran out into the day.

March 6th. Heathrow

I switch on my phone and there are two text messages waiting for me. One is from Maria, reminding me to pick up Rachel and take her to her school play today. The implication is clear: she still hasn't forgiven me for missing the last event. I mean, how many plays and recitals and jamborees and fucking bake sales can a single school put on in a year? I swear I spend more time sitting in that school auditorium clapping than I do at my fucking job. The second message is from Constantina. There are three x's and an o and a picture of her naked. She really does have great tits.

I delete the mobile number the stewardess gave me.

Outside, it's raining, as usual. A grey early morning in London. I need to pick up Rachel, take her to school. The play will only take an hour. Then I have time to get back to the flat and clean up and get to Embankment for the meeting with Gould and Associates, and the dinner after. It's a big contract, and if I can land it, things could start to be good. I'm starting to feel like I'm getting pretty damned good at what I do. Can't help feeling that my old man would have been proud of me if he'd ever bothered to listen. Not like I didn't try, at first. But you tell someone to fuck off enough times and eventually they get the message.

Tomorrow morning, I need to take the early flight to Geneva to see Borschmann. Shit, I wish I could see Constantina before the weekend, but there just isn't time. I don't think I can last that long, though. Just looking at her picture makes me want to jerk off right now. Maybe in the shower when I get home. She'll be pissed at me, though. Likes me to keep it all for her.

During the flight, I reread the letter from my old man's lawyer. Apparently, the will leaves me everything. There is the Calgary house and contents; not sure how much it's worth, a couple of hundred thousand Canadian, maybe. A bank account with a few grand, not much. The letter also mentions some additional stipulations that must be worked out in a final face-to-face meeting. The whole thing has me reeling. After all these years, it's the last thing I would have expected. Still, I'm not going to argue. I'll have to contact the lawyer next week, after I get back from Geneva.

I keep thinking about my old man and that manuscript of his. I've decided I'm going to keep reading the stories in order, the way he had them stacked up in the pile. He never did anything without a reason, without thinking it through. Makes it worse, knowing that. But Jesus Christ, that last story. Explains a few things. Raises more questions, too.

Thinking it through, I can only believe that he wanted me to find it. That's why he left me the house. Must be. I mean, for a long time there were only the two of us, even if he did think he was alone. And now, well, there's just me. Maria doesn't care. She never liked my old man. Too right wing, she always said, a throwback. Too old-fashioned in his views. Not that he was easy to like. Rachel's seen him maybe three times that I can recall, and two of those were when she was too small to remember.

So, that's why he left the manuscript on top of the journals like that. Must be. There was no way he was ever going to present it to me and say: 'Here is this thing I've written, son, to explain everything for you.' No way. That was not the way he ever did things. I can see him lying there in the hospital thinking, If the son of a bitch makes the effort to look around and find it, then he can read it. *Maybe he trusted me enough to get it right, after all. Maybe.*

All these things he never told me. Jesus. Some things you just can't share. I sure as hell would never have been able to. I guess this was the only way.

There is so much that needs to be kept separate. It's only when things collide that people get hurt. That's what lies are for. To protect the people you care about. Secrets keep people safe. My old man knew that, and practised it. And now I'm thinking that maybe I don't want to know any of it. I'm walking along the concourse in Terminal 4, towards baggage claim, and I see a rubbish bin. I reach into my bag and pull out the manuscript. I've lived this long just fine without knowing.

Love

He stood at the bottom of the driveway and looked up at the house and wondered if she would be there. It was the summer of his sixteenth birthday, the year after they'd moved from Toronto to Vancouver. The summer he discovered Thomas Hardy and Ernest Hemingway and Faulkner. The summer Todd was killed near An Lôc.

He filled his lungs, exhaled long and loud, slung his bag over his shoulder and started up the drive. First steps towards a new life. Destiny awaiting.

She was the cousin of his best friend, Scott. A big-boned prairie girl from Saskatchewan, her parents had sent her out west for the summer to work in her uncle's real-estate business as an office assistant. She had long hair the colour of beach sand and a big smile that she turned on him the first time they met. She wasn't like the other girls he knew, the girls in his year at school, Erin and Catherine and Josie, with their home-sewn skirts and peach shampoo hair and their secret and segregated lives and talk of love and marriage and babies. Even her name was different. Shelly.

He stood awhile outside the house, looking up at the windows and over at the pool. Scott's dad drove a Jag. They had a big house and Scott had his own 1976 Camaro. He answered the door. Smiled in that confident way of his, like he knew what life would bring him and it would all be good. As it turned out, he was right, mostly.

'Hi, War,' Scott said. 'Come on in. Want a beer?'

The boy hesitated.

'Don't worry, my parents are away for the weekend. It's just us.'

Us. One word. His heart beat faster.

Scott led him through to the kitchen and living area. It was a new house with long wooden beams spanning high ceilings and a canti- levered front balcony flung high over the sheer rocky slope where you could stand and look across English Bay to Point Grey, and on clear days like today all the way over to the Gulf Islands. She lay sprawled on the sofa in a pair of tight faded jeans and a loose white T-shirt, a beer in one hand. Her hair haloed out around her head like one of those Byzantine illuminations he would see much later, in Cyprus, when he was so much older.

'You remember Shell,' said Scott, opening the fridge.

The boy nodded, swallowed hard. 'Hi.' He turned his head slightly to hide the angry blemish burrowing under the skin just below his jawline.

'Hi, sweetie,' she said, opening up that smile. 'Did you miss me?'

The boy tried to think of a way to reply. *All I have done since I met you last weekend is think of you. My insides ache and I feel dizzy. I have masturbated thinking about you so many times that I am sore.* 'I guess,' he said, finally.

'He doesn't say much, does he?' she said to Scott.

'Naw,' said Scott. 'Like that all the time. I keep telling him. Never get laid if you can't talk to a girl.'

She laughed, raised the beer bottle to her mouth, took a sip.

He'd never seen a girl like this before, so obviously braless, legs splayed, confident. He grabbed a beer and drank hard.

'Can you stay over?' said Scott.

He nodded.

'Oh goodie,' said Shelly, sitting up and patting the couch. 'Come and sit with me, you.'

He stood mute, looking down at her. He could feel it happening, feel the pull. She smiled at him again and it was as if he was being drawn in, by time and history and everything that had come before him. Fear choked up in the back of his throat. He took her hand, sat. She pulled his arm around her shoulder, so that his fingers hovered perilously close to the swell of her breast.

'When you didn't call I thought you didn't want to see me again,' she said.

He said nothing, kept his arm rigid, his fingertips inches from the thin cotton of her T-shirt. He could feel the warmth of her body next to his, the soft fullness of her moulding to him.

'I'm going to the store to pick up more beer,' Scott announced.

'What?' said the boy.

'You heard me.'

'You can't buy beer,' said the boy.

'I know some guys.' Scott grabbed his keys, started for the door. 'You two have fun.'

She squeezed his leg.

They sat and listened to Scott's Camaro start up, the in-line 286 rumbling as it backed down the drive.

Shelly took a swig of her beer. 'I like it here,' she said. 'Our place in Regina is a dump.'

The boy said nothing.

'How old are you?' she said.

He swallowed hard. 'Sixteen.'

'Me too. When's your birthday?'

'It was last month.'

'Just a baby. I turn seventeen in September.'

'I guess.'

'So what are you going to do after high school?' she said.

'I'm going to join the air force. I'm going to travel the world. And I'm going to be a writer.' These were things he had recently decided, in the last few months. He was going to be a pilot, fight in the next war, the war that was coming. He liked to read history and he knew that there was always another war. And, like Hemingway and Faulkner, he would come home scarred and distant and he would be the guy everyone would whisper about – hey, he was in the war, was shot down, but bailed out and survived. And he would write about it. He hadn't told any of this to anyone before.

'My father was in World War Two,' she said. 'He was in the army.

You should meet him. Maybe you can come and visit me sometime.'
She snuggled closer.

'What did he do? In the war, I mean.'

'He never told me,' she said. 'He always wanted a son. But my
mum died giving birth to me, and he never remarried.'

The boy looked at her, noticed for the first time the differing hues
of her eyes, one hazel, the other lake green.

She moved her face close to his, rubbed his nose with her own.
'Kiss me, soldier boy,' she said, closing her eyes.

He reached over and put his lips to hers, tried to be gentle. He
watched her as he did it.

She opened her eyes and laughed. 'Not like that, silly. Open your
mouth and close your eyes. Push harder. Try again.'

He did as she asked. Her mouth opened. Their tongues danced.
She tasted like beer and cigarettes, not like a high-school kid. More
like a woman, or what he imagined a woman must taste like. They
kissed for a long time. After a while, she took his hand, moved it to
her midriff and slid it under her T-shirt, guiding it up her ribcage
towards her breast. And then that contact, skin still, but different,
amazing. She moaned as he explored, squirmed against him. He
could feel himself hardening, pushing up painfully against his jeans.
And then her hand was on him, moving up and down across the
ridgeline of his button fly. He tried to catch his breath, pull air in
through his nose. His head was spinning, his heart hammering in
his chest as if it would explode. And then he was back there, on that
bed in that musty garage with his face pushed into the mattress. He
gasped and pulled away.

'What's wrong, sweetie?' she said, caressing his hair. 'Don't you
like it?'

He cycled air through his lungs, wiped his mouth. 'Sorry,' he said.

She brushed a wisp of hair from his forehead. 'You've never done
this before, have you?'

He shook his head. 'It's not that.'

'What is it, War? Do you want to stop?'

He shook his head.

She pulled up her shirt. 'You like?'

He stared, nodded slowly, deliberately. Yes. God, yes.

She smiled. 'Don't worry. We'll take it easy.' She reached up and put her hand behind his neck. 'Put your mouth on them,' she said, her voice thicker now, deeper. 'Suck.'

He did. She moaned. The sound inflamed him. He grabbed her breasts, one in each hand, squeezed them hard so that the nipples stood. He sucked hard and worked his tongue around the hardening flesh, one and then the other and back again.

And then she whispered in his ear. 'I am on the pill, you know.'

They rose. She took him by the hand and led him to her bedroom. The curtains were drawn. It was dark. She pulled off her T-shirt, snaked out of her jeans, lay back naked on the bed, a pale phantom. He stripped off, stumbled on to the bed with his jeans caught around his ankles. She laughed, pulled him close. He found her mouth, kissed her. She parted her legs, reached for him, guided him in. He had no idea what he was supposed to do. He moved by instinct only, assuming that her sighs meant he was doing it right. It didn't last long. A few minutes later, they did it again. And then, after they heard Scott's Camaro come up the driveway, a third time.

When they emerged from her bedroom, Scott was in the kitchen. He smiled at them, cracked open three beers. They stood around the island and drank. '*Star Trek* is on TV,' he said. 'I've ordered pizza.'

They went to the TV room and watched the episode where Spock's brain is taken by aliens and Bones has to reattach it. Shelly snuggled with him on the couch smoking, while Scott sat in his dad's La-Z-Boy, drinking beer after beer.

I love you. This was what he was thinking. This is what love is, what everyone writes and sings about, what all the girls at school are always gabbing about. Love. So, finally.

They stayed up late watching movies on TV. He drank too much. When she announced that she was going to bed, he followed her to her room.

She stopped at the door and faced him. 'Goodnight, you,' she said, kissing him on the lips. Then she turned and went into her room and closed the door.

He stood a long time, swaying from the alcohol, not sure what had just happened. 'I love you,' he whispered into the crack between the door and the frame.

Later that night he exploded from a dream, covered in sweat, aching hard, gasping for breath. He opened his eyes. A distortion hovered there a moment and he recognised it as Todd, or an image of Todd. He reached out to touch it, but before he could extend his arm, it was gone. He lay in the darkness and surveyed the living room. He remembered stumbling away from her room, finding the kitchen, grabbing another beer, standing out on the back deck, watching the rain fall in staccato time delay until he was soaked.

The cushions beneath him were wet. He must have found his way back here and crashed on the couch. Scott's mum would have a fit. He sat up. Each beat of his heart sent a bullet of pain through his brain, each round tearing into the tissues that controlled his personality, his behaviour, his higher cognitive functions. He clamped his hands around his head as if to keep his skull from flying apart. Waves crashed over him. His guts were churning. He rose, swayed, reached out to steady himself. A lamp crashed to the floor. He cursed, bent double at the waist, stumbled towards the corridor and the bathroom. He felt his way along the hallway, past Shelly's door. And then something made him stop. A sound. He stopped, strained to listen over the pounding in his ears. A cry. Another. A deeper echo, across years. He put his ear to the door. Breathing. Sighs, female. Her. Electricity arced through him, dissolved his spine, the ligaments holding his knees together. He grabbed the door frame, reached for the doorknob, pushed open the door.

Years later, from the cliff edge of time, as existence waned, that moment would return, those images. Her pale butterflying calves. The insistent urging of her sighs. Scott's glistening back. Her pale fingers laced through his dark hair. Her eyes, the lack of symmetry destabilising even in the darkness as she looked right at him. And then her smile.

He turned and ran. Back through the kitchen and out into the rain. He fell to his knees and heaved until it felt as if his stomach would turn inside out. Then he stood, wiped his face with the sleeve of his jacket and started down the drive and towards the highway.

March 7th. On the plane to Geneva

Jesus, Dad. What did you expect? Am I supposed to be sitting here feeling sorry for you, for your sixteen-year-old self? I stuff the manuscript into the seatback pocket, down my whisky, ask the stewardess for another.

I actually did dump the manuscript into that bin. I was almost at baggage claim when I stopped. I stood a moment, thinking about it, about him. I'm still not sure why I went back. Curiosity, I'll call it. By the time I got back, the bin was being emptied out by the cleaners. Breathing hard, I explained that I'd dropped something in by accident. They were very helpful. I rummaged through the bag, immediately regretting my decision as my fingers sank knuckle deep into someone's half-eaten lunch. Jesus, I breathed. The cleaners looked at each other, then back at me. 'You want me to—', one of them began, but I shook my head, kept going. Finally, I pulled the dripping manuscript from the bin liner. The cuff of my jacket was coated with something that looked like egg yolk. My hand was smeared in puke. The cleaners smiled, handed me a rag, watched me blade cold coffee from the cover.

'Lucky,' said one of them. 'We were almost done, about to take all this to the pickup.'

'Looks important,' said the other.

'Not really,' I said.

I swipe my credit card to pay for the whisky. I drink it down in one go, before the stewardess has even finished printing out the receipt. When I ask her for another, she raises her eyes to show her surprise. Or her disdain. Up in business class the whisky is free – as much as you want – and comes with a smile, even at seven in the morning. If I get this contract and the promotion, I can travel up there instead of wedged here in the back where I no doubt belong. I could use the money. I'm worse off now than I was ten years ago. Divorce will do that to you.

I can still feel where Maria open-palmed me, one of her rings opening up the skin over my cheekbone. My right index knuckle is badly swollen, too. I think I might have broken it. Anyone asks me about it I'm going to say I got it sparring at the dojo.

The traffic from the airport yesterday was horrific. Going back for Dad's manuscript cost me more than half an hour. By the time I picked Rachel up from her friend's house we were already forty-five minutes behind. I made up some time between there and the school, broke all kinds of traffic rules, but when we got to the school the play had already started and Rachel was in tears. One of the teachers convinced her to get into her costume and she went on anyway. But she was so upset she couldn't remember her lines and broke down on stage. I could feel Maria drilling holes in my head from two rows back. That wanker of a boyfriend of hers was there too. Troy is his name, a city lawyer, glaring at me in practised solidarity.

After the play finished, I went backstage. Rachel was being comforted by one of the teachers. I started towards her, but as soon as she saw me, she turned and ran. By the time I caught up with her, Maria and her boyfriend were there. Rachel was sobbing hysterically and Maria was running her hands through her hair and kissing her tears. Wanker-boy just stood there in his expensive suit next to them, trying to look suitably concerned. I stopped a few paces away and was about to say something when Maria looked up at me. She locked her hardest fuck-you gaze on me, one I have seen too many times in the last couple of years, and then let me have it with one of her glass-shattering you-are-such-a-fucking-asshole volleys. I know her well enough. I backed away. Went out and stood in the parking lot and lit a smoke. I decided to un-quit three days ago, while I was looking through Dad's place. Health is overrated.

So, I was standing out in the parking lot on my fourth Camel, watching the parents trickle out with their little darlings, and along came Maria and Fuckface. I was going to talk to my daughter. I was going to apologise. I fucked up. I tried, but I was late. I had to try. I started towards them. As soon as Maria saw me, she pulled Rachel behind her, pushed her towards Fuckwit, who put his hand on her shoulder. Maria glared at me.

'I want to speak to my daughter,' I said.

'She doesn't want to talk to you,' Maria said through tear-streaked make-up. I noticed that she was wearing a new dress, one that accentuated her figure. She'd dyed her hair. She looked good.

I stepped to one side, peering past her. 'Rachel, sweetheart, can I talk to you, please? I want to tell you how sorry I am.' I meant it. I could feel myself meaning it.

But before I could finish, Maria was between us again. She glared up at me a moment, and then pulled back her hand and slapped me hard across the face. I should have seen it coming, but I'd let my guard down. The force of it jerked my head sideways. I was more surprised than hurt. I raised my hand to my face. I said nothing, held my ground.

By now, people were watching. I tried again. 'Rachel, please, talk to me.' It was a stupid thing to say. What did I expect her to do? And I was about to turn away when the boyfriend decided to get involved. He pushed in front of Maria, squaring up to me, striking distance. He was taller than me, bigger, but with that soft office look. 'Leave them alone, loser,' he growled.

I stood my ground, looking past him, trying to make eye contact with my daughter.

'Did you hear me, loser?' he tried again.

I ignored him. 'Rachel,' I said. 'Please, sweetheart. I am so sorry.'

Maria shielded Rachel with her body. 'You don't give a shit about her,' she spat. 'You are the most selfish person I have ever met. The biggest asshole I've ever met.' Her voice went up a notch, if that was possible. 'You are such a total loser. I never want to see you again. Ever.'

That's when Fuckwit decided to be a hero. He took a step towards me, trying to impose his size, intimidate. 'You should leave,' he said. 'Now.'

At that point, I'd had it. I coiled up. I knew what I was going to do before I did it, had practised it enough times. It was Dad who got me into it when I was young. One thing I've always been grateful to him for. I brought the sole of my left boot down hard on the top of his right foot, pinning him in place. Startled, he let out a grunt and looked down. As he did, I drove my right fist into his face. Driven back, one foot locked *in place, he fell back and crashed to the ground, blood pouring from his nose. Maria screamed. I turned and walked through the parking lot, Maria and Rachel crying behind me. I got into my car and drove away, 'Findin' My Way' by Rush screaming on the stereo.*

It felt good. For a while.

Peru

From the window of the hotel you could look out across the river that ran through the middle of the city, over to the slums that covered the hills like mange. The young man knew why he was there. She hadn't wanted to go alone. He was tall, towered over her now. Football and hockey had built muscle, and she knew that he could fight and, since the killing, that he did it far too often, coming home bruised and bloody. And she needed someone to carry the bags.

The flight south to the desert wasn't until the next morning, so they left the hotel and walked into the centre of town. It was a place he would return to, years later, with Helena, in that halcyon period before the children came, when they were alone in the world, together. But now the young man knew nothing of that destiny before him, nor of the various points at which he might have changed it, nudged it on to another course entirely. He followed his mother along the narrow streets, watched her step over the crumbling kerbstones and cracked pavement, skip girl-like over the grey puddles that guttered the roadside and drained off into the fetid, stinking canal. They skirted the edge of the *barrio bajo*, felt the stares of the old people who begged from the fringes. The young man, who had seen poverty before, but never like this, walked towards them and pressed small bills, pesos, into outstretched hands until all he'd exchanged at the airport was gone.

In the centre of the city, his mother led him up the stairs and through the entrance of the Gran Hotel Bolivar. After the smoke and dirt of the streets, the lobby was cool and clean, marble and polished wood. A uniformed waiter showed them to a table on the balcony overlooking the street. She ordered a gin and tonic, and he a Coke.

'Rhys would have loved this,' his mother said after a time. Her gin was half gone.

The young man stared at his hands.

'Don't you think?'

'Why do you always say that?' The young man looked up. His mother was staring right at him.

'Because he would have.'

'You don't know that.'

'Yes, I do.'

She tipped back her gin, called the waiter over, spoke to him in Spanish. 'I am having another,' she said. 'Do you want another?'

The young man nodded, looked at her. He realised he hadn't looked at her and seen for a long time. The lines around her eyes and mouth were deeper, longer than he remembered. There was grey in her hair. He'd never noticed it before. His Coke came, a glass of ice, her gin. He pushed a straw into the bottle, drank.

'What are you looking at?' she said.

'Nothing.'

'Nothing.'

'Nothing.'

'You've become as talkative as your father.'

He said nothing.

'Why don't you say something?'

'Say what?'

She shook her head, drank.

'Why do you always—' he began.

'I don't know,' she said before he'd had a chance to finish. 'I'm sorry.'

The young man looked out to the street, the traffic fuming past. After a while, he said: 'Did you see that man, back at the bridge, lying face down in the puddle?'

She nodded, raised her glass to her lips. 'That's the way it is,' she said. 'Not just here, but in so many places. Most places.'

'Why doesn't someone—'

'Do what?' she snapped. And then: 'I'm sorry, Warren. You're right. Someone should. That's why we're here, sweetheart. To do something.'

'Don't call me that.'

His mother smiled. She had a beautiful smile. She reached for his hand, but he drew away.

The next morning, they caught the flight from Lima to Chimbote, four hundred kilometres north along the cold-current Pacific that turned the coastal plains to desert. The small plane landed hard on the dirt airstrip and rumbled to a halt outside a small mud-brick building. Twin propellers spun to a stop and the pilot opened the door. The young man stepped outside. A hot wind blew rivers of sand across the airstrip. He narrowed his eyes, helped his mother off the steps, took the heaviest of her bags. They were the only ones on the flight. The pilot unloaded the rest of their luggage, started the engines and taxied away. Soon they were watching the plane claw its way into the sky, the buff and ice-capped saw of the Andes far off, the cold sea to their backs.

The taxi came not long after, as his mother had said it would. She spoke excitedly with the driver as the car rattled along gravel roads, past dunes and broad washes devoid of green. How anyone could live out here, he could not imagine.

His mother's Spanish was excellent, learned as a girl, at school and for more than a year living with a family in Spain as an au pair. They were here to do a job. This wasn't sightseeing, she'd told him when they had first discussed her plan. A mission, more like, she'd said.

Almost two hours later, they came to the village. She'd never met them before, only corresponded over more than a decade. The mother was short and of matronly girth, but with a big warm smile. Elvira, the original foster child, was fifteen now, still in school. The youngest of her five siblings was two, a smiling, runny-nosed bundle that Elvira carried on her hip like a practised young mother. The two women greeted each other as long-lost sisters, hugging and crying and chattering excitedly in Spanish. They were shown into the house, a one-room breeze-block structure with clean-swept packed-dirt floors. In one corner, a small table and some chairs, and along the facing wall, six stacked mattresses. A sheet hanging from a rope screened off the other part of the house.

The young man sat where he was told to. He sipped the hot, sweet tea provided, smiled at the children who surrounded him and laughed each time they reached to touch his hair and whispered *pelo de oro* to each other. His mother opened their cases and presented blankets, pots, pans, paper and pens, books and toys for the children, clothes and warm jackets for the winter, one after the other, as if it were Christmas. The young man sat and watched her and looked at the faces of the family members as they examined the gifts. They stayed an hour, their driver waiting outside in his taxi. And then it was time to go. His mother chattered through her tears, kissed each of the children and embraced her counterpart. Then she got into the taxi. She waved as they pulled away, the family lined up in front of their little house, laundry flapping on the line nearby, and she kept waving until well after they and the small village they were part of had disappeared in the haze and nothing remained but the long expanse of the cold-current coastal plain.

Eventually, she stopped waving, and then turned back and sat looking out the front window. 'Rhys would have loved this,' she said.

'Would have,' said the young man.

March 7th. Still on the way to Geneva

I push the seat back as far as it will go and try to retreat further towards the fuselage. I am now crammed up against the window. For the past hour, I have been in uninterrupted physical contact with the woman in the seat next to me. The soft dough of her hip and arm flows unimpeded across the frontier of the armrest, invading the small rectilinear space my company is paying me to inhabit for these two hours. In any other situation, this would be categorised as sexual harassment. Me the perpetrator, of course. I should have asked for an aisle.

Now she is watching a movie. I glance over at her screen. Some female superhero is beating the shit out of a bunch of dim-witted villains in a scene of perfectly choreographed emasculation. With her superior strength and skill, she dispatches one with a straight right to the face, decapitates another with one cut of her sword and chokes out a third with a flying triangle between her slender thighs. They are a lot bigger than her, burly Special Forces archetypes with thick shoulders, close-cut beards and dark clothing, but they are no match for her.

I pull myself away from my neighbour's movie and open my father's manuscript to the last story I've read. So my uncle's name is Rhys. Was. It's pretty clear that by the time my dad goes to Peru with his mother — something he never told me about; or if he did, I didn't listen — Rhys is gone. Gone where? Mental asylum? Runaway? Lying in a hospital somewhere in a coma? Dead? I feel as if I am looking at my life through a mirror, as if my father is writing not about his life, but mine. As if our lives are — were — two parallel yet intersecting timelines, one now ended, the other, mine, sputtering along still, into some indeterminate future.

I am suddenly overcome with something I can only describe as melancholy — a word he would have used. Reflection comes, although I do not want it. I try to push it away.

I am forty years old. Divorced. My only daughter hates me. She tells me so each time I see her. She is only ten. I sell insurance products to companies that hope they'll never need them. In six years at the firm, I have received just the one promotion. My back bears the trample scars of the women who've been quota'd up to partner ahead of me, five of them now. Better pay, bigger offices, nicer cars, business-class travel, despite less experience and, in all cases but one, poorer sales performances. Hell, I even covered for two of them a few years back when they went off on mat' leave. Worked time and a half for over a year. It isn't at all how I thought it would be. Not how he said it would be.

And now, of course, there's Constantina. The bright spot. Every time I see her, she tells me she loves me. She wants to get married. She wants to have children with me. Four, she says. Four. Every time I think about it, panic rises in my chest, quakes through the muscles of my shoulders and neck. I take a deep breath, fill my lungs slowly and deliberately. The woman plastered against me glances over at me for a second, then goes back to her movie misandry.

I've tried this once already and failed. The thought of doing it again, knowing what I know now, fills me with dread, even though I know that Constantina is not Maria. Of course, it was different in my dad's time, when I was a child, watching him and Mum and learning how these things worked. But that was a long time ago. After two decades of determined social re-engineering, I am now expected to be something I am not, to perform a function for which I am neither physically built, nor mentally wired. I am not gentle. I don't hear the baby's cry. The sound does not dig through my stomach like Maria always described it doing to her. It certainly does not get the milk flowing. I sleep right through it. One time, Maria came home early one morning from a business trip and there was me sleeping off a dozen rye and Cokes and Rachel bawling her eyes out, not fed and with her diaper full. Maria dumped a bucket of cold water over me and stood there screaming at me for at least fifteen minutes, until I thought she was going to blow a vocal cord or pop a blood vessel in her face. Then she stood there and, step by step, made me change my daughter's diaper, warm the bottle and sit and feed her. And the whole time, all I could think was, You might as well geld me, you bitch. *I have never felt so humiliated. It wasn't the actions, the caring. I'd done all that many times before. And I loved my daughter – I love her now, more than I can express or understand, so much it hurts. It was something else. The enforcement, maybe, the smug oversight. The assumption that it wasn't enough just to do it, I also had to obliterate myself, to become something I was not. I remember leaving the house as soon as I'd finished feeding Rachel, getting on my bike, tearing down to the dojo and beating the shit out of the heavy bag for an hour. Then some bloke came along who wanted to spar and we went at it tooth and tong for at least ten rounds, until he caught me with a spinning side kick to the ribs that stunned me, and a left hook that put me down and had me seeing stars. It was then, afterwards, in the bar, that I said to myself: I am gone. I don't give a shit how much money you make compared to me, or what the expectations of men are now. And I don't care how beautiful you are, or about this fantastic life we seem to lead, with the nice cars and this house in Kew and the holidays to Mauritius and St Barts with all your other banker friends. I am not made for this. OK, so it only took me another three years. And it was Maria who kicked me out in the end. Could never quite bring myself to do it. But it was a relief when she told me to go. Does love only go so far?*

Texas

In the nineteenth year of his life, the young man, who was not yet an engineer but was on the road to becoming one, went south to work in the oilfields of Texas. He lied to US customs officials at the border and two days later arrived in Brownwood on the Greyhound from Abilene. It was a Tuesday in June, and the temperature had hit a hundred and five. He rented a room in the attic of a house in the old part of town down by the river. It was a big wood-sided place with gardens front and back, surrounded by big cottonwoods. The old lady who owned the place offered it him for a hundred and fifty a month, which was what he made in two days working in the oilfields.

On the rigs, the new guys got all the shit jobs. On his first day, the young man scrubbed oil from well heads and valves and risers using a brush and a can of solvent. He scrubbed for eleven and a half hours with a half-hour for lunch. Come evening, he had a raging headache and was covered in oil from his eyeline to the soles of his boots. He tried to wash the oil from his work clothes and purge the solvent from his skin, but no matter how much detergent he used, no matter how much he scrubbed, the oil, the thick green paraffin and the polychlorinated ethylenes clung on. That night, he took a handful of aspirin and lay in the steel-framed bed, listening to the insects in the trees and wondering if he'd made a big mistake coming here.

The next morning, he slid back into the same jeans and oil-soaked T-shirt and waited on the sidewalk in front of the house for his crew chief, Foy Lawson, to arrive and take him to the yard.

'Jeez, they sure have let that old place go,' said Foy, leaning across the bench seat to swing open the pickup's door.

'I like it,' said the young man.

'Where ya'll from again?' said Foy, hunched over the steering wheel. He had fair, greying hair and jacket-leather skin and wore a faded baseball cap that read Charlie Catherell Well Servicing on the front.

'Canada.'

'That's up north, ain't it?'

'North of Washington State.'

'I hear it's winter pretty much all year round up there,' said Foy. His teeth were stained from chewing tobacco, and several were oddly shaped and badly decayed. 'Ya'll got Eskimos and all?'

The young man smiled. 'Where I'm from on the west coast, it snows maybe a couple of times a year. But yes, in the Arctic, we have Eskimos.'

'And ya'll are a separate country?'

'The Queen is our head of state.'

'Queen?'

'Elizabeth the Second.'

Foy ruminated on this awhile. They had had an almost identical conversation the previous morning as they drove to the yard. 'Well, I'll be damned,' he said as they bumped over the rail crossing on the outskirts of town.

'He's like a Messican,' said Rodney, the other roustabout, from the back seat. 'Come here to work illegal.' He had dark hair, strangely pallid skin, and a borderline cleft lip that made him slur his words.

'Hell, look at him, Rodney,' said Foy, spitting from the open window. 'He ain't no wetback.'

'Iceback, more like,' said Earl Lawson, Foy's son and second-in-charge. He was fair-haired like his father, had winter-sky eyes, and looked to be about the same age as the young man.

Every member of the rig crew was missing at least one finger. Foy was missing three: both baby fingers, and the middle finger of his left hand at the second knuckle.

'And you just keep your mouth shut about it, Rodney,' said Foy. 'None of us is wantin' any trouble. You hear me, boy?'

'Well, he sure talks funny,' said Rodney.

'Not everyone talks like you, Rodney,' said Earl.

Rodney tucked his chin to his chest, mumbled something.

That day, they drove to a well site seventy miles west of Brownwood. The country was flat and dry, and there were pumpjacks spaced every quarter of a mile for as far as you could see in every direction. The temperature on the cab's digital display read one hundred and six degrees Fahrenheit.

Foy said the wells in this part of the country were old and were only producing a few barrels a day each, now, but still made money. The oil here was rich in paraffin, which gummed up the piping and slowed production, and so every few months they needed to come and pull out the tubing and the rods, clean them off and surge the well to get production back up.

They pulled into a lease tucked in behind a low rise in the otherwise flat country. Foy positioned the truck-mounted rig and dismantled the pumpjack, and then they tripped out. The completion string was made up of twenty-nine-foot lengths of steel pipe screwed together, end on end. Extracting, uncoupling and laying down a section of pipe took the four-man crew about five minutes.

The young man spent the day catching the free end of each section of pipe as it was removed from the tongs, and guiding it on to the pipe racks. He would then unscrew the lifting stub with a hand wrench, walk the lifting line back to the well head and screw the stub into the next section of pipe. A dozen sections in an hour, hour after hour. Around midday they stopped work and ate lunch, sitting on the ground with their backs against the rig's tyres, pushing themselves into the thin wedge of shade thrown by the derrick. It was tough work, and dirty, but a lot better than scrubbing parts.

Driving home that day the young man asked Foy why they were all missing fingers.

'How long you fixin' to work the rigs?' said Foy.

'Half a year, if I can,' said the young man. 'I'm hoping to go back to university next year to keep working on my engineering degree.'

'Engineers don't know nothin',' said Rodney.

'Don't you pay him no attention,' said Foy to the young man. 'He ain't right in the head.'

'They ain't nothin' wrong with my head,' said Rodney.

'Shut up, Rodney,' said Earl.

Foy drove on for a time and after they passed through Santa Anna, he raised his left hand and said: 'This here finger I lost to a chain wrap four years ago near Galveston. The one next to it got crushed laying down pipe like you been doing today, don't recall how many years gone now. 'Fore I had Earl, I reckon. Tell him, Earl.'

Earl raised his right hand. 'Got caught in the slips and ripped clean off. Never did find it.'

The young man, realising he'd asked a stupid question, thought of apologising, but thought that would make it worse. So he kept quiet, tried to be respectful.

'My finger got chewed up in the tongs,' said Rodney. 'Just last year.'

'Plain stupid,' said Foy. 'I done told you, but you wouldn't listen. Your own damned fault.'

Rodney hunched his shoulders as if to hide his face. 'Six months, you'll be no different t'us, iceback,' he mumbled.

They worked on the same well for the rest of the week, then Foy gave them the weekend off. Saturday morning, the young man slept late, but was finally driven from his bed by the heat. He dressed and went down to the garden, waded through the chest-high grass and climbed the steps to the front door of the old house. The windows were all closed and shuttered. He knocked on the door. After a while, the old lady answered. She held the door ajar and peered out at him from the darkness through narrowed eyes. Morning lit her face. She looked much older than she had when he'd first met her.

'Good morning, ma'am,' he said. 'I'm sorry to disturb you.'

'Yes? What is it?' She seemed not to recognise him.

'Well, ma'am, I was wondering if I could cut the grass for you?' He stood back so she could look past him. 'It's my day off, and I'd be happy to do it.'

'I'm obliged,' she said, clearing her throat. 'But we have a man who comes and does it for us, now that my Emerson is no longer able.'

The young man glanced over his shoulder. 'When was the last time he was here, ma'am?'

'I pay him to tend to the garden twice a month,' she said.

'Pardon me for saying, ma'am, but it doesn't look like anyone's been here for a long time.'

The old lady peered out at him. 'It's Warren, isn't it?'

'Yes, ma'am.'

She opened the door a bit more and peered past him. 'Well, my word,' she said. 'It does look a state.'

'I'd be happy to do it for you,' he said. 'No charge.'

She smiled, revealing straight ivory teeth, and asked him to wait. She closed the door and a few minutes later reappeared. She had donned a wide-brimmed hat with a yellow ribbon, but with the same housecoat and mismatched slippers. She led him through the back garden to an old garage. Like the house, the garage looked as if it hadn't been painted in decades. In places, the paint had almost completely peeled away, revealing patches of bare, worm-tracked wood. The old lady fumbled through a ring of keys, trying at least half a dozen before finding the right one. The young man swung open the door.

'I haven't opened this place up in years,' the old lady said. 'Not since my Emerson died.' Her accent was Southern, but not nearly as broad and difficult to understand as those of the men he worked with.

'Your husband?'

She smiled and nodded. 'Thirty-two years we were married. We met at university in Austin, right after the war. He was an engineer and I was studying English literature.'

'What kind of engineer was he?'

'He was in France with the Army Engineers in the war. Then he studied mechanical engineering. Anything with wheels, he loved.'

'I'm going to be an engineer,' said the young man. He'd become used to thinking this, now that the childhood dreams were all gone.

The old lady smiled. 'Well, you're more than welcome to anything you find,' she said. 'Just a bunch of old junk in here. Could never bear to part with anything, my Emerson. I kept meaning to clean it out, but the years went by – I don't rightly know just where – and, well, I never quite got around to it.'

The old lady reached for a light switch. It was one of the old kind, with a big circular housing and toggle switch and the old insulated wiring he'd seen in his grandfather's cottage on the lake, as a boy. To his surprise, the light came on.

The garage was full of junk. Every square inch of floor space was covered. A vehicle of some kind hulked in the middle of the floor under a dust-covered tarpaulin. There were at least two motorbikes that he could see, tucked away at the back, similarly draped in old canvas tarpaulins. Machine parts scattered the floor, along with stacks of car tyres and what looked to be a big-block V8 engine up on a trestle. Wooden shelving trellised the walls, floor to rafters, stuffed with junk. A workbench ran all along one side, heaped with tools and jars and mouse-eaten cardboard.

'Thank you for offering to do the garden,' said the old lady. 'I expect I've let the place run down a bit. After David was killed, my Emerson spent more and more time in here, and less and less looking after the place. Never knew what he got up to. Just sat here, I reckon, smoking himself to death.'

'I'm sorry, ma'am,' said the young man, meaning it, and thinking that this old lady would understand that he meant it and that he was not just being polite.

'There's a mower in here somewhere,' she said. 'You'll just have to do some looking around.' The old lady smiled and touched his shoulder, then turned and walked away. She walked slowly, befitting her age, but he thought there was a certain grace to the way she moved, an echo.

After rummaging for a while, the young man found some old

shears, a box of rusty files and an old-fashioned oil can. He went outside and sat in one of the old wooden garden chairs, where he got the shears working and sharpened the blades. The tallest grass was too much for any mower, so he set to it with the shears, stacking the sheaves of dry grass in bundles by the fence as he went. It was hot work and he didn't have gloves, and after a while his thumbs were blistered on the inside near the big knuckles. At lunchtime, the old lady brought him a sandwich and a glass of ice-cold lemonade.

After eating, he returned to the garage. He found the old gasoline-powered mower near the back, covered by one of the canvas tarps. To his surprise, it looked in good condition – there was no rust and it appeared to have been stored with care. It didn't take him long to get it running, roughly at first, with big puffs of blue smoke, and then gradually more cleanly. By sunset, he'd finished cutting the front lawn, raked up the cut grass, and swept the now-visible front path.

He showered and was lying on his bed reading *War and Peace* when he heard a car horn blare. He kept reading. Again, the same horn, three times. A jacked-up orange Dodge Charger was idling out on the street. Earl Lawson was at the wheel, Rodney next to him in the passenger seat.

'Come on down, iceback,' shouted Earl. 'It's Saturday night. We's goin' cruisin'.'

The young man, recognising this as one of those times when he needed to overcome his natural desire for solitude, gave the thumbs up and closed the window. He pulled on jeans and a collared shirt, checked his appearance in the mirror above the sink and walked down to the waiting car. As he approached, Rodney got out of the car, and without looking up, opened the back door and sat in the back seat.

'Nice car,' said the young man.

'Big block 440 with dual hemi carbs,' said Earl, gunning the engine. 'Fastest in town.' With an opened beer in hand, he started the car rumbling down the street. 'Place looks different,' he said.

'They should tear that old place down,' said Rodney. 'They say it's haunted.'

'Now who says it's haunted, Rodney?'

'People.'

'Who?'

'People, is all.'

'Well I been livin' in this town my entire life and I reckon you is plain makin' that up, Rodney.'

'I ain't makin' nothin' up, Earl. Old Mister Parkins, for one. He reckons the old lady talks to ghosts. He says he goes on past there sometimes and he can hear her in there talkin' to 'em.'

'Missin' a few planks on the front porch, I reckon. You and him both.' Earl glanced at the young man and flashed a grin. 'Now just pass up a Lone Star, Rodney, and stop talkin' shit.' He said it *she-it*.

Rodney rummaged and passed a can to Earl.

'Not for me,' Earl said, pushing it away. 'For him, stupid.'

The young man took the beer. It was ice cold.

At the lights, Earl nudged up to the white line, stopped the car and took a swig of beer. He revved the big V8. The car torqued, settled.

'Well you gonna open it?' said Earl.

The young man looked at the can of beer. 'What if the police stop us?'

Earl laughed. 'What if they do? This is Texas. I ain't drunk. Not as yet, anyhow. You drunk, Rodney?'

'I reckon I is, Earl.'

The lights changed and Earl gunned the engine. The tyres screamed and the young man was slammed back into his seat as the car fishtailed in a cloud of smoke. Rodney whooped as they accelerated down the street. Earl looked over and grinned. Unlike his father, he had great teeth. The young man opened his beer and took a long drink. Soon, they were cruising down the main strip. They passed a group of girls in tight jeans and halter tops standing outside the movie theatre. Earl gave the horn a blast and the girls flashed white smiles. One of them waved. Earl finished his beer and tossed the can into the back seat. Rodney passed him up another.

'How you likin' it so far?' said Earl, opening the beer. 'Texas, I mean.'

'Good. I like the work.'

Rodney puffed in the back seat.

'Y'all married?' said Earl.

'No. Are you?'

Earl nodded. 'Four kids.'

'That's great,' said the young man.

'Got hitched the year I dropped outta school. Becky-May was sixteen, I was seventeen.'

The young man turned and hooked his arm over the seat back. 'What about you, Rodney, you married?'

Rodney tucked his chin to his chest the way he did and puffed out his cheeks.

'Don't mind him,' said Earl. 'He's sore on account of he can't find hisself a woman.'

'I had me plenty of women,' said Rodney, cracking another beer.

'Yeah, when?'

'In the navy, that's when.'

Earl looked over at the young man. 'Two years at Dee, Texas, in the spare-parts department. Bet the girls were fallin' all over you, Rodney.'

'They sure was, Earl.'

'Sure, Rodney,' said Earl.

They left the main drag and rumbled through a neighbourhood of run-down houses. After a while, Earl slowed the car and turned into a dirt driveway in front of a small wood-frame house. There was a screened veranda out front and a couple of trees shading the driveway. Lights shone inside. A Texas flag hung in one of the windows, lone star up.

'Y'all's invited for supper,' said Earl, getting out of the car. 'Becky-May's especting y'all.'

Earl's wife was petite and pretty. She had long dark hair that she wore pulled back, and lovely dark eyes. She couldn't have been much older than twenty-one, but there were blue half-moons under her eyes and the first lines had started to take hold around the corners. They shook hands and she said 'hi' to Rodney as if she'd known him all her life. The young man and Earl and Rodney sat down at the table. Becky-May set a casserole dish in the middle, brought four cold beers and sat down.

'We is awful glad you could join us,' she said. 'You bein' new here in Brownwood 'n' all. We don't get many visitors.'

The young man thanked her and wished Earl had told him he was invited for dinner, so he could have brought something – a bottle of wine or flowers for the house.

'The kids are all in bed, so we should have some peace.' She served him first, then Rodney and her husband and then herself. 'So Earl tells me y'all is educated.'

The young man, who was fluent in two languages, competent in two others and had excelled in high-school physics and math and chemistry and was two years into an engineering degree, shook his head and said: 'No, ma'am but I'm trying.'

'He's here workin' illegal,' said Rodney.

'Shut up, Rodney,' said Earl.

Becky-May glanced at her husband. 'Myself, I never got the chance to finish my schoolin' on account of my kids comin' along a little earlier than I would'a hoped for.' She reached for the casserole dish. 'When my littlest gets a bit older, I'm fixin' to do a secretarial course down at the college, maybe part time. Would ya'll like seconds?'

'Please,' said the young man.

She helped him to more. 'I reckon you must have travelled some, then?' she said.

'A little.'

'Tell me some of the places you've been,' she said.

'I went to Europe with my parents when I was eleven. France and England and Denmark.'

'You hear that, Earl? He's been to Europe. Ain't he lucky?'

The young man paused, unsure whether to continue.

Becky-May smiled at him, sipped her beer.

'My old man always used to say, we don't have a lot of money, but what we have, we spend on doing things, not having things.'

'I like that,' said Becky-May. 'Doin' things, not having things. You hear that, Earl?' She took another, longer swig of her beer. 'Where else you been?'

'My old man took us to Panama one year, for Christmas, to visit his best friend.'

'Panama. Where's that, exactly?'

'It's in Central America.'

She thought about this a while and then said: 'I ain't never been outside of Texas. Neither has Earl. What do you think about that?'

'I been outside Texas,' said Rodney before the young man could begin thinking of an answer.

'Yeah, where?' said Earl.

'El Paso.'

'El Paso is in Texas, stupid,' said Earl.

'Earl,' said Becky-May.

Earl took a long drink, crushed the can and threw it into the kitchen. 'Well he is.'

'Earl,' said Becky-May.

'Iceback here is lodgin' over at the old Jackson place,' said Earl, forking a mouthful of macaroni and ground beef into his mouth. He held his fork in a reverse grip with the knuckles facing the table and the stub of his missing baby finger pointing up.

Becky-May shook her head. 'Sad what happened to that family. Losin' three sons like they did. Mind you, it was a long time ago now.'

'Does she have anyone left?' said the young man.

'None that I know of,' said Becky-May, a deep frown creasing her face. 'The first one died when he was small. They say he drowned in the river not far from the bridge. He never got a chance to go anywhere, either.'

She was staring right at him. The young man looked away.

'Davey was the youngest,' said Earl. 'He was killed over in Vietnam.' He put down his fork and wiped the corner of his mouth with the thumb and forefinger of his left hand.

The young man said nothing.

'I remember going to the funeral,' said Becky-May. 'The whole town showed up. Fifteen boys we lost over there from Brownwood. I remember feeling so sad for their mothers.'

'Was ya'll's country in the war?' said Earl.

'No, we were opposed to it.'

Rodney grunted, glanced at Becky-May.

'A few Canadians volunteered, though, went to fight.'

Earl cleaned his plate and stood. 'Come on,' he said. 'I'll show you my guns.'

⋀

The next day, Sunday, the young man finished cutting the grass around the house. In the evening, he walked into the centre of town, where he found the Vietnam cenotaph and read the name of David S. Jackson carved into the red granite. In the east buttress of the Main Street bridge, he found a small brass plaque that read: Joseph S. Jackson, born 1946, died 1950.

That week they did workovers on two wells west of town. Foy told the young man to replace Rodney on the power tongs for a spell, so he could learn. Rodney puffed out his cheeks and protested that after all, he'd been roustabout for over six months before he'd been given a chance to work the tongs. Foy told him to shut up, and Rodney spent the rest of the day sulking.

The next day, when they arrived at the site and got ready to trip in, Rodney had resumed his position on the tongs. The young man took station near the pipe rack to continue his role as low man on the team, laying down pipe.

'What you doin' boy?' said Foy.

Rodney looked perplexed. 'You talking to me, Foy?'

'Well I'm lookin' right at ya, ain't I, Rodney?'

'I'm gettin' ready to trip, Foy. Like you said.'

'Now, I don't recall tellin' you to shift back on to them tongs, Rodney.'

Rodney pulled in his neck so that his shoulders almost met his ears. 'The iceback done had his go at it yesterday,' he said.

'Well he's gonna have another go at it today,' said Foy. 'And he'll keep doin' it till I says he stops. You got that, Rodney?'

Rodney thought this through a while. 'Well it just ain't fair, Foy,' he puffed. 'Me bein' Texan, born and bred, and him, well, not.'

Foy took a couple of deep breaths, then stepped down from the control platform and stood glaring at Rodney. 'Born and bred stupid is what you is,' he said.

Rodney hung his head.

Foy frowned. 'Now be a good boy, Rodney, and do as I say, would ya? We got a lot a work to do.'

Rodney shrugged, pursed his lips and puffed out his cheeks again, but he stepped away from the tongs, walked over to where the young man was standing and grabbed the stub wrench from his hand.

Each morning, Rodney would stand at the tongs, ready to work, and each time he and Foy would repeat a new version of the same conversation, always with the same result, the young man taking the higher place in the rig's hierarchy. Their work rate as a crew had improved, Foy said, as they drove home. He kept everyone in the same roles for the rest of the week.

That weekend, the young man asked the old lady if he could paint the house. She seemed surprised, but agreed, giving him two dollars for paint. He walked into town and bought two ten-gallon pails of Cape Cod grey, two gallons of white for the trim and two brushes and a roller and tray at the local hardware store for twenty-eight fifty. He worked through the day, scraping away the old, thickly layered paint, the peelings falling to the ground like years. By evening, the front and one side of the house were scraped clean. The sun set, and a cool breeze blew in from the high country to the north. The young man sat outside and ate some leftover cold chicken and drank a beer. As he was eating, the old lady appeared from the side door with a tray. He jumped up and put on his shirt and went to help her.

He set the tray on a small garden table and pulled up a chair for her. She was wearing a dark dress and had her hair up in some kind of scarf. She had applied lipstick, too, but it looked as if she'd done it without using a mirror.

'There is a letter for you,' she said, handing him an envelope. 'It wasn't posted. Someone must have slipped it through the slot last night.' His name was typed on the front using an old typewriter. There was no return address.

He thanked her and stashed the letter in his pocket.

She poured lemonade and handed him a slice of watermelon. 'It's so nice to have a young man around the house,' she said. 'It makes me feel quite alive again.'

The young man drank. The lemonade was ice cold and not too sweet. He wanted to ask her about her sons, about her husband and their life together, the places she'd seen and the things she'd done, about what she liked to read, who her favourite authors were. But none of it seemed right or respectful. What he said was: 'I'll paint this side tomorrow. And next weekend I should be able to do the front.'

She looked up at the house, the bare wood showing through in big bone-grey patches. 'I see your friends picking you up each morning,' she said. 'And you walking into town for groceries and the like. You don't have a car?'

'No, ma'am. Back home, I ride a motorcycle.'

'My David rode a motorcycle. Emerson got them riding when they were young.' Her voice sounded as if it had come over miles. 'David's motorbike is still in the garage, I think. You are welcome to it, if you want it.'

He took a breath, surprised. 'That's very kind of you, ma'am. But I'm just fine. I like walking.'

She stood and reached for his hand. 'Let's go and take a good look at it,' she said. 'I'd like to see it again. He always looked so dashing on it, so manly.'

He followed her to the garage. She switched on the light.

'That one, at the back,' she said, pointing.

The young man worked his way to the back of the garage towards the dark shape. 'This one?'

She nodded. He pulled the tarp away.

The young man stood for a moment, unable to speak. It was if he had pushed open the slab on a burial chamber, a Pharaoh's tomb. There, in the half light, up on blocks, was an immaculately preserved vintage Harley Davidson. It had one of the big twin-V Shovelhead engines, the old bicycle style seat and big maroon square-cut fenders. He looked up at the old lady. Pride glowed in her eyes.

'I would be most heartily gratified if you would make use of it,' she said. 'I think David would be pleased.'

The young man cleared a path along one side of the garage and wheeled the bike outside into the night. He put it up on its kickstand. The tyres were deflated, but otherwise the bike looked in perfect condition. They stood and admired it in the dim light coming from the open garage.

'David rode it all the way to California and back just before he shipped overseas,' she said. 'It was the last time he used it. My Emerson put it away after...' She paused, breathed awhile. 'After.' The old lady stood there looking at the motorcycle as a crescent moon rose over the rooftops.

After a while the young man said: 'I don't think I could, ma'am. It wouldn't be right.'

She took his hand. 'You hush now,' she whispered. 'I've asked my Emerson and he agrees that it's what David would have wanted.' She nodded. 'Yes. You have it.'

That night, the young man lay in bed and thought about the bike and its previous owner, the circumstances of his death and the old lady's life. He realised that she couldn't be much more than sixty-five.

She looked so much older. And though he was young still, he knew, closely and in detail, how death stole years from the living.

Later, he opened the letter. It was typewritten, like the address on the envelope. It said: *Leave town. We know you are here illegal. If you stay, the cops will hear about it.* There was no signature. He slid it back into the envelope and put it on the table beside his bed. He read deep into the night and tried not to think about the letter or its author or the motorcycle or the old lady's tragedies.

Early next morning, he opened the garage and inspected the bike. He found an old oil pan and some rags, then drained the crankcase and inspected the plugs and the chain. There was an ancient hand pump in the garage which he used to inflate the tyres. He walked to a nearby gas station and bought a can of gasoline and a couple of quarts of thirty-weight motor oil. It was just after ten o'clock when he straddled the bike for the first time. He flipped out the starter lever, gave the throttle a twist and gave it a kick. The engine fired first time. A throaty Harley roar ripped through the quiet Sunday street.

He put the bike in gear and started it down the driveway. It was a big machine, and heavy, but it was well balanced and smooth. Soon he was rumbling down the pre-war streets of the town, past the Eisenhower-era store fronts along Main Street and then, further out, through the bright primary-colour wonderland of Exxon and McDonalds, Burger King and K-Mart. He turned on to the pike and opened the throttle. The bike powered ahead, the cracked and fraying LBJ-era concrete unspooling beneath him, burnt yellow fields a blur to each side, the heat haze on the horizon pierced by the disappearing highway. He came to a bridge over a small creek lined with willows and ash. He stopped and put the bike on its stand, then ran his hand through his hair and stretched his legs a while. It was a beautiful machine. Could he accept it? He didn't have enough money to pay her what it was probably worth, not if he wanted to go back to university in the fall. She'd said she wanted him to have it. But did she even know what she was offering?

He rode on for another half-hour or so and then turned back.

It was mid-afternoon by the time he turned into the driveway of the old house. The old lady was waiting for him, sitting in a garden chair on the newly mowed and trimmed lawn. He rolled the bike to a stop, killed the engine, dismounted and strode towards her. As he got closer, he could see she was crying.

He crouched beside her, took her hand. 'Are you alright, ma'am?' he said.

She looked up at him and wiped her cheeks with her hands. 'David,' she said. 'I heard you leave this morning. I was taking a little nap. When I heard your bike, I thought I must have been dreaming. But it's you.'

'Mrs Jackson, it's me. Warren.' He looked into her eyes, sought recognition, held her hand there in the garden.

'I'm so pleased you've found a nice girl,' she said. 'You know I always wanted grandchildren.'

'Mrs Jackson, I think you've been dreaming.'

She looked into his eyes and squeezed his hand. 'Seeing you ride in just now, well, it's the happiest I've been in years.'

He stayed with her for a while and then walked her back to the house.

⋀

The next morning, the young man again rose early and packed his work clothes and boots into a small backpack and rode the motorcycle to the yard. He went to Foy Lawson's office and asked to be put back on pipe-laydown duty for a while. He was having a coffee in the crew room when Rodney and Earl arrived.

'Whose hog is that out front?' said Earl.

'The old lady I'm renting from,' said the young man. 'It was her son's. She said if I could get it running, I could use it. I'm going to get it licensed and insured this week.'

'Save you walking through nigger town on yo' lonesome?' said Rodney. 'Well ain't that nice.'

'Nice bike,' said Earl.

'Well, it ain't right, to my thinkin',' said Rodney.

'Since when you done any thinking, Rodney?' said Earl, looking at the young man. 'He's just pissed on account of he don't own a car, and can't drive anyhow since he got DWI'd.'

Rodney glared at the young man. 'Takin' avantage of an old lady livin' all on her lonesome. He cuts her grass and she gives him a Harley? No, sir. Sets a fella wonderin' what else he's doin' for her, if you get my meanin'.'

The young man walked up and stood square in front of Rodney. He looked him straight in the eyes. 'Don't say things like that, Rodney. It just makes you sound stupid.'

Rodney tensed, and for a moment, the young man thought he might throw a punch, but instead he hunched up his shoulders and stepped back. 'You hear that, Earl?' he puffed. 'Iceback here called me stupid.'

'That ain't what he said, Rodney,' said Earl. 'He said ya'll is making yo' own self *sound* stupid, not that you *was* stupid.'

'Well they ain't no difference,' said Rodney.

'Well I suppose they ain't,' said Earl. 'Now shut up and start loading the trailer, both of youse.'

They loaded the long trailer, stacking lengths of pumping rod, ninety-four in all, and securing them at each end with belt strapping. Neither spoke. They drove to a well site east of Santa Anna. Foy put Rodney back on tongs. It was mid-summer now and the days were long, temperatures in the high nineties and occasionally well into the hundreds. The young man kept his mouth shut and worked hard; and in the evenings, he rode the Shovelhead back to the old house and showered and read and slept and did it all again the next day.

Weeks passed. There were no more anonymous letters. On his days off, the young man finished painting the house and started on the garage and took long rides out into the flat-baked country of the plain.

And then, one morning, Foy called them together in the office and said that they had landed a special job up near Abilene. A good client of theirs was planning to sell off part of one of their fields. Ten deep wells needed complete workovers. Normally, it would have taken them two weeks. But the work needed to be done in a week to meet the sale deadline. They would have to work eighteen-hour days. He was offering them time and a half for anything over twelve hours a day. They all agreed.

'And Rodney, I'm putting you back on the rack,' Foy said. 'We work a hell of a lot faster with Warren on tongs, and you know it. We don't make the deadline, we don't get paid.'

The first few days went well. They were ahead of schedule and the young man could tell that Foy was pleased. Then, as they were loading up one day, a police car drove into the yard and rolled to a stop outside the office. Two deputies got out of the car and walked towards the work shed.

'We're looking for a Foy Lawson,' one of the cops said. He wore a black gun belt strapped around his waist and a big Stetson. Sergeant's stripes creased his shirtsleeves.

'That'd be me,' said Foy, wiping his hands on a rag. 'What can I do for you fellas?'

The cop flipped open his notebook. 'We have a report of an alien working illegally on your premises.'

The young man could feel himself reddening.

'Well this would be him right here,' said Foy, pointing at the young man. 'He's workin' for us alright, officers.'

The cops took a step forwards. The one with the Stetson started pulling a set of handcuffs from a pouch on his belt.

'But the thing is,' said Foy, tucking the rag into his back pocket, 'we ain't payin' him nothin'. He's studying engineering back in Canada where he comes from, and he's volunteering, so to speak, to get experience. Pays his own way entire. Nothin' illegal in that, so far as I know.'

The cops looked at each other a moment. Silver cuffs dangled in the sergeant's hand.

'Y'all can eyeball our books if you like, officers.' Foy pointed to his office.

'Well, if that's the case, I don't see a problem,' said the sergeant, tipping his hat back on his head. 'We'll check back with the lieutenant. If we need to, we'll call in again.'

'Any time,' said Foy.

After the officers had driven away, Foy turned and faced Rodney and looked at him hard. 'That was just the plain stupidest thing you ever done, Rodney Early.'

Rodney shrank back. 'I don't get yo' meanin', Foy,' he said.

'I mean tellin' the police about Warren here workin' with us.'

'I never done it, Foy,' said Rodney, eyes bulging.

Foy pulled the rag out of his pocket and threw it at Rodney. It hit him in the face. 'You don't get it, do you? If yo' pappy was alive, I'd call him right now, tell him to whop yo' ass. Stupidest thing you ever done and you done a lot.' Foy turned and walked to his office. He was at the doorway when he stopped and faced them again. 'It's our business that gets hurt, if the cops and whatnot come pokin' around. We could get fined, or just plain closed down. Then where you gonna work, Rodney Early? You think anyone else gonna hire you? You like you is? God's truth, if it weren't for that promise I made yo' pappy and us being related, so to speak…' He turned and walked into his office and slammed the door shut.

The young man walked outside and sat on the Shovelhead.

A while later, Foy reappeared, they finished loading the trailer and drove to Santa Anna. No one spoke on the way out. They worked eighteen hours, the young man still on tongs.

After work, back at the yard, Foy called him into his office. 'I'm payin' you cash,' he said. 'So there shouldn't be a problem for you, son.'

'I'm sorry about what happened, sir,' said the young man. 'I'll leave as soon as we finish this job.'

'That would be best,' said Foy, nodding, counting out the cash on his desk. 'Not how I want it, but the way it's gotta be.'

'I understand, sir.'

'You see, young Rodney, he's not right, and he got no one else to look after him.'

'I understand, sir. Thanks for the opportunity. I've learned a lot.'

Foy nodded. They shook hands.

Later that night, the young man woke from a dream. Someone was hammering at the door. He could hear wood splintering, and then a bang as the door broke open. He sat up, ran his hands over his chest. He was covered in sweat. The room was pierced by a strange, flickering yellow light. He stood and went to the window. A fire was burning on the driveway, near the garage. Bright orange flames reached into the night.

He jumped up and flew down the stairs. He attached the garden hose to the spigot at the side of the house, cranked the tap and ran towards the fire with the streaming hose. Twenty feet away, the heat was like a wall. He put his thumb over the end of the hose and directed the water at the base of the flames. The fire hissed as the water hit. Steam billowed yellow, lit by the flames. He doused himself in water and moved closer, keeping the jet of water steady at the base of the fire, hosing down the front of the garage to prevent the wood from igniting. Slowly, the fire abated. Shapes emerged. The square cut of a fender. A wheel rim.

It was the Shovelhead. David's beautiful Shovelhead.

By the time the fire department arrived, the fire was out. He stood with the old lady in the glare of the truck's floodlights and looked at the smoking skeleton. When the gas tank exploded, it had taken most of the front cylinder with it. The frame around the engine was melted, the wheel rims charred and warped. The old lady cried.

The next morning, the young man rose early, packed his few belongings and laid out a month's rent in cash on the dresser. He walked across town to the yard. When Foy arrived in the pickup with Earl and Rodney, he was waiting at the front gate. Earl got out of the truck and unlocked the gate and the young man walked with him to the shed.

'Where's yo' hog?' said Earl.

'Gone,' said the young man.

Rodney was standing near the job board with a cup of coffee. The young man walked up to him and hit him twice hard in the face. Rodney went down, his misshapen mouth leaking blood. The young man stood over him and looked into his eyes. But of what he'd hoped to see, there was nothing. He considered hitting him again and wanted to. But instead, he turned and walked to the front gate and along the pike to the bus station and took the next bus to Abilene.

March 7th. Geneva

It's early afternoon by the time the taxi drops me at the lakeside hotel. I check in, hang up my suit and shirt, stand out on the balcony and breathe in the cold air. The lake is shrouded with mist. A passenger ferry chugs towards the far side.

I think of him there as a young man. I remember vaguely hearing him mention Texas, working in the oilfields. All that's gone now, of course. I drove through there a few years ago, nothing but dead wells and silent, unmoving pumpjacks, miles and miles of them, everything used up and turned to rust, relics from another time.

My phone buzzes. An incoming text message. Maria's number. I open it, read. She wants to meet me as soon as I get back to London. She has made a decision. She has talked it over with Rachel and Troy. But she can't tell me this way. Despite everything, she owes it to me to tell me in person. That's it.

I close my phone and throw it on the bed. There has been a late change of plan and now I'm not due to meet with Borschmann until tomorrow morning. Never a good sign. I pull on my jacket and walk out to the quayside, start walking south, away from the city centre. The traffic along the corniche is heavy now, a countercurrent of white and red.

I have spent most of my life feeling vaguely misplaced, as if something elemental was missing. Let me try again: my life was not supposed to be like this. The conviction is as hard to shake as it is to explain. Wrong people, wrong places. Wrong me. And yet just thinking about it makes me feel guilty. I mean, by the time I was fifteen, I'd been all over, with Dad's work and the holidays we took together, especially when Mum and Adam were still around, and then that first year after Dad sent me to boarding school, we spent Christmas together. We went to Australia and snorkelled on the Great Barrier Reef. All those fish. The layered forests of

coral. We watched a dolphin chasing a shoal of trevally in the shallows.
I can still see the big smile on Dad's face under his mask, hear his cry of
delight as the dolphin came up for air between us. It was less than a year
after my mother went away and I recall thinking: you do not deserve
to be so happy.

I remember we saw a red-tailed tropicbird nesting under the low,
spreading branches of a grove of reef-side octopus trees. I read later that
this species lives at sea, spending weeks on the wing, returning to the
island to breed and nest every few years. The female lays one egg, and
the parents take turns staying with the chick after it hatches, feeding and
protecting it for up to four months. And then, one day, the chick is ready
to fly. Driven by hunger and instinct, it launches itself into the unknown.
The adults follow soon after.

Now, of course, the reef is mostly dead. All that we saw back then is
gone.

The feeling of displacement intensifies as darkness falls. It's colder now,
and I turn up my collar, wish I'd brought a hat. I keep going, walking
quickly now, feeling the cold air flowing through my lungs. I think about
Maria and Rachel. I wonder what she wants to tell me, what she has
decided. Maria is one of the things in my life that was never right.
Problem is, by the time I realised it, I'd lost the courage to do anything
about it.

There was a woman once, not nearly as beautiful as Maria, probably
not as smart. But lovely, so lovely, inside. Sweet and caring. Adventur-
ous in herself and encouraging of it in me. Julia was her name. Julia
McIntyre. It's been a long time since I've thought about her. I didn't know
her long – a year and a half maybe, during my last year of university.
I don't think I've ever been happier than I was then, heading out on a
camping trip, Julia snuggled up behind me on my old Honda 750, arms
around me, head on my back. Late one night, after we'd made love, lying
in that old two-man tent I still have but haven't used for years, she told
me she never wanted to turn off the flame she saw burning inside me.
That's what she said. I know now, too late, that she was perfect for me.
And the more I think about it, the more I realise that I knew it then. It

sure felt like that when we were together. But I wasn't brave enough. I let her go. I know I hurt her. I hurt myself. And now I'm here in Geneva, walking this darkened pathway alone, and while I should be preparing for this meeting tomorrow, the further I walk, the less important it seems.

I stop, light-headed, and look out across the lake, so cold and black now, the lights from the far shore skipping over the surface like throw-stones back when I was a kid and Dad took us to the coast of BC to visit my grandparents. I loved it there. Misty forests rising from the sea. Rocky islands and fjords, so deep and cold and black. Whirlpool Point where Grandpa and Dad would take me fishing for coho and chinook, up before dawn and into the boat, speeding along a coastline so deserted that it seemed the last untouched place in the world. And now I am here, in my fallback job, with my fallback life, and my fallback ex-wife has just summoned me to what I can't help feeling will be the start of an ending.

Yuruk

This morning, like every morning, has come cloudless and clear and scorching, and the sun burns through the curtains, so you can't sleep. Your watch shows just gone five-thirty, but the room is as bright as the long afternoons when the boys from the village sit smoking and talking under the acacias lining the road. Back home, you worship the sun, but here it is Satan, especially when, like now, you're hungover.

The twelve-year-old houseboy brings you breakfast, and you pay him with a hundred-lire note, telling him to keep the change. Eggs and bread and honey and goat's cheese and strong, sweet black tea and tomatoes – straight from the vine, so that the flavour explodes in your mouth. The meal would have cost ten times that back home. You sit on the veranda under the grapevines, listening to the doves in the trees and staring at the refinery. Gleaming distillation towers, storage tanks, miles of cable and pipe, and the two big orange flares that burn night and day. Beyond, the rooftops and minarets of the town, the occasional splash of green. You hardly notice the smell of sulphur and crude oil anymore. You carry it with you now, in your clothes and hair and skin, spliced into your DNA.

Veysil, your Kurdish driver, brings the car and you start the hundred-and-fifty mile drive out towards Şirnak, close to the border with Iraq. The war between Iran and Iraq has been going on for five years now, and millions are dead. You read stories in the Turkish newspapers about Iranian boys from poor families being chained together and forced to advance towards the Iraqi trenches. They walk ahead of the tanks to detonate the mines.

An hour later you come to a small village. It is market day and the main street is clogged with food stalls and people and animals and vehicles of every kind. Boys riding large tricycles weave through the confusion, their oversized baskets piled high with watermelons, plastic sandals, Sony cassette players. Veysil pushes the car into the traffic, blasting his horn, shouting out the window.

'Slow down,' you tell him. 'You're going to hit somebody.'

Veysil keeps going. He is a good driver, but impatient.

'No problem,' he says in Turkish. Like most Kurds, he speaks Turkish, too. 'These are my people.'

You are deep in the traditional heart of Kurdistan. Over the weeks, Veysil has told you much about his people and their struggle for their own homeland, for the right to educate their children in their own language. You suspect he is PKK.

Veysil accelerates, narrowly missing an old man.

You grab his arm. He glances over at you. 'Slow down,' you say again. As you do, the car's side mirror clips one of the tricycles. The contraption tips on to two wheels, balances there for a moment, then rights itself. A watermelon tumbles into the road. You watch the head-sized fruit bounce once, then smash into pieces on the kerb-side. Bright-red flesh spills across the melting tarmac.

'No problem,' says Veysil.

After Hasankeyf, the roads are slick and black with oil from the tanker trucks pouring in from across the border. Because of the war, the Gulf Sea shipping terminals are closed and Iraq must export its oil overland through Turkey. The car fishtails along the narrow road. Veysil seems to enjoy it. Yet again, you tell him to slow down. He bleeds ten kilometres an hour off the speed, keeps going.

By now, you are engaged to be married to a woman you do not love and who you suspect does not love you. The old dreams are nothing but distant echoes. You haven't thought about it for a long time, that other once-impossible life. As the blowtorch landscape speeds by, you remember Shelly and the things you told her you were going to do, the things you never told anyone else. You think of Julia McIntyre, about the fire not going out.

By the time you arrive in Şirnak, the car is black with oil. Everything reeks of Iraqi crude.

Later that evening, you are on the way back to the refinery. You are approaching Hasankeyf when a woman appears at the side of the road. She steps out from the verge in front of you and raises one arm in the air. Veysil slows the car. The woman is holding a little boy in her arms. His head hangs back limp, his mouth open, so that you can see the top row of little white teeth.

Veysil draws the car alongside. The woman speaks to him in excited Kurdish, raising her chin to point to a place on the road. The boy's head jerks loosely as she speaks. He is covered in oil and there is a big red gash near his temple. Blood drips from his head to the oil-soaked tarmac.

'What happened?' you ask Veysil.

'This boy was hit by an oil truck,' he says, then speaks to the woman. She answers.

'The truck did not stop, she says. It just kept going.'

'Tell her to get in,' you say. You recognise this as a time when you might be able to do something good, maybe change the direction of things in some small way. 'Where is the nearest hospital?'

Veysil gets out of the car and opens the door for the woman. 'Mardin,' he says. 'An hour from here.'

'Let's go,' you say.

The woman gets into the back seat and Veysil starts driving. He goes fast. The car swerves and slides on the oily surface. Veysil is enjoying this, you can tell. You think, sitting there in the passenger seat holding on to the door handle, as the dry sun-blasted landscape blurs past, that you are all going to die.

The woman holds the boy in her arms, rocking him gently, whispering to him, stroking his matted hair. Her hands are big and worn, her fingers long and brown with thick, cracked nails. The boy's face is so pale next to her hands. He doesn't move. You think he might be dead already, that the car will go off the road and you'll all be killed, and it will be for nothing.

'What was he doing so close to the road?' you say.

Veysil speaks to the woman. She answers. Her voice is thin, far away.

'One of his goats strayed,' says Veysil. 'They are Yuruk. Nomads. Kurds. They move across the borders between Iraq, Syria and Turkey with their animals. These kids don't understand cars and trucks. They don't go to school. They spend their lives in the mountains.'

They reach the hospital in a little under three-quarters of an hour. You go into the building with the woman and the boy. You're not sure why. Maybe it's because you want to feel like you are doing something, like you may be part of something good, that it may bring some solace, a measure of absolution. But the bastard at admissions doesn't speak Kurdish and can't understand the woman. Veysil translates. They piss around for half an hour taking down names and information. The hospital clerk asks for papers, but of course, they have none. No address, no identity cards. These people don't exist, as far as the government is concerned, says Veysil.

The woman becomes more and more hysterical. She is sobbing, rocking her son in her arms. The asshole behind the desk, you swear he starts to smile. Something goes critical inside you and you walk around the desk, and in your fury and frustration, you grab the prick by the collar and tell him in your best Turkish that he better get the hell moving or you'll go to his superiors. You cram a US one-hundred-dollar bill in the guy's face.

The doctor comes pretty quickly after that. They put the kid in a ward, run him an IV. Clean him up a bit. You hover, watch the staff work. You want your money's worth, goddamn it. The hospital is a mess. Dirt on the floors, flies everywhere. After a while, you walk outside with Veysil and wait in the parking lot, smoking cigarettes. It's about forty-five degrees in the shade.

A while later, the woman emerges from the hospital and walks to where you are standing. She says something to Veysil. She seems composed, has stopped crying. You congratulate yourself. It feels good. Some fraction of balance has been restored.

Veysil says a few words to the woman, and then turns to you and says: 'The boy died of internal bleeding. She asks if we can give her a ride back to her camp.'

Something closes up inside you. Some sense of hope, or justice.

March 8th. Geneva

I'm back in the hotel room after a long day over at Borschmann's offices. Went pretty well. I think I can pull this one off. They want to include a couple of other big assets and lower the deductible threshold, but I think we can accommodate them. I'll run some numbers after dinner. If I can nail this, they'll have to make me a partner. No one in the firm has ever brought in a deal this big.

I pour myself a whisky from the minibar, swirl the contents around the tumbler. The liquid barely covers the bottom of the glass. I open the minibar again and look for another whisky, but all I can find is vodka. I open one and pour it in. Outside, it's as dark as when I left this morning, another sunrise missed, another sunset ignored. I treat them as if there will always be more, rather than the moments of beauty and significance I realise they surely are whenever I actually watch one. I can't remember the last time I did.

I sit in the single armchair that faces the window and grab Dad's manuscript from the side table. I leaf through to the story I read last night in bed – the one about the nomad boy killed by the speeding oil truck in Turkey. When I run my fingers over the page, I can feel the depressions where the hammers of Dad's old typewriter pushed into the heavy paper. It seems fitting that each letter is the product of a physical effort, of metal striking ribbon, of ink smashed into fibre. The whole thing feels like an act of aggression, of repressed combat.

According to the date at the bottom of the page, hand-scrawled, I was three years old when he finished it. I know he worked in Turkey before he met Mum. He would have been in his early twenties then, just graduated from engineering school. Not a pilot, not a soldier, close to a war, but not in one. Playing at being a writer. Playing at life.

And yet, there is that 'you', writing in the second person. Perhaps it is an experiment. But I know it is not. I read it all again. The things you never told anyone else. Something closing up inside you. And then I know. I am the you. He is writing to me.

Helena

The second time he met her, he put a co-worker in hospital.

It wasn't that bad, really. Just a broken nose and a chipped tooth where the guy hit his mouth on the door handle when he fell. But as a result, the young engineer was called to the Vice President's corner office.

'What happened, son?' said the VP, who was youngish and well liked in the company.

'It happened after hours, sir.'

'And?'

'And so, it's none of the company's business what happened, sir.'

He'd been talking to her properly, sober, for the first time. They'd all met in the bar across the street and she'd joined them – a girl-friend of hers worked at the company and had invited her along. He introduced himself and she remembered him from before, said she was happy to talk to him now. She was working as an assistant veterinarian in a local animal shelter and was saving money to get her master's in animal science. They spoke a while and then he went to the bar to order drinks. When he came back, this guy from work was sitting with her, talking to her. She was laughing at something he'd said. The young engineer stood a moment, beers in hand, and watched her. He liked the way she looked. Liked it a lot. The high cheekbones, the girlish blush on her fair cheeks, the pouty lower lip, the big blue-grey eyes like a cloud-strewn sky, the honey and strawberry shoulder-length hair. Such great skin. She was tall and had long legs. She was dressed for work in a demure almost old-fashioned skirt and jacket that hid her figure.

He'd put the beers on the table and asked the guy, who worked in the same department as him at the oil company, to come outside for a minute. 'Got something I want to tell you,' he said. The guy had got up and followed him to the door. He was heavy-set, and had the pale, soft look of someone who watches too much TV. As soon as the door closed, he'd grabbed the guy by the collar and slammed him up against the wall. 'Back off,' he said. 'Just stay away from her.' When the guy told him to piss off, the young engineer had punched him in the face.

The VP's lip started to curl into a smile and then straightened. 'Fair enough,' he said. 'But when it affects the productivity of my staff, then it becomes my business.'

'Yes, sir.'

'And I understand you were drinking pretty heavily at the time.'

The young engineer said nothing.

The VP looked down at his papers. 'You're doing good work, son. You've just got to dial it down a notch.'

'I'll try.'

'I want you to go and see the company doctor, OK? Get yourself checked out.'

'Do I have to?'

'I can't force you, son.'

The young engineer, who liked the VP, admired him for how he carried himself around the staff and the way he kept his cool, nodded. 'I'll think about it.'

The first time he'd seen her, three days earlier, during Calgary Stampede, he told his best friend at the time, who was standing next to him at the bar: 'I'm going to marry that girl.' He was engaged to be married at the time. And so, he found out later, was she.

Much later, in the darker moments of his life, the young engineer would contemplate the nature of this first meeting. He would think back to that first image of her that he was destined to carry in his mind until his final breath, and wonder if this was what people sometimes referred to as *love at first sight*. Certainly, the effect was immediate, highly visual (at first) and strong. He'd approached her, tried to talk to her, but she'd sent him away.

'Come talk to me when you're not drunk,' she'd said with a smile.

For weeks after that first meeting he was physically ill, and no matter how much he drank, miserable.

The young engineer did see the company doctor. He sat on the examination table and the doctor asked him questions about himself and about his parents and poked his back and listened to his chest.

'Were you drinking before you came here today, son?'

The young engineer nodded.

'And yesterday?'

'Yes.'

'How much?'

'Not that much.'

'Tell me, son. How many drinks?'

'I don't know.'

'Take a guess.'

'Ten, maybe twelve. I wasn't counting.'

'And the day before?'

'More. Fifteen, twenty maybe.'

The doctor held back a sigh. 'And before that?'

'Same, doctor. Every day, the same.'

'How old are you, son?'

The young engineer told him.

'You are killing yourself, son,' said the doctor. 'Literally. You have the body of a forty-year-old. Do you understand what I'm telling you?'

The young engineer nodded.

'You need to change your life. And the sooner the better.'

The young engineer looked at a poster on the wall that showed the male and female reproductive systems.

'I'm recommending that you spend a week at a dry-out clinic. There is one in Clairsholm, not far from here.' The doctor produced a brochure and wrote out a referral. 'The company will pay.'

The young engineer looked at the brochure, not quite believing what he was hearing.

It wasn't until a few weeks later, after he'd started going to Alcoholics Anonymous meetings – *Hi, I'm Warren and I've been told I'm an alcoholic and my father is one, but I'm not sure I am really one* – that he saw her again. She was standing in the office lobby, near one of the big marble pillars, when he stepped out of the elevator, one day after work. She was wearing the same outfit he'd seen her in before, but she'd done her hair differently, pulled it back in some kind of braid. She waved, walked towards him.

The young engineer smiled.

'I'd like to have a chance to talk,' she said. 'Without the crowds. Not in a bar.'

'Sure,' he said. 'How about now?'

'That would be good,' she said. 'But this isn't a date.'

'OK.' He didn't care what it was. 'It's just good to see you.'

She smiled. 'It's nice outside. Let's go for a walk.'

They went down to the river pathway and walked under the cottonwoods. It had been a dry summer and the river was running low in its banks. They reached Fort Calgary, walked out on to the footbridge and looked down into the clear river water.

'I heard about what you did at the bar,' she said.

He looked out along the river. It was a clear day, and from here the mountains looked big and close.

'I wondered why he didn't come back,' she said.

'Is that what you wanted to talk about?'

'Not really,' she said. 'I'd like to know what you want.'

'You,' he said.

She gazed into his eyes, shook her head. 'No, I mean what do you want from life?'

'No one's ever asked me that before.'

'Well, I'm asking you.'

'You mean dreams?'

'I suppose so.'

'Yeah, I've got dreams.'

'Like what?'

'Seriously?'

She nodded, looked towards the mountains.

'Go places, I guess. I'd like to go to Africa one day, maybe for work.' There were so many other dreams, of course – fabulous and unattainable and risible, dreams he did not deserve, some already dead or lost, others he could see no pathway towards, many the mere contemplation of which brought embarrassment, and in some cases, shame. Things he would never tell anyone. 'What about you?'

She told him that she wanted to be married by twenty-five, have her first child before thirty, and be independently wealthy by forty. 'And I want to save the planet.'

'What, the whole thing?'

She smiled. 'No. The animals and the good, wild places.'

Her words unsettled him. He could feel it, deep within himself, a cold current eddying with dark viscosity, but he could not tell if it was fear, or admiration, or the grip of something deeper that could only be described as realisation. The sudden understanding that he had been preconditioned to avoid commitment to anything greater than himself. He gripped the railing.

'Why are you telling me this?' he said.

She smiled, ran the tip of her tongue along her lower lip. 'Because this is the time when dreams die.'

He looked out towards the mountains, the glimmer of peak ice. 'I know what you mean.'

'But I'm not going to let them.'

'I'm happy for you,' he said. Now she was just being annoying.

She frowned. But even that was beautiful. 'I'm telling you this so that when you ask me out on a date, you'll understand that I'll only say yes if I think you're marriage material. You'll get three dates. I'll know by then if you are.'

He smiled. He couldn't help it. 'And if I'm not?'

'I don't date for fun,' she said, the sun on the river reflecting in her eyes. 'There is far too much I want to do in my life. So, if you're not, it's over, and I'll move on.'

'An interview.'

'Exactly.'

'What else do you want to know?'

'Why do you drink so much?'

He gripped the railing harder and looked down into the dark clarity of the water, watching the smooth surface flex over the cobblestone bottom. 'The doctor asked me the same thing.'

'Doctor?'

He told her.

She was quiet for a time. Then she said: 'What did you tell him?'

'Nothing.'

'Why?'

'Because it doesn't matter.'

'It matters to me.' She reached for his arm and put her fingers on the sleeve of his shirt. He could feel the warmth of her through the cotton.

'I killed my brother,' he said.

'What did you say?' Her hand closed on his forearm.

'You said you wanted to know.'

She reached for his hand. 'My God. What happened?'

'I was twelve. We were playing with my father's gun. I shot him. Rhys was his name. He died on the way to hospital. In my dreams, he's still alive.' He'd never told anyone before.

They walked a while longer, across to the north side of the river and through the park towards the zoo, close but not touching. She didn't press him further, and he was glad for it, happy just to walk beside her. At the zoo bridge they crossed back to the other side of the river and turned towards the city, and when they reached her bus stop he stood with her and waited until the bus came and she got on and the bus drove away.

A week later, he did ask her out, and, much to his surprise, she said yes. And when she met him at the restaurant, wearing a black leather miniskirt and towering black heels and a low-cut blouse, a part of him nearly died when she walked up to him and kissed him on the cheek.

A Bar Called Mexico

Chris put the bottle to his lips and took a long swig. 'The good stuff,' he gasped, and passed it to Barley.

'What the hell are we doing here?' said Barley. 'We could get into a lot of trouble.' He drank.

'Great view, though,' said Chris.

The young engineer looked out over the town and the serried blue ridges folding away towards the higher mountains in the distance. 'Just keep your voice down, and no one will know we're here.'

'They won't care,' said Toby, grabbing the bottle from Barley. 'We're here supporting the local economy. They want us to be here. That's why they didn't lock the door.'

'It's not locked so people can come in any time they want, fuckwit,' said Barley. 'No telling when someone might have the urge to pray.'

'Religion is crap,' said Chris.

'You have to believe in something,' said the young engineer.

'Why?' said Chris.

'Because even if you believe in nothing, that's still something,' said Barley.

'That's not what I meant,' said the young engineer.

'OK,' said Chris, staring at the half-empty bottle. 'I believe in poetry.'

'Poetry is crap,' said Toby.

'I believe in banana cream pie,' said Barley, who'd returned with a fresh bottle.

Everyone nodded. Coming up through the mountains that day, they'd stopped at a restaurant on the outskirts of a small village. It was run by an American expatriate with long grey hair pulled back in a ponytail, and a grey goatee. He'd married a local girl, and was living in Mexico now for good, he said. He also claimed that he made the best banana cream pie in the world. He was right.

'Religion is crap,' said Chris.

'I'm religious,' said Barley.

'Bullshit,' said Toby.

'I am,' said Barley.

'Is that's why you're here?' said Chris. 'Praying that Lady Brett will be at the bar again tonight?'

Everyone laughed.

Barley grinned. 'She's something else.'

They'd met her the night before, in the bar. She'd walked right up to the four of them and introduced herself and asked if she could join them. She was handsome, but not beautiful. Robust, Toby called her. Her skin was very tanned and her hair was bleached by the sun. And she could drink. Barley ended up sleeping with her that night, while the rest of them drank on the beach outside her hotel. He'd only been up there with her for a little over an hour when they heard someone shouting on the beach in front of the hotel. Some guy was standing there in the sand in his shorts and T-shirt, yelling up at the hotel. A few minutes later, Lady Brett appeared on a fourth-floor balcony. There was a brief exchange, consisting mostly of swearing, before she went back into the room and then reappeared with an open suitcase draped over her arms. A moment later it was falling towards the beach, its contents scattering across the sand. Another case soon followed, and then some smaller things – a shaving kit, a book, an alarm clock. Then she disappeared back into the room.

They'd named her Lady Brett after the character in *The Sun Also Rises*. The young engineer had just read it and had got Chris to read it too.

'Fuck, that was funny,' said Chris. 'I thought I was going to puke, I was laughing so hard.'

'Her boyfriend was pretty nice,' said the young engineer.

They'd all gone over and helped the guy collect his stuff, had invited him to have a drink with them. They'd told him about *The Sun Also Rises* too, that he should read it, but he didn't look the reading type. When dawn came, he was still with them, blind drunk and swearing off women forever.

'Fucking crazy,' said Barley. 'Drinking on the roof of a church.' He took another swig of tequila.

'Stop whining,' said Toby. 'You're the one who got to enjoy Lady Brett while we all slummed it on the beach all night.'

'It was your idea to come here,' said Barley, grinning. 'Lard butt.'

'I didn't even get the chance to pack,' said Chris. 'I'm using Warren's toothbrush for Christ's sake.'

'Bad planning,' said Barley.

'Planning? I thought we were just going to another bar,' said Chris.

'Mexico, idiot.' Toby took another swig of tequila. 'I kept saying Mexico.'

'I thought you meant a bar,' said Chris.

'You ever heard of a bar called Mexico?' said Barley.

Toby laughed. 'Airport convenience store. I told you. But you wanted to hold out for something cheaper, with better selection.'

'What do you know?' said Chris. 'We had to carry you on to the plane.'

Everyone laughed. Toby laughed too, took another drink. The bottle was almost finished.

'There's another one in the jeep,' said Barley, 'I'll go get it.' He disappeared down the stairs.

'What's the bet the bastard takes off, leaves us here?' said Toby.

'He's too drunk to drive,' said Chris.

'What's wrong with you, War?' said Toby, prodding the young engineer with his elbow.

'He's pining,' said Chris. 'And sober.'

'Shut up, Chris,' said the young engineer.

'He's seeing this new girl,' said Chris. 'The one in the bar after work. Vet Girl.'

'Oh, yeah,' said Toby, whistling. 'Helena.'

'Hot,' said Chris.

'Who's hot?' said Barley, returning with a fresh bottle.

'Vet Girl,' said Chris. 'Helena of Troy.'

'Absolutely,' said Barley.

'She asked me if I had dreams,' said the young engineer.

'I have dreams about her,' said Toby. 'Every night.'

'Shut up, Toby,' said the young engineer.

'Dreams,' said Chris.

'You know, things you want to do with your life.'

'Oh, that.' Chris wanted to be a poet. The more he drank, the more he wanted to be a poet. But right now, he was an engineer.

'What about your fiancée,' said Toby. 'She know about this?'

'I called it off,' said the young engineer.

Everyone nodded and was suddenly very solemn. Barley passed the bottle around. Everyone looked at Chris.

'What?' said the young engineer.

'We didn't want to tell you before,' said Chris.

'Tell me what?'

'Well, you know that new guy in drilling? Williams?'

'Mike Williams, yeah.'

'Well, he's been drilling your fiancée for the last couple of months.' Chris looked at the bottle. Barley smirked. Everyone else looked at their feet.

'Fuck,' said the young engineer.

'She was a skank anyway,' said Toby.

'Her eyes are too close together,' said Barley.

'And her tits are too small for her ass,' said Chris.

Everyone laughed.

The young engineer grabbed the bottle from Toby, took a long drink. 'What do you guys want to do tomorrow?' he said.

March 10th. Geneva

I walk back to the hotel from Borschmann's offices. It's a clear afternoon, and the sun warms me, counteracts the cold wind coming off the lake. Despite what's just happened, I think about the two stories I read last night before turning out the light and trying to sleep.

It's strange to think of them there, on that bridge in Calgary, a moment in time so long eclipsed. The younger version of the decrepit and dying man I last saw at the hospital a few days ago; of the woman who was lost to me so long ago I can barely remember what she looked like anymore. The two of them, talking about life, about time, about dreams and the things that kill them. About love and life and finding your way. And now that they are both gone, does any of it matter?

I realise I've passed the hotel. I stop a moment, then keep walking.

We lost the deal. I lost the deal. Borschmann wouldn't accept the terms, the old faggot, and I had run out of room to manoeuvre. A whole week wasted. Months of effort. I had to blow off the weekend with Constantina, too. Shit. Sometimes I don't know why I do it. Why I put up with it all. Why does it matter so much to me? What makes this so goddamned important? The money? The bonus? The status, the possible promotion, the car, the bigger office? Yeah, yeah, all that. Work harder and get more. Get that feeling you have when you walk into the meeting and everyone junior to you is thinking they want to be you, to have what you have. Like showing up at the party in a new BMW and everyone is watching you – that feeling. That's what it's all about, right? Dreams.

I decide to stay here over the weekend and chill. Fly back to London on Monday. I text Maria that I'll meet her on Tuesday. She can tell me whatever it is she has to tell me then.

I need some time to think. The old man's stories have been rattling around in my head for days now, keeping me awake. Damn him. Carrying all this around with him all these years and never telling me. I mean, especially later, when there was only the two of us. Then dumping it all on me like this, when there is no recourse, nothing I can do about any of it.

I keep walking along the lakefront. I turn my phone off and just walk. It's been a long time since I've done this — wandered with no destination in mind, no deadline to turn me around and bring me back, nothing tethering me to the daily avalanche of shit they call responsibility.

The air is cold and there are clouds over the lake and a few squalls and some blue sky. A bit of everything.

I turn forty-one this year. Forty-one. I can't quite believe it, somehow. All that shit about infinity the old man wrote, well I hate to say it, but it's true. No one ever tells you. Or rather, they do, but you don't believe them. When I was young, in my teens and early twenties and even later, when I'd walk past a cemetery and look out at those gravestones, all those lives ended, I'd get a feeling. It was always the same. And you know, I'd never really thought about what it was, that feeling I had. But as I walk along by the lake, I realise. It just comes to me. What I felt was disdain. *That's right, disdain. They were dead, I was alive. They were weak, so they died. I would live forever. I can feel it even now. And of course, the joke's on me. That's what my old man is telling me. I can hear him. He's calling out to me as I walk past, and in his voice, there's disdain.* You are weak and stupid. You think you're different to me. But you aren't. You'll end up like me. And there isn't a goddamned thing you can do about it.

When my old man married my mum, he was twenty-six. She was twenty-four. He was thirty-three when I was born, and Adam was born six years after me. They never told me what happened to Adam, just like they never told me about my old man's brother. All I remember is arriving back at the landing that day with my mum in the car and the old man is standing there on the dock as we pull up, with the long arm of the lake behind him and Adam in his arms. And when he sees us, he stops for a moment and stares at us, and then he starts running towards us and without saying a word he takes the keys from my mum and puts Adam in the car and drives away. That was the last time I ever saw him. The next day, they told me that Adam wouldn't be coming home. I was ten.

War News

The young engineer sat at one of the empty tables in the college's common room and spread his notes and hydrology textbook out before him. Final exams were only a few weeks away now and the room was crowded with anxious students. The TV droned in the background. Outside, spring was coming, and London's street trees were showing the first sap-green buds. He'd spoken to Helena yesterday, back in Canada, made some progress towards patching it up. She'd been angry with him for a long time, upset about him being in trouble with the law when he was supposed to be studying; about other things, too, but over the last few months he'd managed to convince her that he had learned his lesson. He was going to do his thesis in Africa, had secured sponsorship for the work from the World Bank. He would finish his degree, get a job somewhere doing something good. Then he'd ask her. Maybe things would still work out.

He opened the textbook and started work. He was halfway through a difficult derivation when someone turned up the TV.

'Quiet,' a student shouted.

It was the BBC, a special report. Breaking news. Everyone stopped work, turned towards the TV.

'Oh, my God,' he heard someone say.

⋀

Five months earlier, before Christmas, when he'd finally broken it off with his fiancée and started back with Helena, and then lost her again soon after, and the days were short and dark and cold, the young man pushed his way through to the bar. The publican raised bushy, greying eyebrows at him. The young man pointed at the three half-poured pints of Guinness ranked up on the double blue Dublin GAA bar towel, *Áth Cliath* just visible between two glasses. 'A pint of that, please,' he said.

The publican frowned, started to it.

'I'll have a pint of that, too,' said a voice from behind. Laughter broke over the din of a hundred and fifty raised, mostly male, voices. 'You from America?'

The young man turned towards the voice. A broad smile beamed out at him from a face chiselled from the Muskoka granite of his childhood, brown and pink feldspars flecked with muscovite. The guy took a couple of steps towards him, leaned in across the bar, put down a fiver. 'It's on me, Seamus,' he said to the publican, turning towards the young man and offering his hand. 'Seán,' he said.

The young man took the hand, shook, spoke his own name. 'Thanks.'

Seán handed him a glass, raised his own. '*Sláinte.*'

They moved away from the bar scrum, found some space towards the back of the pub.

'What're you doing here, then?' said Seán, wiping foam from his top lip, glancing towards the front door. His forearms were like twisted rope.

'Drinking,' said the young man.

Seán smiled. 'I mean here in London.'

'Studying. Engineering.'

Seán sipped, nodded. 'Oh, yeah. Very good. A man of education.' His accent was very thick, and it was hard for the young man to understand.

'I've only been here a couple of months,' said the young man.

'We like Americans here.'

'I'm Canadian,' said the young man.

'Just as good,' said Seán. 'As long as you ain't a fecking Brit.'

Just then a cold gust swept through the narrowness of the pub as the front door swung open. Two men stepped inside, stood a moment silhouetted in yellow streetlight, then closed the door behind them. Stamping the rain from their dark jackets, they peered in through the smoke.

'Stay for the music later,' said Seán, patting him on the shoulder.

But before the young man could reply, Seán was moving away through the crowd, towards the front door. Every few steps, someone would reach for Seán's hand or nod to him. Women smiled at him, whispered to each other as he passed. He greeted the two men who'd just come into the place. One of them clasped his forearm for a long time, his other hand on Seán's shoulder as he spoke. After a while, the three of them moved off towards the bar.

'Friend of Seán's are you, then?' said a lilting female voice.

The young man turned and looked down at the woman. 'Pardon?'

'Seán Savage,' she said. 'Friend of yours?' Her hair was the colour of an October maple. She was very pretty.

The young man shook his head. 'We just met.'

The woman pursed her lips and held out a slim red-and-black print newspaper. 'Copy of the *An Phoblacht*?' She rattled the tin that hung on a string around her neck. 'Money for the cause?'

'What's the *Phoblacht*?' said the young man, mangling the pronunciation.

'War news,' she said with a you've-got-to-be-joking twist on her lips.

The young man reached into his pocket and dropped three one-pound coins into the tin.

'Bless you,' said the woman, already moving away, canvassing other patrons.

The young man set his half-finished pint on a table and opened the paper. He read that in the aftermath of the bombing at Enniskillen on Remembrance Day, which the IRA described as a monumental error, loyalist paramilitaries were carrying out revenge attacks on Catholics across Belfast.

As he sat reading, the music started. A five-piece band played on a small stage across from the bar, Irish pipes and fiddles. Seán was up there, a flute pressed to his lips. Everyone in the place was standing. Bodies swayed to the music, neighbours linked arms. Voices rose spontaneously in chorus, strange ballads in a language the young man did not understand, melodies of longing and loss, of being far from home. He stood transfixed, carried along. He thought of his own home, so far away, under snow now. He thought of Helena, of what she'd said to him the last time he'd seen her, when she'd ended it.

And then, too soon, the band leader was thanking the audience, and the final number began. Everyone stood. Voices rose together, singing in that haunting ancient language. Old men swayed, hands on hearts, tears streaming across their ruddy, bearded cheeks. The final notes hung a moment in the thickened cigarette air and it was over. The front doors were thrown open. The smell of winter rain and wet city pavement flooded the place, the cold wind carrying in dead leaves and scraps of rubbish. People moved towards the doors, disappeared into the night. The young man folded the paper, slipped it into the inside breast pocket of his jacket and started for the exit.

He was at the end of the bar, not far from the doors, when he felt a hand on his elbow. The grip was strong and forced him to turn. It was Seán.

'Stay for another,' Seán said, still holding the young man's elbow.

'I've got to get back,' said the young man, looking down at Seán's hand, back up at his face. 'Classes tomorrow.'

'Ah yeah, the engineer,' said Seán, smiling. 'Building a better world.'

'That's why I'm here.'

Sean was guiding him towards the bar now, against the outward flow of those leaving. 'Come on. Just one,' he said. 'Never know if it might be your last.'

The young man braced his legs, stopped. He was taller by a few inches, but he was pretty sure that Seán was stronger, and from the look of him could handle himself. 'Look,' he said. 'I really appreciate it. But I've really got to get going.'

Seán smiled and let go of his elbow. 'Sorry, friend,' he said. 'I get a little carried away sometimes. It's like I said. We like Americans here.' He smiled again. It was a big smile, full of straight white teeth. He was a good-looking guy. 'Sorry, yeah. I meant *North* Americans.' He looked down at the floor. When he looked back up his smile was gone. 'We're both a long way from home, yeah. Have a drink with me and then we'll go.'

The young man looked around. The place was almost empty now, and there was no sign of the two men that Seán had been talking to earlier, before the singing. He followed Seán to the bar. Two pints of Guinness were waiting for them, along with a four-pack of tinnies. Seán lit a cigarette, inhaled deep. They drank and watched the last stragglers leave the pub.

'What was that song you were all singing, there at the end?' asked the young man.

'The *Amhrán na bhFiann*,' said Seán, downing his pint. '"The Soldier's Song". My song.' He slammed his glass on the bar. 'Let's go.'

The young man finished his drink and followed Seán to the door. Outside, the rain was coming down hard. It was gone midnight and the street was empty both ways, just the forlorn flashing of the yellow globe light at the pedestrian crossing nearby and the rain sheeting across the lamplit pavement.

'Thanks again for the beer,' said the young man. 'Nice meeting you.' Then he raised the collar of his jacket and crossed the road, turned left and started towards Kilburn Tube station, feeling as if he'd escaped something. He'd just passed the all-you-can-eat buffet Indian place he'd eaten at before going into the pub – all closed up now, its windows barred and doors padlocked – when Seán jogged up beside him.

'Hold up there a minute,' he said.

The young man stopped, faced him.

Seán held out his hand. 'You dropped this,' he said.

The young man looked. It was a Canadian passport. His. 'Holy Jesus,' he said. 'Where did you find it?'

'On the floor in the pub,' said Seán, ripping a tinny from the plastic holder. 'You should be more careful.'

'Thanks.' The young man slipped the passport into the front pocket of his jeans. He had no idea how it could have fallen out. He must be drunker than he'd thought. 'Thanks a lot.'

Seán handed him a can of beer. The young man took it, opened it, gulped down half the contents.

Seán smiled at him, opened one himself. 'Come on,' he said. 'I'm going to the station, too. It's not far.'

They started walking. After a few steps, Seán stopped cold. 'Shite,' he said. A police car was up ahead, crawling towards them, very slowly, high beams on. 'Here we go,' he said.

'Here we go what?' said the young man, watching the car creep closer. It was on the same side of the street as they were, in the nearside lane.

'Fecking cops. Always harassing us. It's been worse since Enniskillen.'

The young man took another sip of beer. 'We're not doing anything wrong.' They kept walking. A second car had appeared now, behind the first, rolling towards them at walking pace, no more. The young man was on the outside of the pavement, closest to the road.

'Step back from the kerb,' said Seán. 'Don't provoke them.'

'Provoke them? Just by walking on the pavement?'

Just then, the lead police car nudged in, so that its tyres were right up against the kerb. The rubber made a squeaking sound as the tyres flexed against the guttersides. The car was less than twenty metres away from them.

Seán grabbed his elbow, tried to pull him back from the edge of the pavement, but the young man jerked his arm away. 'Move,' said Seán. The car was close now.

The young man set himself so that he was walking right on the edge of the kerb, towards the approaching car. He could see the two cops looking out at him from behind the windscreen. They wore peaked caps and black bullet-proof vests.

The car grazed the young man's hip like a slow-motion bull charging a matador. As it did, its side wing mirror clipped him and snapped back on its hinges.

'Shite,' said Seán.

As soon as the car made contact it slammed to a halt. Doors flung open and the two cops were out and facing them, hands on belts. They were big guys, tall and broad-chested, bulked up by their gear.

'You hit the car,' one of the cops bellowed.

'I didn't hit it,' said the young man. 'I was on the pavement. You hit me.'

'Fucking Micks,' said the other cop.

'You fucking hit the car,' shouted the first one.

'Look, we're sorry,' said Seán, backing away.

'What the hell is this?' said the young man, holding his ground. 'We're minding our own business, walking home. We have every right to be here. We've done nothing wrong.' Behind him, Seán was backing away.

The two cops glanced at each other.

'We've got a fucking barrister here,' said the second cop, his mouth wrenched into something that may have been a grin.

'Don't you have anything better to do?' said the young man, getting into his stride now. 'Go and chase some real criminals.'

The second cop pulled out his night stick, palmed it. 'Fucking genius, you are,' he hissed.

'Right, you've been told,' said the first cop. He started towards them.

'What is this?' said the young man, angry now, alcohol fuelling the heat rising inside him. 'We're perfectly within our rights to walk here. What the hell is this? Some kind of police state?'

The first cop was closing on him now. 'Rights? What rights, you fucking scum?'

The young man, who'd played a lot of ice hockey and Canadian football, flung his half-empty beer can at the cop, crouched low and charged. He didn't really know why he did it, didn't think about it.

The can missed the cop's head, but the spray caught him in the face, momentarily blinding him. The young man hit the cop square in the hips with a full tackle, knocking him off his feet and spearing him into the pavement. He heard a crack as the back of the cop's head hit the concrete and then a hiss as the air came out of the cop's lungs.

Half an hour later, the young man was standing before a wooden desk. The second cop from the street stood beside him. Behind the desk, a uniformed police sergeant with a thick grey moustache sat looking through a passport. On the desk were the young man's wallet, a return tube ticket from South Kensington, and a folded copy of the *An Phoblacht*. The young man ran his tongue over his lower lip, explored the thick heat of the split there, checked his teeth to see they were all still in his head. He was pretty sure his nose was broken, could already feel his eyes swelling up. His ribs ached and the handcuffs bit into his wrists.

The sergeant put down the passport and looked up at him. 'What were you doing in that pub, young man?' His voice was like far off thunder, deep and resonant.

'I just went in for a drink, sir. That's all.'

The sergeant picked up the *An Phoblacht,* started leafing through the pages. 'Why are you in the United Kingdom?' he said without looking up.

'I'm doing a master's degree in engineering at Imperial College. My student card is in my wallet.'

The sergeant opened his wallet, found the card, pulled it out. 'And is assaulting police officers part of the curriculum now at that august institution?'

The young man hung his head. 'No, sir. I'm sorry. I shouldn't have.'

'No, you bloody well should not have,' said the sergeant, replacing the student card. 'The gentleman you were walking with at the time of your arrest, how do you know him?'

'I met him in the bar.'

'Did you know him previously?'

'No, sir. We had a couple of beers together is all.'

'What did you talk about?'

'Not much really. He was playing in the band mostly.'

'One of those,' laughed the second cop. 'Fucking queen, he is.'

The sergeant glanced at the cop, leaned forwards across the desk. 'I want you to tell me everything that he said to you, everything he did.'

The young man recounted as much of their conversation as he could. 'Two men came into the place,' he said. 'Seán – that was his name – spoke to them. They knew each other.'

The sergeant reached into a drawer and withdrew a black-and-white A4 photograph. It was grainy and slightly out of focus – two men in heavy coats standing in front of a building. 'Were these the men?'

The young man nodded. His stomach was churning now, that feeling that he was in real trouble creeping through him.

'Put him in the pit,' said the sergeant.

The cell was bare and cold so he could see his own breath. The only light came from a small barred opening in the riveted steel door. The other occupant was a very thin and badly beaten young Irishman who lay shivering on the floor, mumbling to himself. The young man sat in the corner with his arms wrapped around his knees and observed the clear and present slowing of time. Seconds measured in the long contractions of the Irishman's breathing. Minutes announced by the hollow slamming of steel doors, hours thinking about home, about Helena and how he'd fucked it all up, and of the chaos that seemed the only governing force in the world.

Come morning, he was led to a holding room, and then on to a police van. Six other men in various states of dishevelment sat silently as the streets of London rolled past under scattered cloud and shifting islands of bright sunshine. Twenty minutes later, they arrived at a large building with a secure, wired receiving area. The young man was led through a long corridor and down two flights of Victorian ironwork stairs to what could only be called a dungeon – a large arched central space with barred holding cells ranged around on three sides. His cell was the size of a prairie outhouse, so small he couldn't stand and was forced to crouch and lean up against the brick walls.

A kid with fair hair and tattooed forearms watched him from the cell opposite. After a while he said: 'What you in for, guv?'

'I hit a cop,' said the young man.

The kid laughed.

'You?'

'I nicked a motor, didn't I?' he said in a thick London accent.

Just then, the main door to the dungeon opened. A young woman in a navy-blue skirt and matching jacket strode in. She had long legs and dark hair pulled back into a ponytail.

'Phwoar,' said the kid, smiling big. 'Here you go.' Whistles echoed around the place.

The woman stood a moment, checked her notebook and approached the young man's cell. 'I am your public defender,' she said.

'Hi,' said the young man, trying a smile.

'We don't have long,' she said. 'Your arraignment is in ten minutes, so let's get started.' She read the police report to him. He had attacked and damaged a police car, hurled beer cans at officers, and assaulted and hospitalised a policeman. His actions had been unprovoked. 'Prosecution is moving for deportation,' she said, looking up from her notes through a pair of dark-rimmed glasses. Her skin was flawless.

A fizz ran through him, pooled in his extremities.

'Tell me what happened.'

He told her. 'They initiated it. Not me. Ask the guy I was with. He can confirm it.'

'Seán? Seán Savage?'

'Yes. Seán.'

The woman closed her notebook. She looked about his age, mid-twenties. 'After you hit the constable, the other policemen chased him, but he got away.'

His word against that of four policemen. Not good. Still, he was glad Seán had been spared the beating he would surely also have taken. 'Look,' he said. 'I'm sorry for what I did. It was stupid. I was drunk and angry at being harassed. I'm halfway through my degree. I'm paying a lot of money to be here.'

'We should be able to get you off with a year's probation,' she said. 'Keep out of trouble from hereon in and you'll be able to stay. They don't care about you.'

Relief flooded through him. 'Thank you,' he said.

She made to leave.

'Wait,' he said.

She stopped, turned to face him.

'What do you mean, they don't care about me?'

'Don't worry about that. We're going up in a few minutes. Just remember to be contrite. Be honest, but express regret. Be polite.'

/\

By now, everyone was crowding around the TV. The BBC reporter was on location, standing in a sunny street somewhere. Behind her, cars streamed in both directions. The red information bar at the bottom of the screen read: *Breaking news. SAS operatives in operation against suspected IRA terrorists in Gibraltar.* The reporter started her story: suspected terrorists, two men and a woman, were planning an attack on a military installation in Gibraltar. After a tip-off, the group was confronted by security forces in the forecourt of a petrol station. Two of the terrorists, Mairéad Farrel and Daniel McCann, were shot dead immediately. The third escaped and was chased through the streets by the soldiers. When he turned to confront them, he was killed by multiple gunshots to the head and body. He had been tentatively identified, the reporter said, as Seán Savage.

March 12th. Geneva

Walked all day today, south along the lake until I left the city behind, then up into the foothills. Spring is coming now, the first crocuses pushing through the grass, early buds on the trees. If you want to think, if you need to think, walk.

So, I walk. I think about my dad. I know something about losing a brother, about the sheer absence that lives inside you every day for the rest of your life. But to lose a brother like that. And then, with what happened to Adam. My brother, but his son. The weight of it. What happened that day at the lake? Where was he taking him, carrying him from the landing like that? And why did they never tell me what happened?

I think of Rachel. When she was born, I remember holding her little body in my hands and saying, 'Hello there, little one.' And as she grew, I took every day as it came, as if there would be no end to the flow of days. No one ever told me that one day it would be over. Guilt floods me like cold water. I keep walking. Eventually, I find a bistro, order a beer and then another, and when I finally leave, the sun is low in the sky and I am so drunk I don't feel the cold.

When I get back to the hotel it's late. I turn on my phone. Two emails from my boss, asking about the Borschmann contract. Four text messages from Constantina. No photos. Just questions. Questions to which I have no answers.

I stare at the screen for a time, start to grovel out a reply to my boss, apologies, explanations, rationalisations. I stop mid-sentence, reread what I've written, and then delete it and turn off my phone. I call down to the front desk and ask them to bring up a bottle of whisky and some ice. All they have is Bell's and I tell them that's fine. Just fine.

Twenty years ago, I wanted to be an architect. Design fabulous public buildings and sports complexes that people would marvel at long after

I was dead. For a time, I got into carpentry, thought it would be good to make a living with my hands. I was pretty good on a motorbike, too, and for a while I thought I might take up racing, see how far I could get on the circuit. Not sure now, looking back, where I lost the direction. I guess I just slowly convinced myself that those weren't the right dreams, that there were other, more practical, achievable ones to set for. Maybe none of them were the right ones, after all.

The twenty-three-year-old incarnation of my mother stands on that bridge with the damaged but still hopeful twenty-five-year-old version of my father. Her words come to me again, as they have so often since I first read them last night: this is the time when dreams die. *Mine sure did. In the end, hers did too. Maybe we're all better off without them.*

Probabilities

'Are you still coming?' he yelled into the marine radiotelephone handset.

'You have to say "over" and then let go of the talk button,' said the ship's radio operator, unshaven, red-eyed.

'Sorry.' He pushed down the long black button on the handset. 'Over.'

A second later he heard his own heavily distorted voice repeated, filtered and bounced off the troposphere, relayed through Amsterdam into the European phone network and across to Canada. She was there, somewhere, on the other end. The radio operator tuned the dials, modulating the frequency against a background of a thousand conversations that crowded the restless atmosphere. It sounded like a kid's slide whistle, up and back.

'I've lost Amsterdam,' the radioman said. 'Sorry. It's the damned weather. Hang on and I'll try to get them back.'

'Thanks,' he said. He had waited for this moment for so long and yet now that he was about to speak to her again, he was filled with dread. 'It's impossible to make a long-distance call from this country. None of the phones work.'

'No problem. I'll do my best,' the radio operator replied in a thick Dutch accent, guttural and round. 'What are you doing in a shithole like this anyway?' the man added, continuing to twirl the radio's frequency dial between thumb and forefinger as if it were an erect black nipple.

'Trying to help, I guess.' He looked around the cramped radio room and then out of the porthole towards the confused lights of Takoradi harbour. Four and a half months he had been here now, almost twice as long since he had seen her last, waving goodbye as he stepped into the taxi outside the little house she rented with two other veterinary students in Calgary. He was here working to provide clean groundwater to isolated villages, rehabilitating their old and rusted-out wells.

So far, he didn't feel like he had helped much.

Village kids were still as likely as not to drink from the shallow muddy water holes, running the same risk of ingesting the copepods that carried the *dracunculus* larvae. Once infected, their little bodies became nurseries for developing guinea worms, and then, mating grounds. It still sickened him to think of it, parasites coupling inside a living human being, the male nematodes dying after mating, the females absorbing their hapless partners and then burrowing their nether ends through the host's flesh, down along the smooth contours of long bones, through tendon sheaths and around joints, groundward, navigating by gravity. And worst was the result. He should have been immune to it by now: the fiery, weeping blisters at the foot or lower leg where the female worm, now up to a metre long, poked its sex end through the victim's skin, like a piece of spaghetti emerging from a watery bolognese. Strategically placed, head still buried deep within the host, feeding, her sex wantonly exposed, she spurted thousands of fertilised eggs upon contact with water, ensuring her progeny's survival. She had to be pulled out, slowly and painfully over months, a millimetre at a time, or cut out. There was no medicinal cure, and the body created no immunity. Only a safe water supply could break the cycle.

The radioman pulled out a package of cigarettes, duty-free Rothmans, and offered him one.

He took it and bent to the flame of the man's lighter, inhaling deeply. 'Thanks,' he said, pouring the smoke out through his nostrils. 'I didn't smoke before I came here.'

The radioman adjusted his headset, turned a dial. 'This place changes you.'

Of this, he had written to her every day, long letters in which he had tried to describe the asylum ache in his chest – futile attempts to put into words what he was now sure he would never be able to properly express. He told her about the packed-earth and thatch villages, the poor and diseased people, of the smiles of the children, as wide and warm as the continent, of their curiosity and of the crisis of existence they caused him – all of this he poured out in long candlelit pages, entrusted to the uncertain grace of the Ghana Post Corporation.

But of the other things, he had not written. He did not tell of the visit to the clinic, sitting in the waiting room with dozens of sweating Ghanaians, women mostly, dripping with children, anxiety drawn in deep lines across their faces, the sun hammering on the tin sheet roof, the overhead fan immobile, on strike, dead. He had taken precautions. He was not stupid after all, he told himself, and anyway the test had come out negative. The French doctor, a thin, short, balding man whose name he could no longer remember – was it Rene? Rejean? something like that – had warned him that it might be too soon to tell. The probability was low, he had said, but exposure might still manifest itself. He had advised him to return in a month or so. Then they could be sure.

Since then he had received just the two letters from her, written in her looping, rounded hand, one on small, girlish stationery, flowered and perfumed, the other on gridded mathematical calculation leaf. She had forgiven him, she had said. That's what people who loved each other did. That was what commitment was about. It just might work. It would work, she had written.

'I've got them back,' said the radio operator suddenly, handing him the receiver. 'I don't know how long for though, so make it quick.'

'Helena, are you there?' he said, and then: 'Over.' The same whining metallic hiss emanated from the device. His fear was like a virus, now, mutating, multiplying, eroding his confidence. How could such a minute probability suddenly seem so impossibly large, almost *certain*?

And then, through the electronic haze, he heard a voice, almost unrecognisable as the woman he loved, say: 'Yes. I hear you.'

'I'm sorry, Helena. Sorry for what I did.'

The radio operator looked up at him, eyebrows raised. He grinned sheepishly back at the man. The line hissed like a wave on a pebble beach.

'Helena? Are you there?'

'I'm here.'

'The date is set for the twenty-sixth. We have an appointment. The paperwork is done. Are you still coming? Over.'

'I am booked on the KLM flight from Amsterdam a week tomorrow.'

'In a week, then,' he said.

'Warren, I——.' Feedback moaned across the line.

'What is it?'

'Nothing.'

'I miss——' he began, but was cut off as the line was severed.

'Do you want me to get her back?' said the radioman. 'I can try.'

'Thanks,' he said, handing back the receiver. 'No.'

He offered money, but the radioman just smiled and waved it away. He made his way through the cramped passageway and out on to the freighter's deck. The railing was damp in his hands, the night clear and moonless. He looked up at the stars twinkling in the haze. She was not going to come. 'Nothing,' she had said. That's exactly what it was going to be: nothing. He wasn't even sure why she had entertained the idea in the first place, almost two months ago now, through an exchange of letters. It had been rash of them both. That wasn't how real decisions were made. And he had treated her badly from the start. Just weeks before leaving for Africa he had left her waiting right through until morning while he had been with someone else, someone he didn't love, lost in misplaced loyalty, confused, scared. After that, he had lost her for a while and then somehow won her back. And here, he had been unprepared for the warmth of the people and the depth of their thanks, for the girls they had offered him – young, fifteen or sixteen, commanded to disrobe by their fathers, shy smiles under upturned eyes, the men beaming with pride at their daughters' unsullied beauty. It was better this way.

He climbed down the rope ladder to the rowboat tied up on the port side. The riveted steel plates of the ship's hull were rusted and worn, the paint cracked from years in the tropical sun. He waved thanks to the crewmen, discernible only by the red embers of their cigarettes glowing in the darkness, and turned towards the shore. The smooth surface of the water was a carpet of reflected light, the subtle pinpoints of the cosmos obscured by the phosphorous swathes of the port-complex lights. He leaned into the oars and made for shore.

Elephants

He pushed his way through the ten-deep throng towards the railing. Sweating under the five-degree-latitude sun, he scanned the sky, dread rising in his chest. Beyond the runway, the sea stretched out to a muddy-blue horizon.

A light flashed over the water. It hung a while, close to the horizon, strobing in the haze like a star, and then disappeared. A groan shivered across the observation deck. Someone pointed. The light had reappeared. It was turning, lining up with the runway. Soon you could see the wings and the big pendant turbines, and then the stick-like protrusions of the landing gear, the whole thing seeming to hang in the air, defying gravity as it groped towards the runway. Then a puff of smoke and a delayed *chirp-chirp* as first the main gear and then the nose wheel hit the tarmac cold at a hundred and twenty knots. Thrust reversers screamed. The jet taxied to a halt. Motorised stairs rolled up to the front and rear doors. Baggage vehicles circled like attentive service robots. The engines spun down and the aircraft stood silent on the apron in a mirage of rising heat. Within the dark ovals of the windows, he could see tiny faces peering out, and he tried to imagine her among them, searching for him.

The crowd surged forwards. The young engineer, who was now at the railing, braced himself against the weight of bodies pushing from behind.

The aircraft's doors opened. Blue-uniformed flight attendants appeared, stood at the top of the stairways. Then the first passengers emerged into the sunshine, blinking and holding their hands above their eyes, and started to make their way down the stairs and along the apron towards the terminal. A group at the far end of the observation platform broke into shrieks, started jumping up and down, waving their hands in the air. One of the passengers, a big African woman in traditional dress, waved back, her smile growing with every step.

The young engineer scanned back and forth between the front and rear doors and across the column of passengers streaming towards the terminal, the observation platform all around him now alive with people waving, calling out, hugging each other, some crying openly, tears pouring down their smiling faces. Handlers swung the aircraft's huge, curved belly doors open and began unloading luggage. Still the passengers came. Perhaps two hundred had already crossed the tarmac and entered the terminal building. He'd checked every one. She was not among them.

He gripped the rail. Should he be surprised? During that last call from the freighter, her voice had been so unsure, so distant, changed somehow. That was three weeks ago.

He could stop worrying. She had made the decision for him.

A stewardess appeared at the rear door, waved down to the ground staff. No more passengers. A weight crushed down on him from the inside, a mass of regret. They were better off apart. They were too different: driven by different currents, guided by wholly different instruments. She was stronger than him, more practical, more aware.

And then she appeared. There was no mistaking her. She towered pale over most of the other passengers, a white sleeveless summer dress billowing around her like the clouds that dotted the horizon. She stopped momentarily at the top of the front stairs and looked out at the sea. Then she started down towards the tarmac. He screamed her name. He jumped up and down and waved his arms in the air. Helena. I don't believe it. Over here. But she was too far away. She stepped on to the shimmering surface and joined the stream of travellers moving towards the terminal and the fringe of swaying palms.

She was walking directly towards him now with that long, confident stride he had so admired the first time he had seen her. She seemed to be looking right at him, searching the faces lining the observation deck. He waved again and shouted her name. And then she smiled and waved back at him, and for that instant it had been as if he had known her all his life.

M

He woke to the distant sounds of gunfire. Poachers perhaps, or government troops skirmishing with outlaws. He moved closer to her and searched the still-dark sky, listening. She reached for his hand and held it tightly. Through the screened windows of the small caravan, the turbulent symphony of the African night flowed over them. The air was thick with her smell and the deep vapours of the forest. Clouds moved slowly across the earth, obscuring the stars and throwing dark moonshadows over the jungle. Venus appeared, her oceans bright blue, and then was gone. She moved closer to him, moulding her body to his. He could still not quite believe that she was here. Today they would be married.

Gunfire in the distance again, like fat crackling in a fire.

She turned her head on the pillow and looked at him. Her eyes were wide and pained.

'I hope it isn't the elephants,' she said, turning to look at the lightening sky. Dawn was near. 'Animals are better than people,' she whispered. 'Even predators only kill when they must.'

He pulled up his pillow and folded one arm behind his head. The new day was slowly colouring the horizon, and he could make out the hills and individual trees and a pillar of woodsmoke rising from a village to the east.

She turned on to her side and propped herself up on one elbow. 'Do you know how many forest elephants are left?' She paused. It was not a rhetorical question.

'You know I don't, Helena.'

'Well you should. Fewer than ten thousand. That's half as many as a decade ago, and only a tenth of the population at the turn of the century. We're here just in time to see them go extinct.'

'Please, Helena. Not today.'

'It's the truth. What's wrong with the truth?'

He had seen it every day for almost four months, this truth. The huge logging trucks trundling night and day from the forest to the coast, carrying single logs as long and thick as buses, the West African forest being devoured one tree at a time and shipped across the sea. He'd seen the small boys employed as human braking systems, hanging from the running boards. He'd watched the trucks tearing through the villages in clouds of red dust, or, if they needed to stop, gearing down until the boys were able to jump to the ground to swing wooden chocks under the front wheels, pulling them out and running forwards again with each sickening lurch as the truck jumped over the chocks once, twice, four times, the chained log smashing into the bed, until finally the wheels stopped turning.

'You shouldn't be here saving people,' she said. 'There are too many people. You should be saving animals.'

'As long as people are poor and suffering, they will exploit the environment. Helping people is the only way to protect the wild-life.' This was what he had come to understand during his time in London, speaking with university professors and student activists.

'No, Warren, you're wrong. We will never stop wanting more. The richer we get, the more machines we can buy, the faster we can exploit everything. That's not the answer. The facts don't support it. There are just too many people in this world.'

'Lift people from poverty, educate them and birth rates drop.'

'That takes generations. We don't have generations.'

He tried to reconcile her words with what they were going to do today, with what he hoped they would do, one day. 'So, what do you want to do, Helena, just let them die? They're people, just like you and me. They have as much right…' He stopped short. She was sitting up in the bed now, the sheet bunched around her midriff, arms crossed under her bare breasts. He looked into her eyes. He leaned over to kiss her, but she put her palm to his chest and pushed him back.

'This is *serious*, Warren.'

He tried again, but she turned her head. He managed a glancing peck to her cheek.

After a while, he said: 'You know there probably won't be any vows today. It's a civil ceremony, only a justice of the peace.'

'We should we make some promises now, then. Just between us.' She leaned over and kissed him on the mouth. Her hair fell about their faces, and for that brief moment, it was just the two of them, alone in a cocoon of golden silk. 'Promise me you will always tell me the truth,' she breathed. 'No matter what it is, you will trust me enough to be honest, not hide anything from me.'

He moved his head back and away from her, looked into her eyes again. 'I promise.' Even as he was saying it, he was breaking it. It was meaningless, he told himself, impossible. The promise not to lie was itself a lie. A fever waxed through him, warm, protective.

She squeezed his hand. 'Your turn,' she whispered.

'Don't ever use sex as a weapon.'

'Have I ever?'

'I hardly know you, Helena.'

'Since you've known me, then.'

'I'm sorry,' he said. 'It came out wrong.' He kissed her on the cheekbone.

'It's alright,' she said. 'I promise. No pre-emptive strike.'

They lay together, her head cradled in the hollow just beneath his collarbone, her knee drawn up and draped over his thigh, her belly warm and soft against his side, his arm around her shoulders. The sun was almost up.

He pulled himself up in the bed and lay back against the head-board. 'When I was working in Turkey a few years ago, my driver Veysil and I went down to a place called Hasankeyf, near the Iraqi border.' He reached over her to the little side table and picked up the water bottle. 'Want some?' he asked, offering it to her.

She took the clear, blue plastic container and lifted it to her lips. A small trail of droplets ran from the corner of her mouth and dripped on to the bedsheet.

He continued. 'They say the city is over three thousand years old. The people there tell a story of a king of Hasankeyf who built a bridge across the river to join his city with Biltiskeyf, which lay on the far bank. The bridge would take twenty years to build. As he grew older, the king entrusted the project to his only son. Each day his son would ride his stallion to the other side, directing masons and engineers. Evenings, he was the guest of the ruler of Biltiskeyf and his daughter. She had eyes of mauve, like the edges of a sunrise, and every morning the son would stand at the top of the cliffs, waiting for that brief moment when the sky lightened and the sun's edge touched the horizon, so he could catch a glimpse of that colour. Secretly, they became lovers. They dreamed that the bridge would unite their two nations, allowing them to build a life together.' He stopped, self-conscious.

'That's how they tell the story anyway,' he added quietly. The first orange rays of the tropic day broke through the trees and fragmented across the walls of the caravan. She faced him, propped on her elbow again, watching him. Her hair fell over and between her breasts.

He continued. 'But as the bridge moved close to completion, the old king grew increasingly senile and suspicious. He accused the king of Biltiskeyf of plotting against him to take over and rule both cities once the bridge was completed. As the days passed, his paranoia boiled inside him, conjuring ever more improbable conspiracies. One night, in a drunken rage, he ordered the bridge destroyed. That night, his soldiers tore down twenty years' work of a thousand men, pulling out the supports, and undermining the great buttresses. You can still see the remains of the stonework. He forbade his son from ever seeing his lover again. That morning, after watching the sun rise and glimpsing again the mauve of her eyes, he rode his charger off the cliff and into the river gorge. They say it took him a full minute to fall.'

He looked away, and then down at the floor.

She ran her hand gently through his hair and across the back of his neck. 'What do you think about that?' she said in a whisper. 'Dying for love.'

He looked out of the caravan window, into the virid depth of the forest. He had waited for this moment for so long and yet now he dreaded it. Doubt flared within him like a virus, mutating, multiplying, eroding. 'What else is there, Helena?'

'I don't know. Elephants, perhaps.' She kissed the back of his neck and got out of bed. 'Maybe you just have to find what matters most and live for it.'

She got out of bed and stood naked in front of the small mirror, brushing her hair. Her head was tilted to one side as she pulled the brush down with even strokes. He lay watching her athlete's body, the pale skin like water flowing over bleached river stone. He hoped they would be together for a long time.

The morning sun had started to warm the little caravan. She was dressing now, carefully, for her nuptials. He watched her pull a skirt over a long, tanned calf, over the bony knees. The slightest of brassieres.

She stopped dressing and turned to face him. He looked into her eyes. 'Tell me about those girls,' she said. 'The village girls you slept with.' She was dressed now, in a long white skirt and fitted white jacket with white pumps. Her head touched the roof of the caravan.

He looked down, tried to hide the blood burning in his face. 'Girl,' he said. 'Just the once.' He could remember it even now, walking back through the darkened village afterwards, feeling physically ill, promising himself he would never do it again.

'OK. Girl. Tell me. I need to know.'

'I wrote it in the letters,' he said. 'I'm sorry.'

'Was she very young?' She was looking at herself in the mirror, applying shadow to her eyelids.

'I didn't ask her age.'

'What was her name, then? At least you asked her name?'

'Not now, Helena.'

She closed her eyes a long moment. 'I don't understand how their fathers do such a thing.'

'It's a different world, Helena. Don't judge it.'

'I'm not.' She was applying lipstick now, a pale blush. 'I'm judging *you*.' She was staring at him, back through the mirror, a harsh inversion. 'I'm going to Zimbabwe,' she said.

He turned to face her, unsure of what he had just heard. 'What did you say?'

'As soon as the honeymoon is over. I've accepted a position with an NGO there.'

He sat, mouth open, uncomprehending.

'I wanted to tell you, but a letter wouldn't have reached you in time. I'll be working in a wildlife rescue centre in Hwange National Park.'

He sat in the suddenly unbearable closeness of the caravan, all his plans crumbling into red laterite, worthless, barren soil. 'You know that I won't be finished here until Christmas.'

She stood, smoothed her skirt. 'I didn't plan it. I was going to join you, Warren. I was going to drop everything and come to be with you. But after I got your letter, well, I started looking. I've already made the commitment. It's only three months. You can join me when you finish, if you want to.'

'Jesus, Hel, I thought...' He stopped short. What had he thought? That she would come here, forgive everything, marry him, live with him, as if nothing had happened?

'You should dress, we have to leave soon.' She was crying, crying on her wedding day.

A Wedding

'We are here to be married,' he said, pushing the stamped and sealed Notice of Wedding form towards the Justice of the Peace, who sat slumped behind his desk, white-haired head on folded arms. An old rotary phone perched at the edge of the desk, its cord coiled on the floor, disconnected. A ceiling fan clicked slowly overhead. Green hospital paint peeled from the walls, institutional grey beneath. A lizard scurried across the cinderblock, darting between the bands of light and shade streaming through the shuttered windows. And from the schoolyard next door, the shrieks of children playing.

Kwesi said something in Twi and the Justice lifted his head from the desk. His eyes were bloodshot and his breath reeked of alcohol. He looked at the paper, as if in search of some missing approval, and then nodded and put out his hand, the signal to sit.

They sat in chairs facing the desk. Kwesi and the men of his rig crew stood in a semi-circle behind them.

The Justice opened a desk drawer and retrieved an elaborate form adorned with swathes of blue, and a red, black and yellow crest – the Ghanaian coat of arms. He placed the form on the desk and reached out to a glass jar crammed full of pens and pencils. His deeply veined hand trembled and shook, and for a moment, it appeared he would be unable to close his fingers around one of the implements. Finally, he succeeded in drawing a Bic ballpoint pen from the jar. Coagulated blue ink balled around the pen's nib. The Justice looked up and said:

'Name.'

They spelled their names out slowly, the man registering their commitment in unsteady and illegible handwriting. After the form was complete, he opened a small book and read in a deep, gravelled voice:

'Do you, Helena Dubois, take this man to be your husband?'

'I do,' she answered, squeezing the young engineer's hand and looking into his eyes.

'Will you love, honour and obey him till death do you part?'

'I will,' she said, glancing up at him.

And then the Justice asked the young engineer if he would spend the rest of his life with this one woman, or at least give it his best shot, and do his utmost to protect her and provide for her and her children, and care for her and live up to all of her expectations of what life should bring, and stay with her even if she were to fall ill, or go insane and forget his name and slowly grow incapable of even the most basic functions, just as his grandmother had when he was still a boy … And he looked at this creature who he hardly knew and he realised that he felt no fear. The trepidation and hurt of before were gone. There was no panic in him and no urge to flight, and when he said yes, and it was done, and the man pronounced them wed, he realised that it was the easiest thing he had ever done. But he did not know why it was so, only that it was.

They signed the register and then they kissed. The Ghanaians, the men he worked with, their witnesses today, shot big, white toothy grins. He shook each of their hands in turn, in the way they had taught him: grip, clasp, and slip into a snap of second finger and thumb. They laughed every time he did it. She kissed each of the Ghanaians. She towered over the stocky Africans, her ivory skirt flowing in the breeze. Everything about her was contrast, her skin pale against the deep-red earth of the town, wedding white accentuating the black of the men's faces and arms, the arctic blue of her irises reflected in their own murky tannin eyes.

They all drove down to the Elmina hotel, a hopeful collection of decaying buildings built in the 1970s for tourists who never came. Waiters in greying threadbare livery met them in the empty gravelled courtyard and showed them to a table on the outdoor patio that overlooked the beach and the aquamarine sweep of the bay. The breeze carried the smells of the sea, iodine and chlorine, amino acids searching to combine. Palm fronds swayed above them.

Helena sat on his right, the sole female in a system of men. Drinks were poured and toasts made. Kwesi wished them long life and many children and they all laughed and smiled at her. Then Kwesi produced a small figure carved in ebony and waved it above the newly married couple. He offered it to Helena.

'This is from all of us to you,' he said. 'It is the fertility goddess Akua'ba. This is the real one, from the juju-man who has put into it the real power of juju. It will give you many babies.'

Helena took the statue from Kwesi and looked at it carefully. And then she stood and leaned over and kissed him on both cheeks.

After the meal, the men chatted and smoked, each of them glancing almost too frequently at the pale, beautiful woman in their midst. More drinks were ordered and each of the men rose in turn to make a toast, those assembled dissolving into laughter before each speech was finished. Kwesi disappeared and returned a few minutes later with a huge silver ghetto-blaster under his arm, which he deployed on the ground at the far end of the table. He popped in a cassette, and soon the Ghanaians were up, swaying to the African rhythms. It wasn't long before Helena joined them, and the young engineer leaned back in his chair and watched her dance among the black men, their smiles as pale as her skirt, her dilated pupils as dark as their skin.

By the time the Ghanaians made to leave, the sky had already begun its nocturnal transformation, sky-blue to mauve and then star-blasted night. Kwesi wished them good luck and the men wove their way towards the parking lot.

The young engineer signed the bill to the room and tipped the waiters. Fingers entwined, they followed the stonework path, past the main building with its peeling shutters and rusting iron roof, towards the bungalows scattered amid a grove of tall, ring-trunked coconut trees that stretched away along the beach. The lights of

Elmina Fort blinked in the distance. Waves rolled on to the beach, the surf a phosphorescent froth that lit the way to some distant point they could neither see nor sense. Beyond, the sea was as black and imponderable as an imploding star, with only the constellations above to provide reference.

Where the path jogged inland towards the first bungalows, they turned towards the water. They walked along the beach for a while, baby fingers hooked together, shoes hanging from free hands. The water rose to embrace them, the surf flowing cool over their feet and ankles before sliding back down the beach to gather strength for another caress. A rising land breeze blew across their necks and faces, warm and insistent, rich with the smells of earth and woodsmoke. Yellow porch lights shuddered among the arching trunks.

The bungalow was capped with a sloping tin roof and skirted on two sides by covered verandas. He unlocked the door, opened it and searched the inside wall for the light switch. A single lamp in the far corner of the room flickered to life under a dingy yellow shade, a ceiling fan spun in an irregular orbit. The bed had been turned down and the windows thrown open. White curtains streamed and fluttered.

He took her by the waist and pulled her to him. She wrapped her arms around his neck and kissed him. Her body was supple and strong. He slid her skirt down over her hips and let it fall to the floor. With a step and a little kick, she sent it sweeping across the tiles.

'Let's see if the juju works,' she whispered.

The Gulf of Guinea

He woke early, put on shorts and a T-shirt, slipped out into the cool stillness of the morning.

The sky was clear. He looked down along the gentle curve of the white-sand beach, towards the far point, the old Portuguese slaving fort and the outlet of the muddy Pra river beyond. Fishermen sat on the beach next to long dug-out boats, picking through their nets. Small piles of newly caught silver fish flipped on the sand nearby. The fort looked to be about five kilometres away, and he set out at a slow run along the beach, oscillating between the washed-up jetsam of the high-water mark and the edge of the surf, trying to keep to the hard sand, where the running was easiest.

It was good to run again, to feel the oxygen-rich blood pumping into his muscles and the sweat leach the toxins from his flesh. Despite a night where sleep had come only in intermittent swoons, he felt strong and fresh. He passed some fishermen carrying a boat up the beach. They watched as he ran by, called out to him. He kept going. Further on, a group of small boys clustered excitedly around a just-landed net that squirmed and flashed on the sand, its silver prisoners thrashing against each other in futile attempts at escape. The boys looked up and smiled at him. One of them, with dark dreadlocked hair and mahogany skin, much lighter than the others, waved at him. His features were more Arab than African. The young engineer looked away and accelerated down the beach, tried to run his head clear. But the harder he ran, the faster he went, the stronger the images became, until the beach seemed to fill with children running and playing, and everywhere he looked, they stared up at him with eyes full of questions, their hands outstretched towards him, beckoning, crying out to him, *bibini, bibini.*

By the time he returned to the bungalow, he was breathing hard and sweating heavily. She sat in a wood-frame woven palm chair on the veranda with a book in her lap. A long, blue-and-green patterned sundress flowed around her. She looked up at him from under a wide-brimmed white hat. The blue of sky and sea seemed to be gathered and made temperate by her eyes.

'Good morning, baby,' she said as he approached. 'How was your run?'

'Hard,' he said, bent over, hands on knees, breathing deeply. 'What are you reading?'

She flipped the book up to show him the cover. '*Candide*. I read it in school, but I would like to read it again, with older eyes.'

'How are you this morning?'

'Happy and in love,' she said. 'Also tired and sore.' She smiled and laughed. 'How many little deaths can a person endure, I wonder?'

After breakfast, they decided to walk down the beach and visit Elmina Fort. They packed a water bottle each, some sandwiches from the kitchen and the beach towels into their small daypacks. By mid-morning, they stood at the base of the outer wall and looked up at the main tower.

The tour lasted most of two hours. Their guide, a short, stocky man with a pockmarked face and misshapen lower lip who introduced himself as Kofi – born on Friday – led them through the tortured history of the area. The fort provided the stratigraphy and landscape of the story. Kofi spoke an awkward formal English, as if reading from a university history text, full of nested sub-clauses. He said things like, 'In addition to their headquarters at Elmina, here where you stand presently, the Portuguese built forts at Axim and Shama, which, like Elmina Castle, can still be seen today; and also at Accra, though sadly and unfortunately for them, the Ga, a local war-like tribe, not at all like the friendly Akim of this area, of which I am a direct and happy descendant, incidentally, captured and destroyed the Accra fort in fifteen seventy-six,' which made Helena giggle and hide her face in her hands, lest she would offend him or hurt his feelings.

Deep in the bowels of the fortress, the air was cool and dank. Helena shivered in her thin dress. He put his arms around her and held her close. Born on Friday told them how the slaves would arrive shackled in long columns driven by their Ashanti owners and be transferred to the European masters, who would then sex them and herd them into these deep, airless stone dungeons. Here they would stay, with barely enough room to stand, wading in their own filth, the dead expunged every few days, until the slave ships arrived to carry them across the sea. Sometimes they waited months. Kofi pointed to a line that had been painted on the wall of the cell, some two metres above the floor. He said: 'When the fort was restored the year before last, the workers, including my own cousin, found a layer of dried and hardened excrement that had built up on the floor over the years. That line shows the level of the floor before they started digging.'

After the tour, they stood on the battlements and looked out over the small boat harbour and across the water, warming themselves in the sun. They could see the muddy stain where the river discharged into the sea, a huge brown fan of roiling sediment. Towering white cumulus now crowded the horizon and a sea breeze was rising. He thanked Kofi and tipped him a couple of thousand cedi. Helena was quiet and he did not try to speak with her.

After a while, she said: 'I want to be surrounded by the sea. Let's swim.'

They walked to a small cove on the lee side of the point. The water was calm and blue, and in the shelter of the fort, the air was still and hot. They drank some water, shared a banana from her pack, and stripped down to their swimsuits. She wore a microscopic two-piece that she had obviously been saving for him, and mirrored black racing goggles whose raw functionality seemed completely incongruous with the frivolous sex-toy look of her bikini. Despite the depleted ache in his groin, he felt himself harden. But before he could press himself against her and give her proof of his arousal, she was running out into the water, skipping over the waves with long, athletic strides.

Soon they were swimming side by side, out towards the end of
the point and the open sea beyond. Every sixth stroke allowed him
a brief glimpse of her, head down, arms arcing like a windmill into
the water as she powered her way through the waves. He focused
on his breathing and technique, made sure he pointed his toes and
kept his elbows bent on the curve of the stroke, as if the instructor
was walking the edge of the pool beside him, calling out, correcting,
urging him on even as his lungs began to explode. He would not fall
behind. He would keep up and be there with her, even as she found
her rhythm and pushed on again.

By the time she relented and pulled up he was over twenty metres
behind and breathing hard. They must have been going at it for over
half an hour, easily fifteen hundred metres, maybe more, based on his
normal pace. He swam to her and began treading water. They looked
back to the coast. Distance over water is always exaggerated, but it
looked as if they were a lot further out than they should be, two or
even three kilometres. The fort was just a blemish on the white liga-
ment of beach. He pulled up his goggles, rinsed them out, put them
back over his eyes and plunged his head into the water. Suspended
particles of sediment spun in a random dance all around him, a fraction only of the billions of tonnes of red mud and silt ripped from
the heart of the continent by the spring rains and pumped into the
sea like blood. He pulled his head out of the water.

'We should start back,' he said.

After twenty minutes of hard swimming, they were, it seemed,
even further out to sea. He touched her foot and pulled up. She lifted
her head from the water. He bobbed next to her and stretched his
arms out to triangulate on the fort and a small hill to the east that
should have been somewhere not far inland from the hotel.

'We're getting pushed out by the current from the river,' he said
finally. 'Are you OK?'

'I'm fine,' she said, her breath coming in short gasps. She looked
worried.

'We should swim parallel to the current, not against it, and try to break out of it.' He pointed towards the hill and the place where he figured the hotel should be.

They made good progress through the water. Both instinctively slowed their stroke rate and breathing to conserve energy. She was a strong swimmer, but now she was tiring and he slowed to stay with her. The combination of a freshening sea breeze and an opposing current began to build the height of the waves, and they had to work up each steepening wall of water before falling down the long back-side into the trough and then back up into the next face. They were expending almost as much effort working across the waves as they had going directly against the current.

They stopped again to rest and gauge progress. They were now even further out. They had been in the water for almost two hours. Clouds covered the sky, and the surface of the water was no longer blue, but the colour of dull iron. The air was getting cooler. Helena was shivering. She wrapped her arms around herself, frog-kicking beside him. He pulled her to him and rubbed her back and arms with his hands, trying to create some friction to warm her muscles.

'Don't worry,' he said to himself as much as her. 'It's just like a rip. If we keep moving along the shore, we should find a place where the current starts to ease, and maybe flows back in, like an eddy.'

'Physics,' she said, teeth chattering.

'Exactly.'

They started swimming.

By the time the sun was touching the edge of the water, they had been dragged further away from shore; how far he could no longer estimate with any hope of accuracy. Any detail along the coast had melted away, and all that remained was a dark strip of low-lying topography, darker than the churning water, increasingly obscured by the peaks of the building waves. The swell sucked them from crest to trough and then launched them back into the darkening heavens, the first shorelights appearing now in brief, flickering glimpses.

He concentrated on his technique, tried to optimise every movement. Now he swam almost constantly with eyes above the churning surface, keeping her close. They had slowed considerably, perhaps down to a couple of hundred metres through the water every ten minutes. Gone was the powerful technique of a sliced forward entry; her stroke was now slow and deliberate – each arm seemed to hover in the air for a moment before it fell with a splash into the water ahead, to be replaced a while later by the other, equally tired, equally limp, to fall in its turn into the water, as she urged herself forwards, scouring the last joules of energy from dwindling reserves. They were exhausting themselves and losing ground. At least they seemed to be moving laterally along the shore. Somewhere the current had to ease and turn back in on itself.

A faint metallic sound cut through the water, like a steel nail tapping on a tin cup. At first, he ignored it – just the noise of the water playing on his ears. But slowly, it got louder. And then there was no mistaking it – a propeller, closing fast, probably from seaward.

He pushed his head up and out of the water and yelled to Helena to stop. He was in a trough between two waves, dark water in every direction. He waited for the swell to catapult him upwards and, as it did, he swung himself around towards the sound. White spume snaked across a field of corrugated liquid that stretched away as far as he could see. Again, he used the brief seconds on the wave's crest to scan the churning water. He called to Helena to do the same.

'I think there's a boat coming,' he shouted. 'Keep your eyes open.'

Again and again, he rode the swell up and each time he could see nothing but the embers of the horizon and the roiling surface of the Gulf of Guinea.

'There it is!' she yelled from the top of a mountain of water. For the briefest moment, her goggles flashed red and pink before she tumbled down the backside of the wave. Up he went, straining to see in the direction she had signalled.

And there it was, a black sliver bouncing over the surface. It was only a hundred metres or so away, ploughing its way to shore, white spray shooting from its bow as it sliced through the waves. Two figures stood in the boat, rocking back and forth to steady themselves against the roll of the swell, fishermen returning home after a day on the banks.

He called out to them. Each time he neared the crest of a wave he pushed his body up from the water with two strong kicks and yelled and waved his arms over his head in the universal sign of distress. Helena had moved half a wavelength away, so that each time he was sucked back down into a trough, she was on a crest, waving and calling out to the fishermen.

The boat was closing now. But it was making for a destination further west, so that as the craft came closer to shore, it also drifted further away from them. The boat's engine chugged away against the current, puff-puffing little clouds of blue smoke that dissipated quickly in the wind. Every few seconds, a white sheet of spray erupted from the bow and covered the men as the boat lurched from trough to peak, the red, green and yellow stripes along the hull now clearly visible. He screamed louder, pushed himself up and out of the water with all his force. *Please just look over here. Surely, you've got to see us.* Still the boat lurched along, the men intent on home, perhaps already thinking of wives, children, lovers waiting, a warm fire and hot food. He yelled until his throat was raw, until he could produce only a coarse rasp.

And then it was clear that they were not going to stop. He watched in silence as the craft shrank away and then finally dissolved into the cantor set of lights blinking on the shore.

'Assholes,' he breathed.

He sculled his way towards her and put his arm around her waist. She was cold and shivering uncontrollably. He pulled her to him and held her close, rubbing her arms and back, trying to force heat into her body. He looked at his watch. They'd been in the water almost three and a half hours now. The danger of hypothermia was real. If they didn't get out of the water soon, they would be in real trouble. And as he held her and rubbed her arms and back, he realised: *we could die here.* How stupid that would be.

They tried to go on, but after their efforts to attract the boat they were both almost exhausted. Her shoulders and back had cramped up, and she could now only manoeuvre with her legs. 'I'm sorry,' she kept saying. 'I'm sorry.'

She lashed herself to his back, piggy-back style, her hands gripping his shoulders, and he tried to pull her along, breast-stroking like some crippled four-legged mutant frog. It would help to keep her warm, and they had to keep going, east, parallel with the current, away from the mouth of the river.

After what felt like an hour but was probably only a few minutes, he noticed that she had stopped kicking. Her full weight was now on him, and he could feel his strength draining away with the extra effort.

'Hel,' he said between breaths. 'You OK?'

She tightened her arms around him a moment, just a pulse. She was fading. He asked her about her studies, but she just mumbled something about statistics and tailed off into silence.

'What should we name our kids?' he said, labouring beneath her.

'I like Adam,' she said, brighter. 'And Ethan.'

'And for a girl?'

'I'm not going to have girls.'

'What do you have against girls?'

'Nothing. I just know I'm going to have boys.'

'Humour me.'

'Beryl. My mother's middle name.'

'Beryl it is,' he said.

'Ethan.'

'OK. Ethan.'

By now it was very dark. He tried to decipher the clusters of lights strung along the shore, to identify some landmark by which to judge their position, but nothing was familiar or known. Finally, he settled on a jumble of closely spaced white and yellow lights, brighter than the rest, almost dead ahead, and held this point fixed, as if it could provide succour simply by being there. He was near exhaustion. His limbs felt like sag rubber. The lights on the shore, his compass, divided and drifted apart like some back-lit micro-organism asexually reproducing under the microscope, fusing again only when he summoned the effort to refocus his eyes. He knew that he was flirting with the edge of consciousness. Helena had not spoken for a long time.

And then she said: 'It's getting warmer. I can feel it.'

She was right. The wind had dropped. The sea was warming. They must be moving into shallower water. He looked at his cardinal point on the shore. Within the cluster, one intensely bright point of light blinked behind the edge of the waves, a cool Rigel blue, separate and distinct from the smaller stars in the whorl. The lights were breaking up, separating.

'We've hit the back-current,' he said. A final reserve of glycogen pumped into his body from deep within. 'We're being pulled back towards the shore.'

Helena tightened her grip on his shoulders and said: 'I think I can swim now.'

She slipped off his back and began a slow steady sidestroke. Soon they were making good progress towards the shore. The water continued to warm, and the current was pulling them along quickly now. A flat moon peeked out from behind the clouds, splashed molten gunmetal across the surface of the sea.

They made shore on a dark, tree-fringed beach a few hundred metres from a small boat harbour. The wind had died off almost completely now and a gentle surf washed them like drifting corpses into the shallows and up on to the beach. They lay side by side on the sand, prostrate supplicants, chastised but unrepentant.

Λ

The next day, they sat in the hotel restaurant and ordered breakfast. They were the only people in the place.

'It was funny, yesterday,' she said. 'I was quite prepared to die. I was surprised. It didn't seem difficult at all.'

He cracked open the steaming shell of a boiled egg. 'Funny? I don't think so.'

'What I mean is, now that we are together, I am not afraid of the future. Whatever it brings.' She sipped her tea and looked out of the window. After a time, she said: 'Do you think there are sharks here?'

'I don't know,' he said. 'I expect so.'

'We were lucky,' she said.

'We were stupid.'

She smiled. 'Thank you for going back and getting our rucksacks last night.'

He had found them just where they had left them the day before, on the sand near the rocky edge of the little bay at Elmina point.

'My camera was in there. Our wedding photos.'

'I guess we got lucky,' he said.

'Yes, we are,' she said still looking out of the window.

'People here are very honest.'

'I meant we're lucky to be alive. To have found each other in all of this…' she swept her arm towards the beach and the sea '…this confusion.'

'The improbability of life.'

'Impossibility, more like. Boltzmann knew that.'

'Entropy.'

She nodded.

'Please don't go,' he said.

March 13th. Geneva

I drop the manuscript on to the bed beside me. It's still dark out, no traffic yet. My phone buzzes. I reach for it, knock the empty whisky bottle from the side table. I don't remember drinking that much, but it explains the pounding in my head. I pick up my phone and, after a few attempts, get the print recognition to work. The thing lights up, this tether to the way the world wants me to be. It's a message from Maria: Be there. Don't be late. This is IMPORTANT.

I consider calling her, decide I can't deal with another of those conversations right now. About how I am the worst thing that ever happened to her, such a disappointment, about how everything is just so difficult, always a battle. I type out two letters: O *and* K. *Press send.*

I sit a while staring at the wall. Fear creeps over me like the cold air flowing from the window I forgot to close last night.

I Google this guy Ludwig Boltzmann. Austrian physicist, developed the theory of entropy, encapsulated in his (apparently) famous equation S = k Log W, which describes the inexorable tendency of the universe to move from highly ordered states to more disordered ones. This impulse towards disorder or randomness is what drives the apparent forward movement of time, or at least that's what Wikipedia claims. Suffering from bipolar disorder, Boltzmann hanged himself in 1906 in Duino, near Trieste, at the age of fifty-two. Jesus, fifty-two. But who cares, right? We've all got our own lives to lead, our own problems.

Still, it makes me think, all of it. Those stories of my parents in Africa. Guess that's what he intended, reaching out from oblivion like this. I never doubted that he loved her, that they loved each other. You could see they were compatible. Even as a kid I could tell. You could just feel it, whenever you were around them. Everyone did. And then something went wrong. Events just got in the way, I guess. That tendency to disorder.

That's sure what happened with me and Maria. I don't know if we ever were right for each other, not fundamentally, like my mum and dad were. It felt like we were, at the beginning. But it hasn't been like that for a long time. She just doesn't understand me. And looking back, if I'm honest with myself, I don't think she ever did. I sure as hell don't understand her.

Problem is, we never talked about it. We never set out any rules. We just tripped along, day by day, hoping that the physical attraction and the buzz would be enough, but we never established how we would do it together. *Any of it. And then, one day, I realised that we were both just chasing our own ideas of life. And whatever overlap there might have been at the beginning, whatever intersection Rachel provided us, had just corroded away. At least my old man, he had something with my mum, some kind of connection. Some kind of glory.*

I met Constantina on the internet. One of those dating sites. I signed up while I was still with Maria. I wasn't looking for anything other than sex, certainly not any kind of serious relationship. It was a bit of a joke, actually. I never thought something would come of it. All I put on my profile was: Don't want everything to be a f—ing competition. *That was it. That and an old picture of me that I like. Constantina replied the next day and we met a week later at a pub down by the river. She was an absolute knockout, and we talked a long time about nothing in particular, nothing serious. We fucked on the first date.*

But now she wants more. A lot more than I can give her. She's ten years younger than me, for one thing. A different time in her life. She wants kids, a man who will be a good husband. That used to mean something different to what it means now. Well, no thanks. I've fallen into that well, tasted that domestic poison. Felt the fire die inside me.

Jesus, sometimes I sure do wish my mum had been around to talk to me when I was growing up. I reckon she had it all figured. Sounds like my old man thought the same, the things he wrote. So, what the hell happened? What went wrong?

I wonder if Boltzmann ever considered the role of stupidity as a driving force in entropy. God knows, a lot of the disorder I've seen has been a result of just plain stupid things that people did, sometimes knowingly, often not. Maybe that's why the symbol for entropy is a capital S. It's pretty much the one thing I've come to understand. That people are stupid. There you go. A rule to live by. Understand that and you can explain just about everything. A hell of a lot more useful as a construct for modelling the world, I figure, than Boltzmann's equation.

Before the Revolution

The engineer's father was from that stronger generation when being a man was still important, when the differences between the sexes were real and understood and valued.

The engineer had never seen his father, who was a lawyer, cry. Not once, not ever. He'd seen him angry, and bitter, and many times as a boy he'd seen him drunk, stumbling about the house, knocking over furniture and spilling stuff on the floor, and a few times, when he wasn't supposed to and had crept downstairs after bedtime drawn by the shrieks and the hard, brutal whispers, he'd seen his father raise his hand and his mother turn her head and cower in the corner. But he'd never seen him cry. Now there were websites with names like *Man Up* that encouraged men to show their feelings, to blubber like little girls. He wondered what his father would have thought of this, what he would have said. Probably nothing. Just a grunt, or, if he was drunk, he might have said something like, 'Fucking feminists. Trying to cut our balls off, so they can sew them on and pretend they're men.' As a boy, he'd always wondered just what such an operation might entail, and where exactly the scrotum, and presumably the penis, would attach (the feminine form in all its glorious complexity then still a terrifying unknown), and how, once accomplished, that might allow them, over time, to be transformed into men.

The engineer realised now that, to his father, the sexes were involved in a titanic and never-ending struggle for power and control. And sometimes, when he was drunk, his father would rant about his own mother, about how she dominated and bullied his father. And in those skirmishes, the full-out battles, crying was losing.

The engineer was fourteen when his father moved the family west, to Vancouver. He'd gone from a small private school where everyone spoke French and wore uniforms, to an English state high school in a well-off part of the city. On the engineer's first day at the new school, a group of older boys beat him up and stuffed him into a locker. He never wore a tie to school again or carried a briefcase. He blended in, wore jeans and T-shirts and hoodies like the other kids, and when he needed to, he fought back. After a while, he fought even when he didn't need to. The first time, the other boy, who was much bigger, hit him square in the eye with a straight jab. It knocked him down. As he got to his feet, he realised that he was crying. He looked around the hallway, bewildered. A crowd had gathered, and they all stood staring at him. And then one of the girls said, 'Look, he's crying.' And then everyone was laughing and he could feel the shame even now from the remembering, and he shouted out that he wasn't crying, that he had been hit in the eye, but no one listened and so he got up and faced up to the guy again and got knocked down again, and then once more with the same result, and then it was over. After that he followed his father's example. He never cried again.

The engineer often wondered if that made him a bad person. Or just a flawed one. The latter, he admitted. As to the former, he'd tried to be good. Tried to live up to Helena's expectations. He hadn't always been successful. And although he never showed his emotions, it didn't mean they weren't there. It simply meant that they were not anyone else's concern. People would do best to look after their own inner selves, instead of worrying and talking about everyone else's.

The engineer never really knew what his father did for a living.

Whenever anyone would ask him the question, he'd just reply that his father was a lawyer. He knew that his father had dropped out of the equivalent of high school in England, after his own dad died of cancer. He was only fifteen, and he'd gone to work doing some menial job. After a few years of labouring, he'd decided to become a lawyer. He had to finish school at night by correspondence, including learning Latin, which he'd always hated. He'd married the engineer's mother and he'd emigrated to Canada with twenty pounds in his pocket, a new wife and a law degree.

His father certainly didn't do the things he'd imagined as a kid that a lawyer should do. He didn't go to court and defend people or prosecute criminals. He was always travelling. In the engineer's memory, his father is always leaving – his mother in tears – or coming back from some exotic place bearing gifts. One time his father had come back from Sweden and brought him a microscope and slide set. He'd loved it. But his father never talked about what he did. Although the engineer had always had his suspicions.

The engineer knew that his father was smart and that he worked hard. He had, right up until the day he died, an exceptional memory for detail of all kinds. He was especially good with faces and names (something the engineer didn't inherit). He articled in Canada, was hired by the law firm he articled with, and, from what the engineer could remember, must have risen quickly. As a child, one is only ever partially aware of parents' comings and goings. Whatever his father was doing, the family would suddenly and periodically seem to have a lot of money. Soon, they were off on trips to Europe and America. They moved into a nice old house; he and his brother were sent to private school. The engineer's father liked cars, and there was a succession of new models, a big brown Oldsmobile Toronado, and then a series of Chevy Corvettes. His mother's wardrobe exploded, and every night his parents seemed to be out at some party, returning late (he could hear them talking, laughing sometimes, his father crashing into things, swearing). Sometimes they would argue.

And then one day, his mother woke them very early when it was still dark and told him and his brother to get dressed. It was a school day, but it was far too early to go to school. She hustled them down to the front door and helped them with their coats and hats and mitts and handed them each a little suitcase, before walking with them through the snow to a waiting taxi. Next thing they knew they were at the airport and she was explaining that they would not be going to go to school for a little while and that Daddy would be joining them later on. A day later, they were in a hotel room in Panama City. They loved it. He and Rhys spent all day at the pool, ordering hamburgers and drinking cold Cokes and running around the hotel gardens. Later, they rented a wooden cottage near the beach. Their father would come, spend a few days with them, then disappear again. And then, just as suddenly, about a month later, they returned to Toronto. No explanation, just time to go back. A little holiday, they were told to tell anyone who asked.

Not long before he died, the engineer's father told him one story about that time. In a way, it helped him to put some of the pieces together. In some ways, though, it just made everything more opaque. They were sitting in his father's house on a little island off the coast of British Columbia, looking out at the rain angling down across the bay, and his father started talking about Cuba. He used to go there a lot, before Castro and the revolution, before his sons were born. Sometimes he went on business – that's what he called it: business. A few times he took his wife. The engineer still had a faded photo of his parents on the marble veranda of a hotel in Havana overlooking the sea. It is 1960. They look so young, he in a dark suit and tie, she in a white skirt and matching jacket and hat and gloves. The colours are faded, but you can see how beautiful it must have been. And then the revolution came.

Everyone his father had been dealing with – the regime and the big, wealthy families – was either shot or fled across the ninety miles of water to Miami, carrying with them whatever they could. The engineer's father and his business partners had just concluded a big deal (for what, he never said) with one of the wealthy Cuban family conglomerates and feared that they would now not be paid. They had delivered the product a few months before the regime was over- thrown. By the time his father told him this story, he was old, in his eighties, and while he was still sharp, he had a tendency to skip from idea to idea. He described how he and his two business partners had flown into Cuba, just before the Missile Crisis and the blockade, on a private jet. Just out of Miami, they realised they didn't have a corkscrew on board. They told the pilot to divert to Nassau, so they could obtain one. Corkscrew secured and with the wine flowing, they arrived in Havana to an armed escort. They were taken to the presidential palace and a deal was worked out. Castro wanted the goods – they had been confiscated in the name of the new government – but he wanted to be fair, especially because they were Canadians. They negotiated a while, trying to insist on the original cash payment in full, but they got nowhere. The Cubans offered an alternative. It was take it or leave it. They decided to take it.

They were driven in a two-ton military truck to a bullet-riddled warehouse on the outskirts of Havana. A colonel, who was with them, unlocked the doors and led them inside. The entire warehouse was stacked from floor to ceiling with possessions confiscated from the homes of elite members of the deposed regime. There was art, jewellery, furniture, clothes, cars, everything you could imagine. The colonel told them they could take anything they wanted, as long as it fitted into the truck. They had two hours.

The partners, half drunk, couldn't believe their eyes. They agreed on a central collection point near the door, split up and raced into the warehouse.

'It was incredible,' his father said. 'You can't understand the wealth these people had.' He looked out across the water for a while and then continued.

'With ten minutes to spare, we're standing at the collection point, looking at the pile. There was far too much to fit into the truck, let alone the plane. We culled about three-quarters of it, but we were running out of time. Finally, we had what we thought they could take out. One of my partners, Alan, had found what appeared to be an original Picasso and a spectacular diamond necklace. You should have seen the look on his face, holding these things up for us to see. Me, I'd found a collection of rare coins and an entire set of sterling silver tableware. We did a quick tally and figured we might be close to breaking even, worst case, fifty cents on the dollar. The colonel was shouting at us that it was time to go. But we had nothing to carry all the stuff in. Alan ran off and reappeared a moment later with a big carpet. He unrolled it and we threw everything on to it, then rolled it back up and carried it to the truck.'

'Not bad,' the engineer said to his father, refilling his glass. 'Considering what was going on.'

His father smiled. 'But here's the thing,' he said. 'It's always the way things work out. When we got back to Canada, we flogged the stuff, got some pretty good prices for it, especially some of the women's clothes – furs and the like. But the Picasso turned out to be a copy. The diamond necklace was glass. We were going to lose a lot of money on the deal. And I mean a lot. Anyway, Alan, he still had the carpet – the one we carried all the stuff out with – in his garage. A few weeks later, a friend of his was over at his place and he showed it to him. Turns out, this thing was a thirteenth-century French tapestry that once belonged to King Louis IX. The mangy old thing was worth more than everything else we took from that warehouse put together.'

⋀

The engineer's father never spoke to him about Rhys dying. About him killing his own brother. Never once did he say anything about it. He never cried, never blamed. He just kept it all to himself.

March 13th. Still in Geneva

I've delayed my flight back to London for another day. Maria will have to wait.

Haven't turned on my phone for over twenty-four hours now. I just don't want to know. Whatever it is, I don't want to hear about it, don't want to have to deal with it, solve it, broker it, explain it or do it. I just want to be alone, to be left alone. I want to walk by the lake and sit in my hotel room and look out at the mountains and drink, and I want to do it by myself.

I'm pretty sure my mother didn't go to Zimbabwe in the end. My old man must have convinced her to stay with him. Neither of them ever mentioned anything about Zimbabwe that I can remember, anyway, growing up. But then again, they didn't mention much. That's clear now.

Anyway, I know they moved back to Calgary soon after getting married, bought that same house I was in a few days ago, down by the river in Inglewood. It's an older neighbourhood, big gardens, lots of big trees, houses from the start of the last century. That's where I was born. That house.

And from everything I've been told, and the few glimpses of that time I can remember, I think they must have been happy there. Maybe that's why the old man went back there, at the end. Á La Recherche. *He got a job I know he liked – he told me so, several times – with a small consulting company, and Mum finished her degree and started working as a vet. They spent a lot of time in the mountains together, hiking and skiing, just the two of them. After I was born, they always took me along, the boy they named in the middle of a West African sea when they thought they were going to die. I still have a couple of photographs of them, so young, big smiles, my little face poking out of a hooded suit, bundled into a baby carrier on my mother's chest. They look so goddamned happy.*

I met an old drunk out by the lake today. It was early morning, just before sunrise. I couldn't sleep, so I went for a walk. He was sitting on a park bench, sipping from a bottle in a paper bag. You don't see a lot of that here. It surprised me. As I walked past, he said hello, in English. Am I that easy to peg? He didn't ask for money, just said hello. I sat next to him and we started talking. It was pretty obvious that he'd been sleeping rough. His hair was all rasta, tangled and knotted; his beard, too. It's cold here at night, and he was wrapped up in some kind of army-surplus parka with a hood, and had an old woollen blanket draped around his shoulders like someone Van Gogh would have painted in his early period, all dark and miserly. He offered me his bottle and, what the hell, I took a swig. Some sort of foul schnapps. Super sweet.

The old guy asked me where this is, this place. Is this Switzerland? I'm lost, he said. I don't recognise anything.

This is Geneva, I told him. Lake Geneva, out there. He stared out for a while at the water, and then he just shook his head.

'I'm from London,' I told him. 'Canada, originally. I don't know this place either.'

'We're all lost, brother,' he said.

The Chef

It was the chef who'd found him, that first morning, shivering naked on his bed, delirious.

Whatever had infected him, whatever was there now still, ripping him apart, had come upon him suddenly, without preliminary warnings of any sort. One moment he was returning from work, walking back to the guest house along the dirt road that contoured the valley slope, and the next he was doubled up in pain, his body trying to purge itself of every millilitre of fluid it contained.

He had managed to stumble his way to the guest house, crawl to the bathroom. When he awoke later, it was dark. He was on the bathroom floor, covered in sweat and vomit and shit. He stripped himself of his clothes, struggled into the shower. Another bout of nausea sent him back to the toilet, a new level of pain fish-hooking his insides. Wet and shivering, he groped his way to the bedroom, collapsed on to the bed.

The chef had called the doctor, waited by the young engineer's bedside until he arrived and then assigned himself as the patient's chief caretaker. For three days now, the chef had brought him water and sweet tea, administered the medication the doctor had prescribed. He'd helped him navigate the fifteen steps between his bed and the toilet every time his guts started to liquefy, sometimes carrying him in his arms. He washed the shit from his sheets and bathed him when he was too weak or delirious to do it himself. And in all of this, the older man was gentle and patient, respectful; and when the young engineer woke from his dreams and opened his eyes, the chef would be there, nodding to him, smiling.

He wasn't sure if it was the dehydration or the drugs, but the chef now started to appear in the young engineer's dreams. His broad, dark face would materialise among images of home and displaced persons and the violence of poverty, the things he had started to understand about this place, the acute longings of loss and regret. Emerging from a dream, deep in the night, he'd lay panting under the ceiling fan, covered in sweat. The chef would be there, in a chair near the bed, eyes closed, his head titled to one side, mouth agape. In the moonlight streaming through the shutters, the young engineer would trace his gaze along the deep, L-shaped scar that ran from the man's eye to the corner of his mouth. Over the pitted, cratered skin of his face. Across the folds under his chin, and over his big, smooth, powerful forearms. And he would wonder who this man was.

Five weeks the young engineer had been here. And each morning, and every evening, at 07:30 and 19:30 precisely, the chef would arrive at the guest house, dressed immaculately in his white uniform, his traditional stovepipe hat perched proudly on his big head, a crisp white napkin folded over his left arm. His two assistants, young boys from the village dressed in white collared shirts, black trousers and ill-fitting shoes, would follow him in, each wheeling a trolley.

The boys would set the table under the watchful eye and direction of the chef. One place, as if for a state dinner. Crisp linen. Two forks, three knives, two spoons. A sparkling glass, side plate, main plate, soup bowl. Evenings, he would snap his fingers and one of the boys would produce a candle in its holder. The chef would place it on the table, light it. Then he would bow and pull out the chair. 'Dinner is served, sir,' he would say.

It was not what he had expected. Not at all. This was, by all measures, one of the poorest countries in the world. Civil war raged in the north, in Eritrea, and the rebels were moving steadily south towards the capital. But the World Bank had deemed the dam and the hydropower it delivered to the capital important enough to fund their work, and so here he was. Living alone in a palatial guest house with a view across the valley, the dam just three kilometres up-river. Twice a day, the chef appeared with his two helpers and provided him with meals as varied and delicious as he had ever tasted. And every day after returning from work at the dam, walking through the little village that had grown around it, passing workers and their families, hangers-on and hopefuls, he would think about all of this and the disparities and the sheer blind luck that had put him where he was, and all of them there.

Now, on the third day of the sickness, the chef lifted the young engineer's head and raised a bowl to his lips. 'Drink,' he said. 'You are much better now. This will make you strong.'

The soup smelled wonderful, tasted even better. He drank down a few mouthfuls and let the chef lower him back down.

'Thanks, Hakim,' he breathed. 'It must have been the street food I ate. Or the water.'

The chef nodded, gave him more soup. He was a big man, and his uniform – brilliant white and perfectly starched – stretched across his chest as he leaned in with the bowl. 'Not good food there,' he said, in accented English. 'I told you to take care.'

'You did.'

The chef smiled, put a hand on the young engineer's shoulder. 'But you are young. You want to try everything. I understand. This is the time for trying.'

The young engineer winced as a fresh wave of pain sawed its way through his guts. The whisky probably hadn't helped either.

The chef patted him on the shoulder, rose, stood by the bed. 'You are feeling a little better, yes?'

'Thanks to you, Hakim.'

The chef's face creased into a big smile. 'I will go home now. But I will come back and check on you this evening. I will bring you some more soup. Perhaps some fresh bread.'

The young engineer nodded, watched the older man turn and leave the room. The thought of food sent his stomach reeling again. As soon as the chef had gone, he dragged himself out of bed and started towards the bathroom, swaying on unsteady legs.

That afternoon, he managed to sleep. When he woke, it was dark, and through the big windows he could see the lights coming from the cooking fires across the valley. He switched on his bedside lamp, drank some water and trudged to the bathroom. He still felt weak, but the pain had receded.

The young engineer dressed and moved to the living room, sat on the couch. He was trying to concentrate on Robertson Davies' *The Manticore*, when the chef arrived.

'A very light meal tonight,' said the chef, ladling soup into his bowl, his movements precise, expert, no drop wasted. 'Tomorrow you will be much better, and breakfast will be special.'

The young engineer tried the soup. A chicken broth with vegetables, a lovely taste of pepper, perfectly salted. The electrolytes and protein his body was craving. The smell of freshly baked bread filled the room. The chef placed a steaming roll on his side plate, offered him butter. The young engineer broke the roll open, carved out a big chunk of butter and watched it melt into the bread. Never had anything tasted so good. And as he ate, the chef stood silent by the sideboard, the napkin folded over his arm, watching.

When he'd finished, and the table had been cleared and the boys dispatched back to the kitchen, the young engineer stood and shook the chef's hand. The chef made to leave.

'Stay a moment, please, Hakim,' he said.

The chef turned and faced him.

'I wanted to thank you, Hakim. What you have done, over the last few days, well, I don't know what to say.'

The chef smiled, waved this away. 'No matter, no matter,' he said.

'Please, is there some way I can thank you?' said the young engineer, reaching for the fold of US dollars he'd put into his trouser pocket for just this purpose.

The chef glanced down at the young engineer's hand, fixed his gaze, shook his head back and forth. 'No, Mister Warren. Absolutely not.'

The young engineer withdrew his hand, empty. Of course. Of course.

'Thank you, Mister Warren.'

The young engineer nodded. 'What are you doing here, Hakim? In the middle of nowhere. You could work anywhere. The best restaurants.'

The chef glanced down at his shoes a moment. 'This is my home now, Mister Warren.'

'Where did you live before?'

'In Addis.'

'And what did you do?'

The chef glanced over his shoulder, back towards the door. He stood a moment looking straight into the young engineer's eyes, as if making a decision, coming to some determination. After a moment, he said, voice lowered: 'I was head chef at the presidential palace. It was a long time ago.'

The young man drew a breath. 'You were Haile Selassie's chef?'

The chef nodded. 'The emperor and his ministers. State dinners for two hundred people, three hundred sometimes, I cooked for. The very best china, silverware, ingredients shipped from around the world, Russian caviar and French cheese and wines. Ministers, ladies, generals.' He sighed. 'But ten people owned eighty percent of the land. And then there was a terrible famine that the government hid from the world.'

'What happened?'

'The socialist revolution came. Eighty ministers were shot. Many of the staff at the palace, too. The emperor was strangled, God rest his soul. I was captured, held in prison for more than a year. My wife and baby girl almost starved. Finally, I was released, banished to the country. I came here ten years ago, with my family.'

The young engineer, whose life in comparison had been without such tumult, closed his eyes, searched for words that might be adequate, but could find none.

'Please,' said the chef. 'Tell no one. It is still very dangerous for me.'

The young engineer closed his eyes a moment and nodded, offered his hand. 'Of course, Hakim. You have my word.'

The chef shook his hand and left by the back door, as the rules stipulated. The young engineer watched him close the door behind him, then a few minutes later, caught a glimpse of him through the front windows as he turned along the road leading to the village, dressed in dark trousers and jacket. Under his arm, carefully folded, ghostly white in the rising quarter-moon, were his uniform and chef's hat.

The young engineer waited until the chef was almost at the first bend in the road, then he slipped out through the front door and climbed the slope behind the guest house and started through the dark trees and across the fraying rhyolite towards the village. Still weak, he struggled through the darkened ridgeland, panting in the cold, stopping frequently to rest.

The chef wasn't moving quickly. Just ambling along the roadside. The young engineer kept to the trees, close to within about fifty metres of the other man, keeping as quiet as he could. He could hear the chef humming some village tune, his voice deep like a waterfall. Soon they were approaching the village, the chef there on the road, the young engineer tracking him along the high ground of the ridge, a shadow among the trees and the boulders.

And then the chef stopped, stood a moment as if listening for some far-off call. He looked down the road, back along where he'd come, and then turned down a narrow footpath towards a small hut on the edge of the village. Yellow light glowed in a small window, shone warm from gaps between the mud walls and the sloping thatch of the roof. Smoke wisped from the chimney. In the moonlight, the young engineer could make out a little garden out front, vegetables and sleeping sunflowers, a bicycle leaning against a tree, small outbuildings.

The young engineer scrambled down the slope, stopped behind a large boulder not far from the roadside, and watched the chef approach the hut. As he neared, the door opened. A woman stood in the doorway. She was dressed in a long, flowing cloth and an elegantly piled headdress. He reached for her hand, kissed her on the cheek. She smiled at him, kissed him back, took his uniform. Then he slipped his arm around her waist and led her inside. As he turned to close the door, he stopped and gazed out across the road until he was looking right at the young engineer. Then he smiled, raised his hand a moment and turned away and closed the door.

Blue Nile

'Mengistu is a dog.' Teferi swayed in the wavering lamplight, turned his empty glass over and placed it rim down on the table between them.

'Your president's reputation is…' The young engineer paused, aware of his position as a guest. 'Controversial. The project was almost cancelled because of it.'

'I would use a stronger word, but I do not know it in English,' said Teferi.

The young engineer found the tabletop with the base of his glass, grabbed the edge of the wood stool, steadied himself. Sweat slurried down the gutter of his spine, pooled between his buttocks. 'Describe it to me,' he said, shifting on his stool. His words circled around the mud-brick walls of the hut, came back as a distortion.

'It is when you are…' Teferi paused, moved the middle finger of his right hand in and out of his left fist '…to someone already dead.' He raised his hand, signalled towards the darkened end of the hut.

A man emerged from the edge of the lamplight carrying a bottle, shuffled to their table, refilled the young engineer's glass with a trembling hand. Some of the caramel-coloured liquid spilled on to the tabletop.

'*Ameseginalehugn*,' said the young engineer, the Amharic brutal in his throat. Thank you. The first and most important words to learn in a new country.

The old man nodded, disappeared back into the darkness.

'He is hungry,' said the young engineer with a tip of his head.

'Everyone here is hungry.'

'Not everyone.' The young engineer recalled the place on the outskirts of Addis Ababa where they'd stopped weeks before, at the start of the journey to the dam. While Teferi had bargained for supplies with the shop owner, he'd wandered the store, found his way to the back aisles. There, on a shelf against the back wall, sacks of grain piled high, dozens of them, fifty-pound bags of flour, plastic gallon jugs of canola oil set out in ranks. All emblazoned with the handshake logo of USAID, and the words *Gift of the People of the United States of America* stamped in black beneath. All for sale.

The young engineer felt the first tremor, the now familiar destabilisation of the ground under his feet, the lurch of gravity, a reversal of Coriolis, ten times stronger. He walked his fingers to and around the glass, spilled more of the stuff they were calling whisky on to the table.

Teferi sipped his drink. 'When will you finish your work?'

'Soon.'

'And then the dam will be fixed?'

'The dam is not broken, Teferi. The penstock is the problem – the pipe that carries water to the turbines. It was built on swelling soils, and it's shifting.' The young engineer lifted his right forearm, tilted it to an angle, pushed it upwards with the fingertips of his left hand. 'If it shifts too much, the pipe will rupture.'

'And then?'

'The lights go out. For a long time.'

Teferi nodded, scratched the top of his head. 'What remains for you to do?'

'The drainage galleries we've been installing will keep the penstock's foundations stable. The last one is going in tomorrow.'

'How many more days do you need?'

'Two or three.'

Teferi nodded. 'You must finish quickly.'

The young engineer did not reply, took a slug of alcohol.

'And then you must go home.'

A distant concussion shook the hut, thrummed in his chest a moment.

'The rebels are close,' said Teferi.

'Will they cross the river?'

'Soon, yes.'

'What will happen if they win?'

Teferi grinned a moment, as many teeth as not. Then his lips closed and pursed and his gaze flicked away to the right, towards the entrance. Sensing movement, the young engineer swivelled on his stool. A man stood in the doorway. Kerosene lamplight lit one side of his face, left the other in shadow. Sweat stained the front of his uniform, dark wedges in the centre of his chest and under his arms. A handgun hung from a belt around his waist. He was small, his clothes outsized, like a boy playing at being a man. The soldier nodded to the barman, said something in Amharic. There were only four small tables in the place, each with a pair of stools. The soldier walked to a table set against the opposite wall, sat down, looked at them.

Teferi glanced at the glass on the table between them. 'Finish,' he said. A whisper. 'We must go.'

The young engineer shook his head. 'Always it is this way.'

'You do not like our country.'

'I like most of it very much.'

'But not this?'

'Not how it is run, or who runs it.'

Teferi frowned. 'And yet you are here.'

'Please understand,' said the young engineer. 'I hope there is more good than bad.' That is what he told himself, had convinced himself he still believed.

'Finish your drink. We will go before there is a problem.'

The young engineer drank. He stood, the mud floor shifting beneath his soles, and started towards the doorway.

'*Koom,*' said the soldier. Stop.

The young engineer stopped, turned and glared at the soldier. He may have been young, but it was hard to tell. Lines gullied the skin around his eye sockets. Sweat beaded on his forehead, greased his temples. Like everyone here, his bones seemed very close to the surface.

'Necrophile,' the young engineer said.

Teferi glanced at him, a question in the flex of his left cheek.

'That's the word.' The young engineer stared at the soldier, made the same motion with his finger and fist as Teferi had. Then he raised his voice. 'Fucks the dead.'

Teferi grabbed the young engineer's arm, started guiding him towards the door. 'Please, do not provoke.'

The soldier called out in Amharic.

They were almost at the doorway now. Outside, the living din of the African night, the dark earth radiating the day's heat, the desperate, transpired humidity of a thousand days without rain, all of it accelerating the vortex in his head.

'Keep going,' whispered Teferi.

The young engineer stumbled, gripped his friend's shoulder.

'*Koom*,' the soldier repeated, louder this time.

They stopped, turned to face him. He was on his feet now, moving towards them, speaking rapidly. Teferi held his palms out and open, responding. The young engineer could make out a few words among the tones of conciliation – *aznalehu.* excuse me; *i'bakih*, please.

The soldier was close now, a fist's throw away. His voice was shrill, constricted, loud against the night. He waved his hands in the air, alternatively pointing out into the darkness and at Teferi's chest. The young engineer planted his feet, stared back at the soldier, adrenaline cutting through the booze. He was a head taller than the soldier and almost half as heavy again. He leaned in, stared down at the man.

The soldier pointed at Teferi, said something the young engineer could not understand. Anger boiled in his words. Teferi took a step back. The young engineer did not. The soldier was yelling at him now, jabbing his finger at him as if this alone could somehow translate, explain, solve. And the young engineer realised that it was no longer about the things he had seen since he'd arrived in the Horn of Africa, the war raging closer every day as the rebels moved south, or even the simmering anger inside himself that he had brought with him to this fevered continent. It was something altogether more basic, this exothermic proximity, the heat generated when fight overcame flight.

'Fuck you, asshole,' the young engineer shouted, forcing the syllables out from deep within himself. 'He has as much right to be here as you do.'

Teferi grabbed his arm, started pulling him towards the door.

The soldier, initially taken aback by this foreigner's outburst, renewed his attack.

'Please,' said Teferi, hauling on the young engineer's arm. 'There is no need. Come.'

The young engineer twisted away from Teferi's grip, bunched his fists at his sides, and took a hard step towards the soldier. Surprised, the soldier lurched back. His foot caught a table leg, and he toppled backwards over a stool, hands clawing at dead air. He hovered there for a moment, and then came down hard, the back of his skull striking the edge of one of the rough plank tables. It sounded like a car door closing. That hollowness.

They stood looking down at the soldier, waiting for him to get up. But he didn't.

'Jesus,' said the young engineer. 'I didn't mean to…' He stepped forwards to help the soldier, but Teferi grabbed him.

'He's not moving.'

Teferi shook his head. 'We must leave. Now.'

'We should help him.'

'Please. Before someone comes.'

They ran to the car. Theirs was the only vehicle in the small dirt clearing under the dark shadow of a sprawling mango tree. Soon Teferi had the car hurtling towards the main road, the dim myopia of the headlights jetting through the hacked bush that crowded both sides of the red earth track.

They didn't speak for a long time. After a while, they left the main road and moved through darkened fields and sleeping thatch villages, the country increasingly rocky and covered in stunted trees. By the stars – Dubhe and Merak pointing to Polaris – the young engineer knew that they were heading north, towards the river.

'Where are we going, Teferi?' he asked, still shaking from the encounter at the bar.

'Before you leave, I must show you.'

'Show me what?'

'Not far.' Teferi guided the car up a narrow track through the brush. The vehicle lurched over the rutted, uneven ground, the suspension groaning. After a while, the track ended. Teferi stopped the car, turned off the engine. They sat a moment, blinded. Slowly, the world reappeared, lit by precarious stars. 'Walk now,' he said.

The night was very still. The silence of a billion screaming insects. The young engineer followed Teferi up the rocky slope. Sweat ran cold at his temples, across his chest. A chill shuddered through him.

'That soldier…' he said.

Teferi stopped, turned back to face him. 'It was not your fault,' he whispered. 'You must be quiet now.'

'If the police find out…'

Teferi shook his head. 'Come, we must hurry.'

They climbed. Ahead, the dark silhouette of a ridgeline, constellations behind, the dust of nebulae. A sudden flash erased the stars, revealed a silvered landscape of crags and boulders, a hacked-out geometry of shadows. As quickly, it was gone. The young engineer stumbled, disoriented, the ground flexing like hot rubber beneath him. Seconds later, the distant shock of thunder, felt as much as heard.

He kept moving, Teferi there ahead of him, almost invisible in the darkness. The slope had died away now, and ahead he could see some sort of precipice, and beyond that, the edge of a cliff, a pale fluttering sheet of rock. After a while, Teferi stopped and dropped to the ground and signalled him to do the same. Side by side, they snaked their way towards the precipice.

The young engineer gripped the rock, felt the world spin beneath him. He closed his eyes, but that only made it worse. He pulled himself forwards and looked out over the edge, down into the canyon. Far below, the Blue Nile, dark and scattered with stars. And beyond, across the divide, a million cooking fires strewn like glowing coals across the darkened sweep of the Eritrean plain.

'Somewhere out there,' whispered Teferi, 'is my home.'

And a million and a half Eritrean troops waiting to cross the river and crush Mengistu. 'Family?' said the young engineer.

'My wife and three children, God bless them.'

It was the first time in the eleven weeks they'd spent together that Teferi had spoken of such things. They lay still for a time and peered across the river.

Teferi touched his arm, said, 'Wait here. I will be back soon.'

'Where are you going?'

'Do not move from this place. Do you understand?'

In the distance, how far away he could not judge, a string of tracers arced red across the plain. And then the sound came, the raptor trill of automatic gunfire. He turned to answer, but Teferi was already up and moving away, towards a draw in the valley. The young engineer watched him until he disappeared.

For a long time, he lay among the rocks and gazed down into the canyon at the dark surface of the water. He could hear the river coursing through the rocks, feel it cutting its way down into the flesh of the highlands on its way to meet the White Nile at Khartoum and then on to Egypt and the great delta and the Mediterranean. In this, he felt insignificant and small. And then he thought about the soldier in the bar, and if he was OK, and if he would report what had happened, and if the police would be waiting for him when he returned to the dam.

When Teferi returned more than an hour later, he was very quiet and would not answer any of the young engineer's questions. They walked back to the car and drove to the dam in silence.

Λ

Three days later, they arrived in Addis Ababa. Abandoned vehicles choked the roads. Smoke veiled the city, pillared hot into the sky from the hulks of burning tanks, smashed buildings. Dead animals littered the roadside, bloated carcasses of horses, goats, dogs. Soldiers streamed into the capital, many without weapons or leaders. Children wandered naked and aimless, lost in the confusion, crying for their parents.

The young engineer sat in the front passenger seat, stared out of the open window at the world gone crazy. Before leaving the dam, he'd supervised the installation of the last drainage gallery, stayed another day, testing its performance and evaluating the data. There had been no trouble, no sign of the police, no mention of the soldier in the bar. The next day, he'd reported his findings to the dam manager, proclaimed the penstock safe. The dam manager had thanked him and advised him to leave the country immediately. The rebels had crossed the Blue Nile that morning and were bearing down on Addis. Mengistu's troops were in full retreat.

Teferi guided the car through the melee towards the airport. 'Not far now,' he said, easing past an abandoned fuel truck.

'That soldier, the one who hit his head.'

Teferi said nothing, kept driving.

'He died, didn't he?'

Teferi shook his head. 'Do you have your tickets, passport?'

The young engineer patted the breast pocket of his jacket.

'Thank you for helping my country,' said Teferi. 'It has been good to know you.'

'Likewise,' said the young engineer, meaning it, feeling something else too. It felt vaguely like cowardice.

Teferi reached into the back seat, produced a small package, handed it to him.

The young engineer opened the newspaper wrapping. It was a small, stringed musical instrument, like a crudely made ukulele.

'It's a *kra*,' said Teferi. 'The instrument of my people.'

The young engineer plucked one of the strings. 'Thanks, Teferi. It's not necessary. But thanks.' Yes. Cowardice.

Ahead, an army checkpoint, the airport terminal building a couple of hundred metres beyond. The sound of a jet powering up for take-off. Car horns blaring. Teferi slowed the car, stopped at the barrier. A harried-looking officer peered inside the car, checked their documents. He'd just handed the young engineer's passport back to Teferi when he looked up in the direction of the city and froze. The young engineer just had time to spin in his seat before the shock wave hit. The blast knocked him back, sucked the air from his lungs, blew out the windows in the building across the street. He caught his breath, looked back towards the city. A huge pillar of brown smoke mushroomed into the sky.

'Jesus,' he said, turning towards Teferi. 'You alright?'

Dust billowed in the air around them like fog, as if the ground were an old rug that someone had picked up and snapped.

Teferi nodded and jutted his chin towards the roadblock. 'Look.' The soldiers were picking themselves up from the glass-strewn tarmac and walking away. 'They are going home. It is over.'

A convoy of Mercedes Benz sedans flashed past towards the airport, four cars in all, police escort front and back. Teferi handed the young engineer his passport, slammed down on the accelerator, sent the car hurtling after the convoy. They pulled up in front of the terminal just behind the last Mercedes.

Teferi turned to him. 'Go quickly,' he said. 'The airport could close at any time.'

People were piling out of the Mercedes, big men in superbly tailored suits, gold flashing against dark fingers and wrists, equally big women swathed in multi-coloured cloth and elaborate headdresses, half a dozen overweight children. Porters loaded mountains of luggage on to waiting trolleys.

Teferi spat. 'Our government.'

The young engineer hoisted his pack and stepped on to the pavement. He looked out across the city, counted eleven, twelve, thirteen columns of smoke rising into the sky. A jet screamed by overhead. He wanted to remember it, all of it.

He closed the car door, leaned back in through the open window. 'Where did you go, Teferi, that night at the river?'

His driver looked at him a moment, clenching his fist around the steering wheel. 'We are a poor country, my friend,' he said. 'The dam is very important. No one else could have fixed it.'

The young engineer nodded, understood.

Teferi smiled. 'This,' he said, waving his hand towards the city, 'is the beginning, God willing.'

March 14th. London

As soon as I walk into the place, I know it's going to be bad. I am fifteen minutes late. I blame the Tube, but I didn't try all that hard to be on time. I can hear the rebuke already, delivered with that half-sigh and twist of the head, accented by the slightest upward roll of the eyes. She's chosen the ground carefully. A coffee shop in the open, marble-vault foyer of the big Canary Wharf tower that is home to her esteemed merchant bank. All traces of 2008 are long gone. As I walk through the big rotating doors, I can smell the money, feel the power here, the sheer disdain. Now this is entitlement.

I look around the place, my eyes adjusting to the glare of the polished surfaces – all that expensive cut stone and moulded chrome. Maria is waiting near the reception desk, looking impatient. It's Maria the hotshot banker, severe in a navy-blue suit with her dark hair pulled back and no make-up. Troy is with her, his pudge squeezed into a pair of super-tight light-blue jeans and a pink shirt – to show confidence in his reconstructed masculinity, no doubt. He completes his ensemble with a short fawn sports jacket that looks two sizes too small. The effect is one of a fabric designer off on a Caribbean cruise. Except for the swollen, busted nose and the dark swathes under his eyes.

As I approach them, I can't help cracking a smile, but it withers almost immediately under the blowtorch of Maria's scowl. It's that scowl. The you're-late-you're-inattentive-and-stupid-and-inconsiderate-and-childish scowl that she wields with martial precision and devastating effect. I can't imagine working for her.

'This is the man who was late to his own wedding,' she says to Troy as soon as I am close enough to hear. 'It's true.'

Troy smirks at me.

'Turns out I shouldn't have shown up at all,' I say, immediately regretting it.

'You see, I told you,' she says, still speaking to Troy. 'Can you imagine *if Rachel heard that? For a child to know that her father wishes she had never been born.'*

'*That's not what I said, Troy,' I say, addressing myself directly to Fuckwit – I prefer calling him that. 'Children can be produced out of wedlock these days.'*

'*I told you,' she continues. 'He's like this all the time. Everything is an argument.' She has yet to look at me, acknowledge my presence in any way.*

'*Yes, it's true, Troy. I should have been a lawyer. But then again, the world doesn't need another parasite.' I lock Fuckwit's gaze a moment, watch him squirm. He does that puff-up thing, sucking in his gut, standing a bit taller.*

'*Just ignore him,' Maria says, reaching for Troy's arm and pulling him back.*

I hold my ground. 'Yeah, Troy, you don't want that nose broken again, do you?' I am enjoying this now, my earlier trepidation fading as I hit my stride.

'*I want you to know that I will be pressing charges,' Troy says.*

My stomach flutters. 'Is that why you asked me here?' I hear myself saying. 'Well, press away,' I say, trying to look unconcerned. 'As I recall, you were the aggressor. You came at me. I was only defending myself. See you in court, asshole.'

Troy looks as if he is being strangled. His face has turned the pulsating, blood-filled shade of an erect dick. He's a dickhead. The realisation makes me laugh. It's part nerves, of course, but it drives him crazy.

'*That's not true,' he says, looking back at Maria. 'I have a witness. You hit me.'*

'*Self-defence.'*

'*We'll see what the judge says.'*

Maria pulls him back again, a dog on a leash. Lapdog. 'Stop it, Troy,' she commands. 'That's not why we're here, Warren,' she says, looking right at me for the first time. Her gaze stops me dead. She hasn't called me by my name for years. She has my attention, and she knows it.

'*The bank has offered me a senior vice-president role,' she says. 'I've decided to accept.'*

I exhale. 'Congratulations.'

She glances over at Troy. 'I've decided to accept,' she says again. Her look softens a moment, hardens again, a momentary lapse. 'The position is in New York.'

She pauses there, lets it hang. Her timing was always impeccable.

'I'm taking Rachel with me,' she continues. 'Troy is coming, too. He will be looking after her while I'm at work. There will be a lot of travel.'

I don't know how long I stand there, mute, but it's a while, a minute or two at least. By the time I speak, Troy's face is almost a normal colour again and that smug grin has returned. 'I have visitation rights,' I blurt out. 'You can't take her away.'

'Don't make this more difficult than it needs to be,' Maria says. 'I am going, and Rachel is coming with me. There is nothing you can do about it.'

Anger rises inside me, bitter hot. 'Did you ask her what she wants?'

'Yes, I did.' She stands a moment, jerking me on a wire. 'She wants to come to New York. She's excited. I have already enrolled her in an excellent school. Besides, she doesn't want to see you anymore.'

It's as if I've been hit by an NFL linebacker. I stagger back, dazed. 'She's ten years old, for Christ's sake,' I manage, choking on the words. 'You can't expect her to make decisions like that.'

'She's very mature. Not that you would notice. I respect her views.'

'Look,' I say. 'Being late for a school play doesn't warrant—'

But Maria cuts me off before I can finish. 'Is that what you think this is about?' she hisses. 'The play? You really have no fucking idea, do you?'

'It's pretty hard to be Superdad on alternating weekends,' is the best I can come up with. Lame.

I can see her soften a moment. If you didn't know her you would never know. 'You should have thought about that sooner, Ethan.' She checks her ladies' Rolex, jams her hands on her hips. 'Anyway, I'm done here. If you want to fight this, go ahead. See you in court, as you say. But I don't think the judge is going to side with a physically abusive father.' And then she pivots on her heels and strides towards the elevators.

Troy smiles at me, mouths the word 'loser' and hurries after her.

New Year's Eve

Helena was four months pregnant. You couldn't really tell. She carried well, on that tall athlete's frame of hers.

It was cold, minus twenty-five, and it hadn't bottomed out yet. They piled into a taxi, the engineer and Helena and one of her friends, a ditzy brunette they called Planet (Janet), and headed south along Macleod Trail, the strip-mall ugliness softened under a smother of still-falling snow. Helena looked fabulous. Under her floor-length winter coat, she wore a tan mini, black stockings, glamour heels and a black scoop-necked blouse. Her hair was up, the way he liked it. She was beautiful. He was already glowing, knowing that she would be the best-looking woman in the place, some party that a friend of Janet's – a restaurateur – was throwing.

He helped her across the frozen, ice-packed parking lot from the taxi to the glass-fronted restaurant. That great feeling was going through him, of her leaning on his arm, of being strong and capable and of her trusting him. He held the door open for the two ladies, helped them with their coats once they were inside. He'd been brought up that way, and he was glad.

The place was packed. Planet led them through the crowd towards the bar, introduced them to the host. He was a short guy, broad and gym-muscled, slightly off-kilter, as if he'd worked the front of his body – the part you could see in a gym mirror – to the exclusion of the back. His dark, narrow eyes seemed far too small for his fair, broad-boned face. He kissed Planet, eyes open, not interested, then looked Helena up and down, smiled wide and offered her his hand. He said something cheesy like *and hello to you, beautiful*. She towered over him. She shook his hand, withdrew hers quickly. He was still staring at her when Planet introduced the engineer as Helena's husband. That got his attention.

'Warren's an engineer,' she said. 'He's just got back from Ethiopia.'

'Well, isn't that great,' said Restaurant Owner, booze breath wafting over them. 'Where the fuck is Ethiopia?' He smiled at Helena. The engineer was about to explain just where the Horn of Africa was when Restaurant Owner leaned forwards and stared into his eyes and said: 'Who gives a shit, right?'

There was no figuring some people. What they think will impress others. Still, this was Calgary.

'Nice guy,' the engineer said after Restaurant Owner left.

Helena poked him in the ribs, frowned. He ordered drinks at the bar, paid cash. Rum and Coke for Planet, ginger ale for H, a beer for him. They drank. After a while, Planet wandered off. They didn't know anyone there, and they didn't care. Just stood close and sipped their drinks and held hands and swam in each other's eyes, the rest of the guests just flowing around them, as if they were a rock in the middle of a river.

Until the screaming started.

At first, they ignored it, and after a while, it died down. They kept talking, finished their drinks. He was about to go to the bar to order another round, when a high-pitched wail split the room, followed quickly by a loud crash, like pots and pans clattering to a tile floor, and then a man's voice, deep and angry, bellowing. The commotion was coming from the back of the restaurant, where the kitchen was. Everyone in the place stopped dead, listening as the tirade continued.

'What the hell is going on back there,' said Helena.

'Who knows,' he said. 'Drunks.'

Then another shriek came, louder than before, higher-pitched still, a different voice, fear and pain there. Before he could stop her, Helena was striding towards the kitchen. He followed her as she rounded the door and disappeared around the corner. She was always like this, Helena. Never could leave any injustice unchallenged, turn away from any cruelty, trust that someone else would act. If it matters, you don't wait for someone else, she always said. It was one of the things he loved about her. One of the many things.

Actually, he loved everything about her, even the things he hated.

When he caught up with her, she was already in the kitchen. Drunk Restaurant Owner was there, at the end of the service run. His poorly developed back, strangely slack under his tight T-shirt, a protein-powder arm raised above his head, he seemed unaware of their presence. He was brandishing some kind of stainless-steel kitchen implement. Beneath him, wedged back against the far wall, curled on the food-strewn floor, a small Asian man dressed in a chef's smock cowered on his knees, whimpering. Blood streamed from his face.

The engineer grabbed Helena's arm just as she yelled out 'STOP!' at the top of her voice. The owner did exactly that, pulled up the spatula in mid-stroke and spun around to face them. For a moment, he stood there staring at them, eyes wide, hyped-up. A mist of blood covered his face and the front of his shirt.

'What the fuck?' he screamed, recovering now. 'Get the fuck out.'

The engineer was shaking his head now, knowing what this guy was going to get, talking to H like that.

'Stop what you are doing,' she said, her voice even, authoritative. 'That man needs medical attention.'

'Fuck off, bitch, and mind your own business,' the owner shouted back. 'Get out of my fucking kitchen.' And then, as if to emphasise the point, he spun and let go a withering kick that caught the cook in the jaw, sending him crashing head-first into the steel panelling. The cook slumped limp to the floor.

'If you don't stop, right now, I'm calling the cops,' shouted Helena. 'I mean it. Right now.'

The owner turned to face her again. A grin creased his face. 'You think so, cunt?'

By now, the engineer was trying to pull her back to the door, but she was strong and he didn't want to hurt her.

'I'm going to call the ambulance,' she said, standing her ground. 'Stop now and I won't call the cops, too. I mean it, asshole.'

H never swore. Hardly ever. It took a lot for her to betray herself like that. She hated foul language.

For a moment, it seemed as if the owner had considered Helena's threat, had assessed the consequences, and determined that it was time to back off. He stood there slack-jawed, obviously awed by what he was seeing.

That's right, the engineer thought, just walk away now, idiot. This can still end well. But it never did go that way with them, him and Helena. They never seemed able to find the easy path. If there was a hole to fall into, a trap to spring, they'd do it. And so, when the guy started moving towards Helena, hand raised for a strike, part of him wasn't surprised at all, had been expecting this from the moment he saw her disappear into that kitchen.

Helena drew in a breath, coiled back her head and shoulders, braced herself.

Restaurant Owner seemed surprised that this woman hadn't backed down as soon as he started moving towards her, but again, bullies are always like that. He hesitated a moment, stopped dead.

And then she let it go. The force of it seemed to blow the guy back in his tracks. A hurricane of sound that tore from her lungs, silencing the whole place. One word. No.

Before DRO could recover, the engineer grabbed Helena by the arm and dragged her out of the kitchen, pushing her coat into her hands. 'Put this on and let's get out of here,' he said, hustling her towards the door.

'Did you see what he was doing?' she said, still pulling against him, reaching for a payphone on the wall near the entrance. 'I'm going to call the cops.'

'Please, Helena. Let's go, now,' he said, pulling back.

They were almost at the door when the owner appeared. He was standing at the kitchen entrance, chest heaving, crazy-eyed. 'You fucking cunt,' he screamed. 'Coming into my place, telling me what to do. Get the fuck out.'

That's what did it. She'd had enough of the language, the attitude, the cruelty. She never could tolerate stupidity and ignorance, Helena. She whipped her arm away from the engineer's grasp, paced back to the payphone, picked it up, started dialling. 'I'm calling the cops,' she shouted, so everyone in the place could hear her.

'Put that down,' he said, moving towards her. By now, everyone in the restaurant was watching.

At this point, he didn't really have a choice. What else could he have done? He'd tried to be the peacemaker, get them out of there before anyone else got hurt. But now she was punching the numbers in on the pad with one hand, the telephone receiver held to her ear in the other, her hair wisping elegantly across her bare neck. DRO was closing fast, fists bunched at his sides, glaring.

The engineer stepped between them, blocked his way. He was quite a bit taller than DRO, probably about the same weight.

The owner stopped dead in front of him. 'Get the fuck out of the way,' he growled.

'If the lady wants to make a call, that's her business,' the engineer said. 'Not yours.' He may have added an asshole there at the end. It was all he could think of. He remembered thinking at the time it sounded like something Bogart might have said, minus the asshole, of course. He may have smiled then, because of it, and it was like a trigger switch. The guy charged. Just put his head down and came on like a bull. The engineer's back was to the front entranceway windows. The guy caught him in the hips with his lowered shoulder and ploughed him back, legs pumping. When the engineer's back hit the glass, he felt the pane flex behind him, just for an instant as it took the combined mass, and then explode as they flew into the parking lot.

They landed on the ice-covered tarmac in a shower of glass, DRO on top. The force of the impact knocked the air from the engineer's lungs, and for a moment, he lay gasping for breath, his body adjusting to the sudden onslaught of minus thirty. But the other guy had taken the worst of it. Facing the window as they went through, he'd caught the shard edges on his arms and face. As he staggered to his feet, enraged now, whatever drugs he'd been doing really starting to kick in, he looked at the blood dripping on to the snow from his face and arms and he laughed.

The engineer pushed himself up, leaned against a car, steadied himself, tried to breathe. He decided to laugh, too. 'Look what you did to your restaurant, you idiot,' he said, pointing at the blown-out window.

The guy looked up, all the guests now crowded at the windows looking out at the two morons in the cold. 'You're a dead man,' he bellowed, a little melodramatically, the engineer thought. Then the idiot stripped off his shirt and stood there flexing his bare torso in the cold.

'You've got to be kidding,' the engineer said. A couple of people in the restaurant laughed. DRO glanced up at his guests plastered up against the windows, and then he charged.

The engineer let him come. The snow was hard-packed and slippery. It was difficult for him to accelerate. Just as he reached the car, the engineer sidestepped him and drove his lowered head into the car's front bumper. The guy hit with a blunt thud, collapsed to the ground. The engineer jumped on top of him, in mount position, hips pinning his midsection, and pounded his face. At least four rights connected. On the second one, he felt the guy's nose go, that raw cauliflower crunch as the cartilage shattered. His face gushed blood. It was over.

The engineer jumped up. Helena was there with Planet, standing in their coats in the snow, staring at him with open mouths.

'Let's go,' he said, not wanting to risk any of the guy's friends having a go.

'Jesus, Warren,' said Planet. 'What'd you have to go and do that for?'

He ignored her and led Helena across the parking lot.

'How are we going to get home?' Planet continued, trudging after them. 'It's New Year's Eve, for God's sake.'

That's when he spotted it. A taxi cab, filling up at the gas station across the street. 'Come on,' he said, upping the pace. The driver was just getting back into his car after having paid for the fuel when they strolled up. 'Can we get a ride?' he asked.

'Sure,' the cabbie said, his breath thick in the sub-zero air. 'Climb in.'

And that was it. The engineer gave the guy Planet's address. He started driving.

After a while the cabbie said, 'Pretty crazy, eh? New Year's. Did you guys hear about the riot at that pizza place back there?'

Helena smiled at him, reached for his hand. It felt good, that smile.

March 16th. London

Had to get out of the office. Fucking Robertson, hypocritical bastard. I can't believe he did it. I really can't. I mean, all that shit he's always spouting about this being a meritocracy. Numbers don't lie, he says. Whoever delivers the goods, gets the rewards. The only thing that matters here is results. The problem with aphorisms is that people start to believe them. Memes. They make things easy. Perfect for the lazy idiots who roam the social-media wilderness in sleepless discontent.

I like it here, by the river. I come here sometimes when I need to think, get out of the office. The water flows past me, smooth and brown. There are buds on the trees. We should get away this summer, me and – I was going to say Maria and Rachel, but no, I can't think that way. Those days are over. I have to think about Constantina. She really is great, in so many ways. We can go up to the Lake District, do some walking, stay in little B&Bs, eat in pubs. Maybe drive to France, go to Normandy. Always liked it there. I can't even remember the last time I took a holiday.

Robertson picked Grobelink for the senior partner role. Fine, he's the boss. I just wish the bastard had at least had the balls to tell everyone the truth. But that would have exposed all his bluster about performance as the bullshit it is. And that smug look on her face when he made the announcement. She knows that I brought in the most and the biggest deals last year. And the year before that. So does he. He even told me so. Brought me into his office just three months ago, and said it himself. Ethan, he said, you've got the best record in the firm. Keep it up, son. The rewards will come. Yeah, right.

Well, you know what? Fuck him. OK, I lost the Borschmann deal. But her sales and profits are still less than half mine. If that's what he wants, I'm gone. That's what my old man would have done. My mum, too. I know that, now. It's his loss. I can work anywhere.

If I am honest with myself, I've seen this coming for a long time. Like everyone, I've been hearing the rhetoric, the steadily increasing pressure from boards and watchdogs, seen colleagues in other companies go down for the same reason. I know I'm supposed to agree with it all, suck it up, and say nothing. Most blokes do. Hell, I'm even supposed to applaud it, support it. As a father, I get it. I want Rachel to have a good life, to get all the opportunities she wants. But I also hope she's strong enough never to accept anything she doesn't deserve. One thing I know is that somewhere along the line, if it keeps going this way, it's all going to break. People, women and men, are just going to finally say, enough bullshit. And I worry for her that way, too. That it's all going to break on her. Wasn't it Tolstoy who wrote: 'if anything is possible, then nothing is true'? *Always liked Tolstoy.*

I realise now, as I watch the clouds darken to the north, that the only reason I've stayed with the firm as long as I have is because of the money. When did I get like this? Something happened to me. When I was in my early twenties and just starting out, I had nothing. I never worried about money. There always seemed to be enough, somehow, to do the things I wanted to do. But now that I have had it and lost it, I worry about it all the time. It's as if, suddenly, the money owns me.

I've read ahead. Just now, sitting here on this park bench overlooking the river, like some old guy contemplating his life gone by. I promised myself I would read all the stories in order, as he had arranged them. Until now, I have. But I read the first few paragraphs of the next two stories and decided to skip ahead. They were about Yemen, where my old man worked a lot when we were living in Cyprus, me and my brother, in the early days, before he died, when my mum was still around. I remember it was a happy time. Maybe I just don't want to be reminded of that now, of the good times we had. It was the title that grabbed me. I read it, and I just knew. 'Muskoka'.

And now, I can't quite believe what I've just read.

The rain has started, and I watch the drops opening little black holes in the pavement, dissolving the ink on the front cover of the manuscript and spreading it blue through the fibres of the paper. I brush the water away. My heart is beating so hard I think it's going to blow my chest apart. I put my head back, look up at the clouds and let the rain fall on my face, drop into my eyes and run like tears. Slowly, my breathing steadies.

I will sit here awhile and then go back and read the two Yemen stories. And then I'm going to go back to the office and talk to Robertson.

Time Bomb

The pumps ran night and day, pulling life from the ancient aquifers under the city. Water which fell as rain during far-off thunderstorms in centuries past, and then found its way into the deep Cretaceous sandstones of the basin, now fed a growing city. Without it, no one could live here. This is a land of stone and rock and barren hills. There are no rivers or lakes. In this time, it rains rarely, perhaps once in a year. The few trees and shrubs that dot the hillsides cling to clefts in the rock, driving their roots deep, and in the old city, there are still the palms and gardens of the oasis.

The engineer stood on the balcony of his room and listened to the diesel pumps chugging in the distance. The sound echoed from the nearby cliffs. As the sun moved behind the hills, he undressed, hung his dusty work clothes over the back of a chair, and walked to the shower. In the mirror, he saw what he wanted to see – skin tanned from weeks in the sun, broad shoulders, trim torso, still free of fat, the heavy pendant testicles and, if he turned his head to just the right angle, he could think for a moment that he was reasonably good-looking. He was still young, he supposed.

Today he had walked the old wadi through the centre of the city. A dry cobblestone riverbed choked with garbage. Plastic bags, old car tyres, dead animals, more plastic. There were old, hand-dug stone wells all through there. Ismail, his guide from the UN-sponsored Water Commission, said that some of the wells were more than a thousand years old. 'Until about twenty years ago, they were the only source of water in the city,' he'd said. 'But the city was small then, a town, full of gardens. You can still see some of them, but most are gone, now.' He'd pointed towards the sprawl of new buildings outside the old city walls. 'All of this was gardens,' he'd said. 'Orange groves, fields of vegetables and watermelon, palms, orchards. All of it was irrigated with shallow groundwater. It was very beautiful.' He walked on, seemingly lost in the memories.

They took water samples from a few of the old wells, marked their locations on a map. The water was murky and foul and smelled of chemicals and rot. 'Twenty years ago, we first noticed this,' said Ismail, holding his nose as he decanted a sample. 'We warned the government, but nothing was done. Now it is all like this, unusable, even for watering gardens. That was when they started drilling down to the deep aquifer.'

They kept going, through the old Jewish quarter, the mud-brick buildings largely abandoned, and came to the *suq*, the old market. They stopped at a small teahouse, ordered tea. The proprietor spoke to Ismail a while. His tone was hostile. After a while, he reappeared with two glasses of black, sweet tea. Ismail paid him. The proprietor took the notes, inspected them a moment, as if he suspected they might be counterfeit. Then he closed his fist around the bills, threw them to the ground and disappeared back into the shop.

'What's his problem?' the engineer asked.

Ismail pointed to the blue logo on his shirt. 'The UN is very unpopular here,' he said. 'The people here believe Saddam is the saviour of the Arabs. They are still angry that the UN supported the Americans in the war.'

They had finished their tea and kept going. By the time Ismail dropped him off at his hotel, the sun was low in the sky, blood red in the dust and woodsmoke haze. Back in his room, he'd packed the water samples on ice from the hotel kitchen, checked his notes and field measurements and marked the location of each well on his map.

The engineer turned on the shower and stepped under the stream of twelve-thousand-year-old water, felt it wash the sand and salt and diesel from his skin and hair. He watched the water run down the drain. It was not hard, this water, despite flowing through the rock for centuries, and it lathered readily. And because this was rain that fell long before the start of atomic detonations and testing, it was free of deuterium. He stayed longer in the shower than he should have. Guilt gnawed at him as he towelled himself dry.

Tonight, he would write Helena. He wrote her letters, pen on paper, and waited sometimes three weeks for hers to get to him. He would ask her, as he did in every letter, to kiss Ethan for him, and, as he wrote he would look at the photos of them he carried with him everywhere he went. He would tell her how it felt to be here, in this place, to marvel at this ancient culture and see its beautiful relics and to know that, after centuries, it was dying. He had completed his modelling, he would tell her. He was pretty sure it was accurate, given the data he had to work with.

Since the Gulf War, when Yemen supported Iraq, and Saudi Arabia kicked out more than a million Yemeni workers (mostly young men) in retaliation, the population of the city had skyrocketed. Discontent walked the streets, lurked in the darkness at night, looking for someone to blame. There were more guns here than people, and more than half the people were under the age of thirteen. It was a demographic time bomb waiting to go off. And they all needed water. This was how revolutions were born.

New water wells were being drilled every day. He could see the rigs everywhere when he walked around the city. According to the finite-difference modelling he had done, if nothing changed, the Tawhila sandstone, the city's fractured wet nurse, would run dry in fewer than twenty years. And then, the two-thousand-year-old city would die. It made him sad to think of it, that it was happening now, not in some distant past or unknown future time. He would write that to her. He would say how it made him feel, that he was vaguely ashamed that this was happening while he was alive and that he knew that, despite his small efforts to help change things, it was unlikely he would have any effect, and that the destruction would continue. And he knew what she would think when she read his words. She would think him naïve and would write back that people were, after all, parasites. A parasite of the mining, tearing, consuming variety that eventually killed its host. But he wouldn't write her about the nightmares he'd been having, the ones where, somehow, he was married to his first fiancée.

In those dreams, he would wake and he'd be lying beside her, and he would try to explain to her that there must have been some mistake, that he was married to Helena; but she'd just laugh and reach for his swollen penis and tell him that it was no mistake and not to worry because she'd never loved him either, but that it was all too late now. The dreams were so real that he would wake up covered in sweat, blinking at the deception of walls and windows and the sun-blasted rhyolite cliffs in the distance. Maybe it was the duty-free whisky, he thought, or the altitude. Or just the loneliness.

A few days later, he was sitting in a café near the old city. Ismail had parked the UN-badged Toyota Land Cruiser out front. The engineer ordered tea and Ismail said make it two. They were at the back of the café. It was early evening and most of the tables were occupied. A few women, some unveiled, sat nearby. Through the front windows, he could see the traffic flowing past on Taiz Road, the people in the cars, the shoppers browsing the stores across the street.

That morning, he'd submitted a draft report on his findings to the director. It felt strange, being there in a city that did not see its own death coming in its furious growth. The people here felt half dead to him, he thought. This thought came into his head: *The time of the individual has passed. And for the best. People like you would have us all die like wild dogs, fighting for the last scrap.* And as it did, he saw a flash of movement outside on the street, near the front of the café. A young man dressed in a light-coloured *thaub* jumped out of a car. He stood for a moment on the pavement, looking at the café. There was something in his right hand. He looked both ways and then raised his hand and threw what looked like a black baseball towards the windows of the café.

The engineer dropped to the floor. He did it instinctively. He didn't have time to think about it.

The explosion ripped out the front of the café. Broken glass and debris hurtled through the room. It was like an ocean wave passing over him. After a while, the energy had passed and there was quiet, just a moment. He opened his eyes. Ismail was beside him on the floor. Dust enveloped them. His ears were ringing, and now he could hear the far-off, muffled sounds of people murmuring and then the screams.

Ismail reached for him, grabbed his arm. 'Are you OK?' he mouthed. There was blood on his face.

The engineer nodded. 'I think so.' What about you, he was about to say when a second detonation ripped through the air. They both hugged the ground, covered their heads with their arms. Sirens wailed outside, faint, distant. Ismail scrambled to his feet, pulled him up. The place was a wreck. Dust-covered bodies lay scattered in the glass among broken tables and overturned chairs, chunks of masonry. Red light strobed through the smoke and dust. Outside, a car was burning. Thick orange flames and black, oily smoke billowed into the sky.

Ismail grabbed his arm. 'Come on,' he said, pulling him towards the back door. The engineer couldn't hear him, but could see his mouth saying the words. 'Before the police come. Or worse.'

A Day in Aden

The country was everything he had always imagined a distant land would be, and some of it was beyond his imagination. There were ancient terraced hillsides and mountain villages perched high above deep, vertical canyons, and sometimes there were oases notched into the narrowest part of a valley, where the springs welled up clear and cool from thick Palaeocene limestones and dolomites. The people of the country – tribesmen of the Wadi Hadramawt, of the Tihama plains, of the northern mountains of Saba – were tough and independent, qualities he had been taught to value as a boy, and had come to appreciate of his own accord later in life. Sometimes there were bombs. And always, there was war.

There were many wars, in fact; overlapping conflicts over water and land and *qat* and the ancient blood feuds between tribes. And now, too, there was the oil.

At first, there had been excitement among the people, the promise that the wealth beneath their land might be shared. The oil companies brought technology and changes the people had never had to cope with before. For a few, there were jobs as cooks and guards and cleaners and drivers. The government negotiated with the oil companies, and soon royalties began to flow. But the president kept the money for himself and his close circle of family and advisers and friends and business associates, and the people saw none of the promised riches. Soon the government sent the army to protect the oil workers from the people. A new war was coming.

After the work on the water in Sana'a, it was the oil that brought the engineer back to Yemen. Western oil companies had made big new discoveries in the Masila, in the south, near the Empty Quarter,

the long, poorly defined border with Saudi Arabia. The engineer
came to help the oil companies manage the wastes that they produced. Mostly, the waste was heavy brine that was pumped up with
the oil. This had to be separated out, before the oil could be pro-
cessed and exported. The more oil they pumped from the ground,
the more brine they had to deal with. At first, they dumped it in pits
scraped into the dry ground. Then, as production increased, there
was no more room for pits, and they started releasing the brine into
the dry wadis, letting it flow down the ephemeral riverbeds as far as
it would go before it evaporated and what was left soaked into the
ground. It was a *cost-effective* solution. After a year of production,
some of the oil companies were pumping out five barrels of brine
for every one of oil. The engineer tested the brine and found that
not only was it saltier than seawater, but it contained hydrocarbons
and metals and was toxic to humans and animals. The normally dry
riverbeds, which might see rain once a year or, in some places, once
a decade, now ran like rivers, day and night.

He started walking the wadis, miles and hours alone under the
heavy sun, tracing the flow of the brine overland, and its likely sub-
terranean course. Wherever the brine went, the hardy natural trees
and scrub that clung to the wadi slopes died. Though the oil opera-
tions were far from the nearest villages, such was the rate of pumping
that he soon determined the brine would reach the villagers' wells if
something did not change. When it did, their water would be ruined
forever. And with it, their lives.

The engineer, no longer young, still believed in the fundamental
good in men. He was not a cynic, as so many of his friends were
by this stage in their lives. He worked hard at not being a cynic,
despite what he knew of himself and what he had seen of others. It
was difficult, but he did not want to be like them. It was too easy to
believe only in the bad, to claim that the world was shit. It was dis-
missive. It was a coward's way. Some of his friends called him naïve.
Helena understood. It had been her influence that had helped him
understand the need to fight against it. He wasn't naïve. He'd seen

more of life, more shit, than most of his acquaintances back home who practised their world-weary contempt from the safety of their suburban country-club bubbles. He chose to be positive. To believe. It was his version of faith.

The engineer went to the oil company's in-country manager and told him of the impending risks to the villagers. The manager thanked him and told him to put it in his report. It would be taken into consideration back in Europe, at headquarters. The manager shook his hand and thanked him. He was an American, a good man with a wife and kids back home. Something would be done.

The engineer completed his report two weeks later and submitted it to the manager, reminding him again of the seriousness of the situation. The next day, he packed his things and caught the flight back to Aden. From the little Twin Otter, he sat and watched the barren desert highlands give way to the deep-cut canyons of the Hadramawt and then, later, to the dark-stained lava fields and cinder cones of the Aden plain. Sometimes there were patches of life, the green thread of a shaded valley, the spate terracing of fields in a spring-fed wadi. And, three hours in, the first flash of Indian Ocean blue. The marks of men were few here. The occasional stone and mud village perched high on a mountainside or nestled into the flank of a wadi. A road scraped from the stony plateau. Otherwise, the country was as it had been since long before the oil, or the wars or the prophets of men.

The in-country manager was on the same flight. They were both leaving on the Air Egypt flight to Cairo the next afternoon. They ate dinner together at the company guest house in Aden, and again, the engineer reminded the manager of the findings of his report and the urgency of the situation. The manager smiled and assured him that it was at the top of his priority list. He would be back in the office in a couple of days and would talk to the VP about it personally.

After dinner, the manager, whose name was Bill, invited him to come out for a drink. They got into the back seat of a waiting Land Cruiser. Two Yemeni men sat in the front. The driver was bearded, wore the traditional Yemeni headdress, the *keffiyeh*, a loose *thaub* and a brown tweed jacket. The man in the passenger seat was dressed in a dark Western suit and white collared shirt and was clean shaven. His dark, wavy hair accentuated his hewn-sandstone jaw, his rare blue eyes. He put his arm across the seatback and nodded to Bill.

'Salim,' said Bill. 'What do you think?'

The man Bill had called Salim smiled. 'The dens, I think, for a start.' He spoke good English with a noticeable American accent.

Bill nodded. 'I was thinking the same. Show our friend here some of the famous Aden nightlife.'

Salim said something in Arabic to the driver, and the Land Cruiser started out of the compound gate. Night air came cool through the windows. After weeks in the desert, the smell of the sea cut him open, as if he were halfway home. The lights of Aden strobed in the distance. The Crater loomed dark against the star-silvered grey of the harbour. He thought of home, of Helena, of his sons, on that beautiful little island in the Mediterranean.

Soon they were in a part of the city he'd never seen, a neighbourhood carved into the tuffs and basalts of the volcano. The streets became too narrow for cars. The driver stopped the vehicle and they got out and walked. Salim led them deeper into the maze, past shop stalls carved into the rock of the volcano, night-lit dwellings cut into black basalt. Eyes peered out at them from every recess and shadow.

Salim turned into an opening and disappeared. Bill leaned forwards and followed him in. It was a tunnel. Lights hung from a wire that ran along one side of the excavation, suspended from metal spikes driven into the rock. It went in a long way. Bill and Salim were already far ahead. The rock was hand-hewn. The engineer could make out the individual chisel marks. He took a deep breath, bent at the waist and followed them in.

Arched pillars of rock divided the cavern into a series of poorly lit dens. The place was packed, the air thick with swirling blue smoke. The crowd parted for them. Salim led them through, and they fronted up to the bar. There were two big steel vats against one wall and a stack of beer kegs nearby. On the wall behind the bar was an old *Playboy* centrefold, the colours faded, the edges curled. Miss July had large pale breasts and pink nipples and long blonde hair. Someone had folded over the top corner, so you couldn't see her face.

Salim ordered three glasses of gin and three beers. He didn't pay for the drinks. He raised his glass. As he did, his jacket opened slightly. 'Cheers,' he said.

They raised their glasses, drank.

The gin was industrial, burned the engineer's throat. After a few sips, he turned and faced the young and old men who had crowded in around them and now stood staring. As he did in the villages, the engineer picked out a face, a youngish man with a dark complexion and deep-set eyes. 'Merhaba,' he said to the man, using the secular greeting made common in the south during the Marxist regime.

The man appeared not to have heard, stood unmoving, expressionless as before. The engineer smiled. '*Merhaba. Ismee Warren*,' he said, putting his free hand over his heart.

Salim touched his elbow. 'Do not,' he said.

'They are looking right through us,' said the engineer.

'They are not here to talk.'

'What's wrong with them?' said the engineer, still staring into the young man's eyes.

'These men have been replaced.' Salim pulled him away. 'This is the real story of the Gulf War.'

'I don't understand.'

'Many of these men were working in Saudi Arabia, sending money home to their families. Because Yemen supported Saddam in the war, the Saudi government revoked their work permits and sent them home. There is nothing for them here.'

'And they blame us.'

Salim nodded. 'Before the war, Saddam was America's friend. He was an ally. For ten years, Saddam fought a war against Iran, with America's support. Then a deal was made. Saddam would invade Kuwait, and guarantee America a supply of cheap oil. America wanted to counteract the increasing power of the Saudis. But they didn't anticipate the global outrage. Who would have thought that so many people would care that much about a tiny country populated by a few super-rich oil sheiks and their harems? When it all went tits up, America betrayed Saddam and retook Kuwait.'

'That's crazy,' said Bill. 'Everybody knows that's not what happened.'

Salim smiled. 'Who is everybody, my friend? These people, this is what they all believe. Is it really so crazy?'

They drank in silence. Salim wandered off.

'He's carrying a gun,' said the engineer. 'I saw it when he raised his glass. He's got a holster under his jacket.'

'Everyone here carries,' said Bill. 'This is Yemen.'

'Do you?'

Bill smiled. 'Me? Hell no. Against the rules. Back home I do, though.'

Salim returned, ordered another round. Again, he offered no payment. After a while, the engineer again turned to face the men who continued to press in around them. The same young man was there still. The engineer smiled at him, raised his glass. He wanted to break this barrier. He wanted to see some glimmer in the man's dark, heavily veined eyes, some acknowledgement of sameness. But there was none.

They finished their drinks and left. The tunnel was longer than he remembered it. The first breath of night air came to him, cool on his face. He stumbled on something underfoot, righted himself, hit his head on the tunnel roof. He stopped, doubled over, held his head in his hands. He was drunk. And despite the imminence of his flight home – five hours to Cairo, a three-hour wait before his flight to Larnaca – the distance now seemed impossible, a fiction. A journey of years, lifetimes.

Outside, the sea mist had cleared. Stars shone.

Bill was there, waiting for him. 'You OK?' he asked.

The engineer nodded. They followed Salim to the car. Soon they left the old city behind and drove out past the salt flats and the swirling lights and dark water of the harbour.

Ⱥ

The bar of the Mövenpick hotel was plush and cool. They sat in a cushioned booth in the corner and Bill ordered whiskies.

'Why do you come here?' said Salim, scanning the room. 'Is it for the money?'

'You bet,' said Bill.

'I want to go to America,' said Salim. 'I like it there. Yemen is shit.'

'Did you study there?' said the young engineer.

'I studied three years in Virginia. But then the war came.'

The drinks arrived. Bill dropped some Yemeni rials on the table.

'What about you?' said Salim.

'Me?' said the engineer. 'It's not just for the money, no.'

A couple came into the bar. They walked across the little hardwood dance floor and slid into a booth set against the far wall. The man wore a light-grey suit. He had grey hair and a grey moustache. The woman had thick blonde hair and wore a knee-length dress and heels. A big silver crucifix hung on a chain around her neck. She was young enough to be his daughter.

Salim sat looking at the pair for a while, sipping his drink. 'So, you are here to do good, then? To civilise us?'

'No,' said the engineer.

'Is this not what Christians do? Civilise?'

'I'm not Christian,' said the engineer.

Salim adjusted his jacket. 'Nevertheless.'

'I'm an engineer. I build things, fix things. If I can do some good, then why not?'

Salim drained his glass, set it carefully on the table, twisted it a half-turn to the right. 'And you think this is good, what you are doing here?'

'Don't look at me,' said Bill.

The engineer shot Bill a glance. 'That depends.'

Salim was staring at the couple across the bar. 'On what?' he said.

'On what the big shots decide to do,' said the engineer. He tried to catch Bill's gaze, but he looked away.

'Always this,' said Salim. He flashed a smile, pushed back his chair, stood, smoothed his suit. 'Excuse me a minute,' he said, then turned and walked across the bar to where the man and the young woman were sitting.

'Shit,' said Bill.

Salim shook hands with the man, and then with the woman. Her bare arm flashed pale in the dim light. A conversation ensued.

'Who is he?' said the engineer. 'Salim.'

'He's with the government,' said Bill. 'Liaison.'

The engineer was about to ask from what part of the government when the older man in the grey suit burst to his feet. Drinks spilled. A glass fell to the floor, smashed. The older man was shouting at Salim, pointing across the room, waving his hands. Spit flew from his mouth. Veins bulged in his neck and forehead. The young woman sat in silence, her head bowed. Salim stood staring back at the older man, unmoving. After a moment, he unbuttoned his jacket, stood with one hand on his hip, the other free at his side.

'Shit,' said Bill.

'What's going on?' said the engineer.

Salim turned and walked back to the table.

'Jesus, Salim,' said Bill.

'Iraqis,' said Salim. 'Christians. Both of them.'

'What were you doing?'

'I asked him how much.'

'For what?'

Salim waved the waiter over. 'For her.'

'Shit,' said Bill.

'A man brings a woman into a place like this, dressed like that. What does he expect? A Muslim man would never do that.'

'And so?' said Bill.

Salim laughed. 'She's his daughter. Can you fucking believe it?'

'Jesus, Salim.'

'A lot of them here,' said Salim. 'Rich Iraqi Christians who fled Saddam. They live here because it's cheap. To them, Yemenis are dark-skinned, uneducated scum.'

The drinks came. Bill made to pay, but Salim waved this away, nodded to the waiter. The waiter left. They finished their drinks. It was late. The place was almost empty now. When they left the bar, the older man and the woman were still there.

The driver was waiting for them in the hotel parking lot. They got into the Land Cruiser. The driver started the engine, rolled the car towards the exit.

'Stop,' said Salim, reaching over to touch the driver's arm. 'Go back.'

'What is it?' said Bill.

The driver reversed. Salim pointed to the far side of the lot where big trees cast dark shadows across the tarmac.

'What are you doing, Salim?'

The driver turned off the engine. They sat in the darkness.

'Salim, what the fuck?' said Bill.

Salim reached inside his jacket, turned to face them. The pistol was in his hand. It was some kind of automatic, blunt and black and mean-looking. Salim ejected the magazine, inspected its contents, pushed it back into the grip, worked the slide.

'No, Salim,' said Bill, reaching for the driver's shoulder. 'Take us back to the guest house, now.'

Just then, the couple from the bar appeared at the hotel entrance. They stood there awhile, under the lights, as if expecting someone. The woman's hair glowed yellow in the bright overhead light. Then her father took her hand and they started across the parking lot.

Salim tapped the driver on the arm. They rolled slowly towards the couple. They were within fifteen metres when Salim told the driver to stop. He got out of the car and walked up to the couple.

Bill jumped out and ran after Salim. The engineer followed.

The older man had put himself between Salim and his daughter, was backing away, one hand raised, palm open. Salim was speaking to him in Arabic.

The older man shook his head, mumbled some reply.

Bill reached for Salim's arm. 'You've made your point, Salim. Let's go.'

Salim ignored him, kept on at the older man. When Salim levelled his gun, the older man froze, eyes wide. The woman shrieked, tried to pull her father away.

'Put that away, God damn it,' said Bill.

Salim looked back. 'Don't worry, Bill.'

Then he turned and aimed his pistol and fired.

Salim walked back to the car, got in. The engineer stood and looked down at the man, his daughter on the ground beside him, crying, pawing at the blood seeping from his leg. He stood and watched the man bleed. He watched the woman cry. Bill was speaking to him, pulling at his elbow.

'We should do something,' the engineer said.

'Get in the car, Warren, for Christ's sake.'

Bill opened the door and pushed him inside, crowded in behind him. A few minutes later, they were flying along the causeway towards the city.

Salim howled, waved his pistol out of the window.

'What the fuck, Salim,' said Bill, shouting over the noise of the engine and the wind buffeting through the windows. 'Put that away, you fucking maniac.'

'No trouble,' said Salim. He pointed his pistol out into the night and fired off three shots.

'Jesus,' said the engineer. 'We are in deep shit.'

'Don't worry,' said Bill. 'He's the police.'

Salim turned and put his arm across the seatback. He'd put his gun away. 'No problem, my friend,' he said. '*Ma'afi mushkilla*. It is nothing. This other was garbage. Nothing will happen.'

The next day, the engineer woke with a hangover. He ate a late breakfast in the company guest house and caught the flight to Cairo that afternoon. The wait in Cairo airport was more like six hours than three, and he ended up missing his flight to Larnaca.

March 16th. London

I stop reading, take a deep breath. Pure chaos, here, in my hands, all around me, now and then. It's as if my skin has been hacked open and peeled back, revealing the wormed and decaying randomness beneath. Entropy, yes, but so much more. He never told me about any of it, never prepared me.

I stack the pages of the manuscript, snap the elastic band around all of it and start back to the office. I know what I have to do. It is as if I have been grappling with a mathematical equation for which I could find no solution, no essential balancing, and then, suddenly, terms cancel and the whole thing simplifies down to something so elegant I wonder why it took me so long to see it. Truth is, it was always there. Just took me this long to understand it.

I heft my father's manuscript in my hands, as if it has taken on some new mass, an invisible density. I reach the bridge and start across the river. Halfway over, I stop and stand at the rail, looking down into the flowing Thames slate. Torn strips of grey cloud squall past, close enough to touch. A few drops of rain dot the pavement, touch my face. There is meaning in everything, even if you can't see it. That's what he is telling me. Meaning where there is none.

I keep going, reach the office. I brush the rain off my coat, take the stairs. I go straight to the fourth floor, Robertson's corner office. Lorena, his PA, tries to wave me off, but I go straight in, closing the door behind me. Robertson is on the phone, sitting behind his desk. He opens his eyes wide and shakes his head at me, trying to concentrate on whatever is being said on his call. I stay where I am. He shakes his head again, points to the door. Get out, *he mouths. I shake my head, stay put. He frowns. A few moments later, he says, 'I will call you back', and puts down the phone.*

'What do you want, Scofield?' he says.

I cycle a breath. 'I want that promotion. I deserve it.' As I say it, I realise that I don't want it at all.

'I told you, Grobelink got it.'

'Yeah, I know. You told me. But what you're doing, it's not right. What happened to the only thing that matters here is results?'

Robertson looks down at the papers on his desk, scalps his hand across the polished dome of his skull, front to back. 'There are pressures,' he says without looking up.

'Clearly.'

'And you lost the Borschmann contract.'

'The terms he wanted were outside our standard guidelines. Your guidelines, Andrew. I couldn't push him any further.'

'Still.'

'Fix it or I'm leaving.' As I say it, I can't quite believe the words are coming from my mouth.

Robertson looks up, frowns. 'What did you say?'

'You heard me.'

'Yes, I did.'

'Well.'

'You know I can't do that, Ethan.'

'Bullshit.'

Robertson puts his face into that flatline smile look of his. 'Look, I'll tell you what. Put your head down, keep working hard. You had a good year, despite Borschmann. Maybe next year we can get you that promotion.'

'That's what you said last year, and the year before.'

'It's the best I can do.'

I stand there, recognising the edge, scared to jump.

'Well?'

'I'll think about it,' I say. Habits have a way of betraying you.

'You do that.'

I start towards the door, another fucking capitulation. I get to the door, step out into the open-plan area, head for my cubicle. And then I *think of my old man in that café in Yemen, how close he came to being blown to pieces, trying to do the right thing by the people there. I stop, gaze across the ordered cells, combs in a hive, towards the far windows. The rain has stopped and the sun is shining on the wet metal roof of the building across the street. I turn around. Go back to Robertson's office. Step inside. He looks up.*

'I'm off,' I say.

Robertson looks up. 'Good idea. Take a few days.' He's not a bad guy, really.

'No, I mean I'm out. You can hire yourself another woman.' I turn and walk away without waiting for a reply. And as I walk back to my cubicle, collect my few things and head for the stairs, all I feel is pity. For all of them.

Muskoka

The summer of that new year they rented a cottage in Muskoka, in the northern lake country of the Canadian Shield in Ontario, where the engineer had spent summers when he was a boy. To help Helena with the kids, and give her some time to herself, they hired an au pair, a pretty French-Canadian girl from Chicoutimi.

The cottage was on a small island of pink granite that sat in the crotch of a big L-shaped lake. There was a wooden dock and an old boathouse with a sloping roof made of cedar shakes, and a swept pathway that led through the trees up to the cottage. The island and the cottage belonged to a friend of his from university who had inherited it from his father. He was working abroad so offered it them for the summer.

They arrived in the second week of June when the lake was starting to warm. They had met Francine, the au pair, at the bus station in Toronto, and driven the three hours north to the lake country, the last of it on gravel roads through forests of maple and white pine. The engineer's friend kept a boat in a small shed at the southern end of the long arm of the lake. They parked the car under an ancient, sprawling maple. It was quiet, after the noise of the city and the highway. The smell of sap and warming pine filled the air. Helena eased Adam out of his car seat and lifted him to her chest. She put a finger to her lips and mouthed: *He's still sleeping*. Francine unloaded the groceries. Ethan jumped from the back seat and before anyone had noticed was running down towards the water.

'Ethan, wait,' said Helena. It was a half-shout. She didn't want to wake Adam.

But the boy was already at the boathouse and was sprinting along the uneven planking towards the far end of the dock.

'Slow down,' shouted Helena again. 'You'll fall. Warren, do something.'

Before the engineer could reply, Francine dropped her bags and sprinted after the boy. She moved like an athlete, with long, powerful strides. Just as the boy reached the end of the dock, she swooped down and took him in her arms.

'Leave the boy be, Hel,' said the engineer, lowering his voice, so it wouldn't carry. 'He's excited.'

'He's only ten, for God's sake.'

'Give him some rope, Hel. Please.'

'Easy for you. You're never here.'

'Please let's not start that. Not here. Not now.'

'No,' she said. 'You're right. Not here.'

They carried the bags of food and the cases down to the boathouse. Soon they had the little flat-bottomed boat loaded up. The engineer pulled the starter cord on the small ten-horsepower Evinrude outboard, and the motor coughed to life. He closed the choke, pushed the boat away from the dock, put the motor in gear and turned the throttle. They started down the lake. The boat was heavily loaded and deep in the water.

Helena sat in the bow with Adam on her lap and one hand trailing in the water. Francine sat in the middle bench with Ethan beside her.

'Isn't it lovely,' said Helena. 'So green and cool.'

The engineer, just back from Yemen, closed his eyes and breathed in the cool lake air.

'Can we go fishing, Daddy?' said Ethan, leaning over the gunwale to reach the water. Francine had one hand hooked into the waistband of the boy's trousers.

'You bet, Etho. We'll go this afternoon, after we've unpacked.'

'What kind of fish are there here, Daddy?'

'Pickerel, and bass, and sunfish and some big pike.'

'How big, Daddy?'

'Bigger than you, Etho.'

The boy pulled his hand from the water and sprang away from

the side of the boat. The engineer laughed. 'Don't worry, son. They don't eat children.'

Francine smiled at him. Her eyes were very pale, and in the sunlight, took on the aspect of a sandy lakebed. Helena was still trailing her hand in the water, gazing out at the shoreline. The engineer smiled at Francine and opened the throttle a little more. The little boat surged ahead.

'Slow down, Warren,' said Helena. 'The water's almost coming over the side.'

The engineer slowed the boat. The lake here was very deep.

He stayed with them for a week. The weather was perfect. Cool in the evenings, when they slept with the windows open and the breeze flowed through the flyscreens, carrying the smells of the forest, and sunny during the day, when they would warm themselves on the pink rocks after emerging cold and goose-pimpled from the dark water of the lake. In the mornings, the engineer would take the second, smaller motorboat and go fishing with whoever wanted to come with him – always Ethan, sometimes Helena. They caught pickerel, which was good eating, and on the fifth morning, a big long-nosed pike, which he released. On the Sunday, he said goodbye to his boys and to Francine and walked to the dock with his small day pack. Helena walked him to the boat.

'I wish you didn't have to go,' she said, holding his hand.

'I'll be back as soon as I can. A week at the most. We have all summer,' he said.

She squeezed his hand. 'Don't forget to bring more food,' she said. 'You have the list.'

He patted the pocket of his pack. 'You'll be OK?'

She smiled. It was her 'of course' smile. She was a very competent woman. It was one of the things he loved about her.

'The MacDougalls are just down the lake, about a mile. If you need anything, take the boat. They have a phone there, and a car.'

She nodded, kissed him on the cheek. 'Work hard,' she said.

He pulled her close, threaded his arm around her waist, reached his hand up inside her shirt and put his hand on her breast. He held her like that for a long time.

'You'd better go, before I end up keeping you here,' she said.

She stood on the end of the dock and waved to him as he started the boat along the lake. He looked back, watching her for a long time. Then he raised his hand and turned away. A few minutes later he looked back again, and she was still there, standing on the dock, staring out at the water.

As so often happens, the urgent meetings of critical importance to the project turned out to be not so urgent, and even less important. After three days, he had done what was needed, and was preparing to drive back up to the lake country when the phone in his hotel room rang. It was his boss, phoning from Calgary. The Yemen client was requesting an urgent meeting with him, at their head office in Oslo.

'What, Norway?'

'Yes, Norway.'

'Jesus. When?'

'The day after tomorrow. Get yourself over there.'

'Jesus, Fred. I'm supposed to be on holiday.'

Silence. He'd had to say it. He knew he had to go, that he would go. But it had to be said.

'Do you know what it's about?'

'They want to discuss your report. The produced water-disposal issue.'

That night, he phoned the MacDougalls and left a message for Helena that he would be delayed. The next morning, he flew to London, and then to Oslo.

Three days later he was back on the lake, the little boat loaded with groceries, everything on Helena's list carefully packed and double-checked. It was late afternoon, and the shadows of the trees reached out across the water. A breeze was blowing down the lake, pushing up little waves that buffeted the boat's bow and occasionally sent spray flying over the gunwales and into his face.

When the island came into view, it was almost dusk. Little pink clouds dotted the sky, ranged out in high-blown rows. He could just make out the boathouse and, through the trees, the flicker of lamplight from the cottage windows.

He killed the motor and glided the boat to the dock. The aluminium gunwale bumped the big, tarred log upright, and he reached the stern line over the cleat on the edge of the dock. It was dark now, and he could see Helena moving about in the kitchen, silhouetted in the yellow kerosene light, her long hair down. Voices came faint and disaggregated through the trees, the soft voices of women and the laughter of children. He sat in the boat for a long time, watching and listening.

He would tell her, later that night, about the meeting in Oslo. He hoped she would be proud of him. He was proud of what he'd done. Whatever the consequences might be, he knew it was what she would have done. It made him happy to think of it.

When he finally walked in the front door, three bags of groceries in each hand, Helena jumped up and threw herself into his arms. Ethan hugged his leg. Adam sat at the table, beaming, a spoon in one hand and apple sauce all over his face. Francine, too, in shorts and an apron, turned from the stove and smiled. He had never been so happy.

Ten days later, Ethan caught a fever. They put him to bed, nursed him, but he got worse. Helena decided to take him into town to see a doctor. She left early the next morning. The engineer stood on the dock and watched them go, waited there until they were nothing but a distortion on the horizon, an aberration of light. He stripped off and went for a swim. The water was cold. He swam across to the other side of the lake and climbed out and warmed himself in the sun a while, and then started back.

As he neared the island, he could see Francine standing on the big granite outcrop near the dock. She waved, pulled off her top and stepped out of her shorts, then dived into the water. After a while, she broke surface, pulled back her hair, smiled and started breaststroking towards him.

He waited for her. Through the dark water, he could see her long, tanned legs and the pale skin of her buttocks, and as she kicked and raised her chest and head to breathe, the pale crests of her breasts.

'It is so beautiful,' she said, breathing hard through her accented English. 'Shall we swim?'

'Where is Adam?' he said.

'He is still sleeping.'

He smiled at her. She was very young and very pretty. It made him feel strong, being here with her like this. 'OK,' he said. 'Let's go. But we can't be long.'

She was a good swimmer. He struggled to keep up. Soon she was three, then five body lengths ahead. All that sitting in meetings and planes and cars was making him soft. He determined to start exercising hard again. He would swim each morning that remained of the holiday, and when they got back to Cyprus, he would join a triathlon club again, get back to some serious training, do a few races.

When he climbed out of the water she was lying on the rock. She was on her side, facing him, up on one elbow, one leg crossed over the other, accentuating the curve of her hip. Water beaded on her skin, dripped from her nipples, rivered across her thighs and stomach to pool on the rock around her.

'I heard you talking about your meeting in Norway,' she said. 'What happened?'

'I fired my client.'

She frowned. She looked good like that, he thought. Naked and frowning. 'Why?'

The engineer stood looking at her. 'You're beautiful,' he said.

'So are you,' she said, smiling now.

'We should go back,' he said.

'Don't worry,' she said, smiling.

'I love my wife,' he said.

'I know. You have a very beautiful family.'

He sat facing the water, pulled his knees up to his chest.

She shifted, sat beside him. He could feel the warm softness of her hip against his.

'Are you OK?' she said after a while.

'We should get back,' he said. He stood and started towards the water. She followed.

Later that afternoon, after they had fed Adam and put him down for his nap, the engineer was sitting in the living room, reading a book. Francine came to him. She took off her clothes and stood naked before him. He did not tell her to go away, to put her clothes back on. He sat and looked at her face and breasts and her long, tanned legs. When she stepped closer, he reached up and explored the topography of her body with his hands. She parted her legs and moaned. And when she kneeled in front of him and started undoing his shorts, he did not stop her. When she took him in her mouth, he closed his eyes, and when she mounted him, he did not tell her to stop, nor did he tell her that he loved his wife. And when she shuddered and cried out, he bucked into her as if he were a man of twenty again.

They stayed like that a long time, holding each other in the coolness of the afternoon breeze. After, when they went to check on Adam, he wasn't in his room. They looked through every room in the house, the sand box where he liked to play, the woods around the house. When they finally found him, he was standing on the lakebed beside the dock, looking up at the surface of the water, his mouth open in a little round 'o', his blond hair gently swaying in the bottom currents, his face pale and strangely coloured by the lake water.

The engineer jumped in and pulled his son out of the water and lay him on the dock and administered CPR for more than an hour, pounding the little boy's chest until the ribs broke, shouting his despair to the empty heavens. Then he carried the boy's lifeless body to the boat and laid him inside and started the engine and started down the lake.

March 17th. London

I wake up early. I'm nearly halfway to work by the time I realise I don't work anymore. This whole thing with Dad's manuscript and Maria threatening to take Rachel away has got me rattled. Last night I made the mistake of rereading that last story, the one about Adam dying. All night I dreamed about it, him standing on the bottom, looking up through that green water, and no matter what I did, I couldn't get to him. It was as if my limbs had turned to hardwood.

I get off at Kew, and it's a nice day so I decide to walk around Kew Gardens for a while. I haven't been here for years, not since Maria and I brought Rachel. She was seven, I think. Three years ago, then. Makes you think. About time and all. It's all you have, and yet you can never hold on to even a small piece of it.

We are all weak. No one is strong. Not even the people you look up to because you think they somehow have strength where you have not. I know my old man was weak, that he was flawed. No wonder he and Mum never talked about it, about how Adam died. Jesus fucking Christ. I can't even imagine. I really can't. To live with that inside you. There must have been a big part of him that didn't want me to ever read this. I can imagine him wrestling with it. Wanting to create a legacy, a memory of the way he would have wanted to be remembered, rather than being straight with the truth. Because the truth is hard. It hurts. People don't want to tell it about themselves, and they don't want to know it about others. Much preferred is the pleasant fiction, the confirmed bias, the mainstream ideal. No one wants to admit that we are all fucked up, that we are all imperfect, vain, frightened, too easily flattered, so readily tempted. Christ, I sound like the Old Testament.

And yet we go on with our fictions, our made-up lives, trying to mirror some television or internet ideal of who we should be, what we should look like, how we should act. It's worse now than when I was a kid, I can see that with Rachel. Everything is instantaneous now, universal. Twenty million views in an hour. A hundred million likes. Groupthink has arrived, only a few decades late, and in a more perfect form. It crosses borders and knows no barriers of language or time. And even in the coarsening of every message, the same artifice prevails, stronger than ever. This is how I want you to see me. Not how I really am. I am neither as mean, as screwed-up, as perfect, as strong or sexy or rich or smart or victimised as I would want you to believe. Everything is an exaggeration, a fabrication, a portrait for the king. Trust no one. Not even yourself.

I am inside the big glasshouse when my phone rings. It's Maria. I answer. I listen. She hangs up before I have a chance to reply. There's not much for me to say, anyway. I close my phone, drop it into my pocket, keep walking.

It's not until I reach the exit that I process what's just happened. Maria has filed for sole custody of Rachel. Somehow, she knows I've quit my job. And Troy has filed assault charges against me. I don't stand a chance, and she knows it.

Red Sea

The day the work was to begin, the engineer rose before the sun. The camp was dark and quiet. He dressed in shorts and a T-shirt and walked barefoot to the rocky cove to snorkel the reef for the last time. The salt crust of the sebkha was cool under his feet. As he walked, the sky lightened. Beyond the low dunes, a barren desert coastline stretched away towards Arabia and the red edge of the world as day came.

The sea was flat and calm and not yet as blue as it would become later in the day when the sun was at its highest and the breeze would come up and carry the mauves and violets and deep aquamarines arcing from the surface to his eyes. All of this, the blueing sky and the mirror white of the flats and the blue surface of the sea, he determined he would never forget. And of everything else that lay hidden like some childhood treasure beneath that surface, he would make it so he would remember it for the rest of his life.

By the time he reached the water's edge, the first radians of the sun's disc had pierced the horizon. A lone freighter tracked across the mirage, heading west, bound, he guessed, for Suez. He thought of Helena, wondered what she was doing, who she was with – but as he had so many times over the past few days, he pushed the thought away before it could be answered.

The engineer pulled on his fins and mask and slipped into the water. In the shallows, the water was warm. As he waded out, he could feel the cooler, deeper water envelop his legs. Then he was in and swimming hard. After weeks of this, his shoulders were strong, his technique improved. He surged ahead, felt the power in his body. His breath rasped through the snorkel tube as he cut the tense morning surface. The sea churned and swirled in his ears. The water was very clear, as clear as any he had seen anywhere, here or in the Med or the Caribbean. Beneath, sand gave way to the first corals, scattered, fist-sized blooms of soft crimson and polyp green.

Fish approached, inquisitive and unafraid, nibbled the skin of his arms. At the reef slope, where the water deepened, he lifted his head and looked back towards the shore. Morning sun lit the rocks of the point. He could see the new orange survey flags fluttering on the near shore, and beyond, the work camp, the generator, the portable cabins, the excavators and water tanks, men and equipment stirring now; all of this come overland from Cairo and already covered over in a layer of Sinai dust so thick that for a moment he imagined that the desert had reclaimed these intrusions, pulled them in and swallowed them up.

He took a deep breath and plunged down into the cooler water below.

A swarm of pink-and-lilac basslets engulfed him. Silver mackerel shimmied past, too many to count. He reached out for them, fingers searching through the blue, but they slipped deeper and filtered away into the coral canopy below. He followed them down, the weight of the sea pressing in his ears, the coral reaching up towards him. A prehistoric leatherjacket peered out at him from its staghorn hide, mouthing words he could not hear, then retreated into the darkness. All around were trumpetfish, wrasses of every colour and pattern, transparent skeletal cardinalfish, schools of yellowtail scad, damsels so exquisite as to have been crafted by genius. And hovering in the dark water just beyond the slope, their eyes lambent and cold, a pair of reef sharks, separate as the sea itself.

He burst to the surface, filled his lungs. He had drifted out and towards the point. Plenty of time still. He took off his mask, spat into the visor, ran his fingers along the glass, rinsed it out and sealed it back to his face. Then he breathed deep, exhaled, sucked in another lungful of air and dived down until he was just above the pitted stems and branches of the canopy. Face down, arms and legs splayed wide, he floated in the brine and peered down into the swirling maze.

A trance of blue and yellow flashed past his mask and, for a moment, he thought he would lose his balance and tumble out to sea. After the sand and rock and monotonous desert sky, it was as if the solar spectrum had ruptured and spat its photons into the ocean to be made flesh and scale. Above, the sky-lit surface rippled and warped in the breeze he knew was there, but could not breathe. And what struck him, this last morning, as he felt the oxygen in his body burn away and his mind start to drift, was that all of this life, this wealth, this fierce display, was impossible, and the workings of it all, the delicate, ever-changing equilibrium of light and energy and matter, he could not fathom. As with so much in his life, he saw everything, could describe its physics, the workings of its growth and reproduction and death even, but of its essence, he understood nothing. Here, in this small cove on the southern coast of the Sinai Peninsula, he swam within a small and perfect mystery whose secrets he was about to destroy.

/\\

Three weeks before, he'd stood outside the boardroom and run through the presentation in his mind one more time. Under his arm, the charts and graphs summarising two months' work, all that he'd learned and seen reduced to the compact and precise language of his trade: bathymetrics, monitoring points, distributions of species of concern, predicted impact zones, proposed mitigation measures, development options.

He ran his finger under the collar of his shirt, rubbed away some of the dead skin from the back of his neck. When he looked up, the secretary was watching him. She was dressed in a spotless grey hijab. Her face was young but severe, wrapped tight in an off-white headscarf that lent her complexion a greyish pallor that reminded him of shark skin. She frowned. He smiled at her, aware of his own appearance. He hadn't had time to cut his hair since returning from Sinai, and its unruly curl had been bleached by thirty-one days of salt and sun. That morning, he'd cut himself shaving with the cheap, plastic disposable razor, and the two nicks still oozed blood. His suit was wrinkled after weeks folded in his case.

'You are the engineer?' she said in English.

He pulled out one of his business cards, placed it on the desk before her. '*Aiwa*,' he said. Yes. '*Ezeyika*.' Hello.

She glanced at the card a moment, raised her eyes again. 'You are expecting someone else, also?' she replied in English, ignoring his Egyptian slang.

'Someone else?'

'Your senior.'

'No. Just me.'

She stared at him for a time. Looked right into his eyes. It was unusual for a Muslim woman to challenge male authority with such brazen and forceful eye contact. He looked away first.

She waited another moment and then she said: 'The board is meeting now. Wait, please.'

He nodded and sat, feeling suddenly alone in the world.

In the end, they kept him waiting for almost two hours.

When he was finally ushered into the room, the first thing that hit him was the smell: half-eaten falafel and the sharp waft of Egyptian cigarettes mingled with an overpowering odour of stale sweat. It was a fifth-floor office, with grimy metal-framed windows that looked out across a narrow street to a row of Nasser-era apartment buildings, their afterthought balconies strung with drying laundry, the walls studded with the buzzing hives of dripping retrofit air-conditioning units. He couldn't see the sky. The room was hot – hotter than the waiting room, despite the single ancient AC system wheezing in the corner.

Eight faces looked up at him from around a long conference table. Ahmed, his direct contact, the one he'd negotiated the contract with, stared up at him from the far end of the table. The engineer smiled. Ahmed sat expressionless.

The chairman raised his eyebrows, puffed out his cheeks and lit a cigarette. His skin was pitted and shone with sweat. 'Welcome, young man,' he said, exhaling smoke, waving his cigarette towards an empty chair at the end of the table.

The engineer, who no longer felt young in any way, placed his folio of charts on the easel nearby and sat in the indicated place. Sweat bloomed in the backs of his knees and at his temples and soaked his shirtfront. Nothing about this project had gone to plan. The field work had been much more difficult than he'd expected. Approvals from the ministry had taken more than twice as long as he'd allowed for, and now he was more than two weeks late and well over budget. He'd only just finished the last graphics for the presentation a few hours earlier. They were rushed and inexpert.

'Please,' said Ahmed.

The engineer stood, took a breath, flipped over the first page. He faced his audience. Other than Ahmed, they were complete strangers.

The chairman butted out his cigarette, looked down the length of the table at him. 'Begin,' he said.

There were to be no introductions.

He tried his best. He presented all the data, described the predicted impacts. He offered alternatives. A cove ten kilometres further east where the coral was much less dense, with a natural channel out to sea. That one he'd swum half a dozen times, verifying the details himself. And another natural harbour, or the start of one, five kilometres further along again, larger than the primary site and almost barren of coral. Both of these alternatives would provide similar levels of shelter during winter storms. The further option had larger capacity, and in both, the damage to the reef would be much less, almost negligible for the further option. He had also secured preliminary approval for these options. As he turned over each page, the tick of the AC grew louder, the silence in the room deeper.

He flipped over the final chart. 'Questions?' he said.

There had been none.

M

After almost three-quarters of an hour in the water, he clambered up on to the rocks and towelled dry. The sun was higher in the sky now and it was already hot. Out by the reef edge, the cutter-suction dredge manoeuvred into position, a rusty spoil barge in tow. A thin line of black smoke rose from its grey funnel into the flawless blue sky. Voices skipped out over the water, crewmen preparing the ship for the day's work, and then the clank-clank-clank of the anchor chain running through the hawser pipe. The engineer stood on the shore and watched the dredge drop its great spider-like stanchions into the water. The cutter suction head, a gaping maw filled with rotating blades and grinders, dropped into position. Stanchions were secured. The spoil barge was tied alongside and the slurry hose attached and made fast. They were ready.

Thick black smoke belched from the ship's funnel and drifted inland on the sea breeze towards the rocky hills. The sound of the engines rose and fell as the cutters bit into the reef. Not long after, he watched the first spoil, a thick slurry the colour of vomit, spew from the discharge pipe and shudder into the barge.

He turned away and walked back up across the *sebkha* towards camp. The groan of the dredge followed him on the sea breeze. He felt faint. It would not take long. By the end of the day, he would be back in Cairo and on the way back to Cyprus, the money they owed him deposited in his account. And the reef would be gone, the cove dredged out to make way for the new marina. Maybe she would still be there waiting for him, but he doubted it.

March 18th. London

I've just read my old man's story about the reef in Egypt. This one was handwritten, and was dated October 25th, 2002, Egypt. He doesn't write another story again for a long time. Ten years until the next one, and then only three more in the sixteen years before he dies, all in the last week of his life. It's as if the fire went out, whatever was pushing him to write.

The reef story has a sketch of the coastline at the bottom of the second page, with what seem to be sampling points shown with arrows. He coloured it, too, with areas of sebkha and reef shaded in yellow and blue pencil. The word 'slut' is scrawled across the bottom of the page. The letters are pressed into the paper from repeated tracings, so that its mirror is embossed on the back of the leaf. I've been sitting here with my eyes closed, feeling the ridges on the back of the paper with my fingertips.

I brought up satellite images of the Sinai on Google Maps, zoomed in, made my way along the coast. I think I found the place he was describing. There is a big marina with three hotels clustered around it, and you can even see ranks of sunbeds covering the beach just beyond the rocky point. There are reefs a kilometre offshore, patches of lighter blue showing through dark sea blue.

What follows is not another of Dad's stories, but a newspaper clipping, faded a deep yellow, the paper brittle, poor quality, taped to a sheet of A4 writing paper. It's from the Cyprus Daily Mail, the island's English-language newspaper, dated the next day, October 26th, 2002. It reads simply:

A man and a woman were killed yesterday near the village of Kakopetria when their car left the road. It took emergency services over three hours to reach the car, which fell almost three hundred metres into a steep wooded valley. The dead have been identified as Mr Velimir Kontosky, twenty-six, the son of a Russian aristocrat and distant cousin of the last tsar, and Mrs Helena Scofield, forty-four, Canadian, the wife of an expatriate engineer working for a Cyprus-based offshore company.

I shiver as the memories come hurtling back. I was thirteen. The man from the embassy came to the house. I haven't thought about it since the day it happened. I'd certainly never seen the newspaper clipping. But now I can see it so clearly. Him standing there in the hallway in a white shirt and tie, whispering to our Filipino maid, her bursting into tears. I'd seen the man she was with in the car around the house, when my old man was away, but at that age of course you don't understand. He was just a nice man who came round now and again. I remember him being very tall and good-looking, and my mother smiling a lot when he was there.

How can two people be so clearly in love, so compatible, and yet hurt each other so? I mean, my old man changed his whole life for her. They always say you can't change a person, but that's just bullshit. All these platitudes we accept as truths. All bullshit. She changed him. He stopped drinking. He changed his worldview, his profession. All he wanted to do was make her proud, be worthy of her. He wanted to change. That's the secret. You have to want to change. The only thing was, she couldn't change him enough.

Maria wanted to change me. Nothing I ever did was good enough. She wanted me to be someone I wasn't. OK, I was happy to go along with it at the start, pretending to be this man of her dreams, and for a while it was fun. I mean, it was wild. I've never had better sex. Really. But, Jesus, who is this guy she thought she wanted? Be all the things a traditional man is supposed to be: strong, protective, financially secure, generous, all that shit. But she also wanted me to be, well, what can I say? Basically, she wanted me to be Troy.

At first, before Rachel came along, it was OK. We both worked hard, made some money, did what we wanted. After Rachel was born, Maria took a short maternity leave – eight weeks – and then started back to work. Her career started taking off, promotion after promotion. I was working my ass off to try to keep up, do my share, seventy-hour weeks. We had a full-time maid and a nanny for Rachel, so it worked OK, for a while. But then things started to change. Of course, I knew that with a child, they couldn't stay the same. But it wasn't what I expected.

It started with the laundry. She decided that I should start doing my own laundry. Told the maid not to do it. She said it was right that I should do it myself. I argued, but the maid took instructions from her, and my shirts and underwear piled up in the laundry room. I started sending my stuff out, dropping it at the cleaners on the way to work. When Maria found out, she was furious, ranting on about male privilege, about how things were different now, that men should realise it, accept it. By now, she was making double what I was, and letting me know it whenever she could. She started leaving all these little Post-it notes all over the house, telling me to dust this room, make this bed or clean and polish this floor. Of course, I ignored them. We went on like that for months, dancing around each other, her leaving notes, me picking them from whatever surface they were stuck to and throwing them in the bin.

Finally, she confronted me. Told me that this was who she was, that she was just coming into her own, that she needed to be the alpha, had always needed it and thought I had realised that at the start. I'd had no idea. None.

So, there it is. We never stood a chance, her and me. I was never the man she thought I could become, and she wasn't the woman she pretended to be. What a couple of idiots. And the crazy thing is, there is still a piece of me that loves her anyway, her crazy, dark-burning soul.

Kingfisher

They'd only been on the river two days and already he knew it was a mistake. A mistake coming back to Africa in the first place, taking this job; a mistake thinking that anything would ever change, that *he* could change it.

The old engineer rubbed his aching shoulders and watched the young man feed a mopane limb into the fire. The dry wood flared and caught, casting a sunset glow across the young man's face. The old engineer did not like this face, the girlish symmetry of fine, high cheekbones, the wavy too-long hair the colour of reed chaff, the burst plum lips, those yellow topaz eyes that could have belonged to a white man, the copper-coloured skin as smooth and perfect as a Himba woman's painted breasts. The kid looked like one of those impossible male models in the airline magazine ads for cologne and designer clothes, the ones with the peacetime eyes and keyboard teeth, far too young for all that stuff they were trying to sell: stuff he would never be able to afford, even after thirty years of work, especially now, since the divorce.

The young man spooned a steaming heap of *poike* from the cast-iron pot on to a tin plate. He wore a beaten silver ring on his right thumb. 'I think the helicopter is better for you, old man,' he said in a smooth tenor. 'From here we can still go back.'

The old engineer shifted on his camp stool and looked across the fire at the young man. He pointed to the night sky. 'What I am looking for, you can't see from up there.'

The young man looked up at the stars, gazed a moment. The galaxy light brushed his face pale, star-white against the darkness of the river and the hills rising from the far bank and the forest beyond. 'There are things you will never see, old man.'

The old engineer just shook his head at this, this arrogance.

'The helicopter is easier for you, old man. No hard work. No danger. There has been much rain. The river is running strong.'

'Fuck you,' the old engineer muttered under his breath, his voice swallowed by the *Quadrophenia* of river and rapids and wind and the night voices of a universe of insects.

'The other project people, they are only coming in the helicopter. Never standing on this ground.'

'Bunch of assholes,' said the old engineer. 'Incompetents.'

The young man held out the plate of food. 'What is it, this thing you are looking for?'

The old engineer took the plate and set it on his lap. At the last meeting, held in the tin-sheet cinderblock project office on the edge of town, the project leader, a young Namibian engineer from a South African university he had never heard of, had set out the expectations of those in power – that this be done, and be done here. No discussion. Find a way. 'None of your goddamned business,' said the old engineer.

The kid – that's what he was, couldn't have been more than nineteen or twenty – looked at him a moment and then sat down in the sand and stared at him. 'And you are not afraid?' he asked after a couple of stars had disappeared behind the edge of the hills.

It was an interesting question, one with many answers. Travelling through a Cygnus of time, alone, without her, without their sons – what the hell was he supposed to feel? Of course he was scared. Living in an air-conditioned trailer inside a chain-link and razor-wire compound since he'd started here didn't help. There had been trouble reported in the news, demonstrations, a couple of pipe bombs gone off in the town, jumpy, red-eyed conscript soldiers everywhere. 'No,' he said.

'Not afraid of the crocodiles?'

'I was told the crocodiles had all been shot.'

'That was in the war. A long time ago now. Some have returned.' The young man looked down at his hands and then into the fire.

'But war is coming again,' he said after a long time. He looked tired, resigned.

'Bullshit.'

'Do you know of the war, old man?'

'I want you to stop calling me that.'

The kid looked at him, frowned, said nothing.

The old engineer grunted and sniffed the stew: vegetables and meat, some kind of broth. 'The Border War,' he said. 'Back in the eighties. South Africa fighting the communist insurgency from Angola.'

The young man pointed to the far side of the river, the silver thread of the bank and the dark weight of forest. 'From there.'

The old engineer pushed a fork into what looked like a chunk of potato and brought it up to his mouth, blowing through pursed lips to cool the food. Not bad. He tried some of the meat. 'It was the Cold War. A different thing.'

'War is always for the same reason,' said the young man.

The old engineer took another mouthful and fixed the boy with a stare. 'What the hell is that supposed to mean?'

But the young man just smiled, helped himself to the stew and moved off to the edge of the firelight. His limbs were long, his movements languid, almost careless, like the lope of a painted dog the old engineer had seen in Etosha a few weeks before. 'Lucky to have seen one,' he had been told by the guide. 'Almost gone from here now.'

The young man sat on the sand and leaned back against the fibreglass hull of one of the boats they had drawn up on to the shore. He ate in silence. Upriver, the rapids churned white in the starlight. The sound they made was like a city street, a river of cars hissing along wet pavement. After a while, the young man stood, walked over to where the engineer was sitting and reached for his plate.

'Explain to me, old man, why you do this.'

The old engineer grunted and thrust out a tin mug. 'How about some coffee instead?'

The young man filled the mug with steaming water from the

kettle, reached into one of the plastic packing boxes and passed him a tin of instant coffee and a spoon.

The old engineer stirred in the coffee, took a sip and spat it out. 'It's not me,' he said, pushing himself to his feet and wedging his hand into the small of his back to straighten his spine. He looked out across the river to the dark forest on the Angolan side. 'It's you,' he said. 'Your people, your government.' He dumped the coffee into the fire, turned away and started across the shadowed sand towards his tent, knees stiff from sitting, calves sore, gait uneven, glad of the darkness.

'And there is no problem for you?' the young man called after him.

The old engineer stopped and turned to face the voice. 'None what so goddamned ever.'

'I think you are empty, old man.'

'I really don't give a shit what you think, *boy*.' The old engineer turned and walked back to his tent, the African night passing through him like an X-ray.

The next morning, he stood on the bank and watched the dawn sky blush pale over the dark mountains. Earlier worries about handling his boat in the rapids had gone. Yesterday he had run both sections of whitewater without incident, enjoyed it even. And he had slept well, better than in a long time, deep and tired and black and without the dreams. He pulled on his fleece jacket and walked to the fire. The kettle was nestled up against a small pile of glowing coals, steam wisping from its spout. The boats, two-man Canadian canoes, had been pulled down to the water's edge and most of the gear was loaded and strapped down. The old engineer stood looking out across the water as day came.

A shriek skipped across the water like a flat stone, the river a couple of hundred metres wide here. A pair of vervet monkeys playing in a tree on the far bank, tumbling like circus performers high above the water. Something caught his eye, downriver, in the shadow of the far bank. It was a head, low in the water, just submerged, blistering the surface as it surged through the current. A crocodile. He'd never seen a crocodile in the wild before. The kid had not lied.

The old engineer watched the thing carve a disturbed wake through the green surface. The monkeys had gone quiet and now sat perched in the tree, staring down at the water. Suddenly, the crocodile changed direction and began traversing the river towards camp. As it moved out of shadow, something flashed about its head, pale in the sunlight: a limb, a leg. A burst of white spume rose and fell, a flurry of splashes churned the surface. The old engineer's heart spiked – it was the boy. He was fighting for his life. The old engineer took two quick steps towards the water's edge and stopped dead. He thought of the sat phone buried deep in the kit in one of the boats. Another spasm, a flash of limbs, an explosion of whitewater. And then it was over, and there was just the green river running laminar towards the sea. The boy was gone.

Time slowed, and then stopped. The old engineer stood on the bank and gazed out across the river as the reality of what he had just witnessed calcified and set hard, a moment moulded and driven into the catacomb of his bones along with the other moments he would never forget. The wind dying and the trees like rows of silent crosses when they came to tell him about Helena, all those hours and years ago. Even the clouds had stopped then, shocked into frozen mourning.

The old engineer watched time re-establish its dominion. The river was moving again, swirling thick and green, as if nothing had changed. Eddies were born and twisted in the current, carried along before disappearing again, random lives extinguished and replaced. This river had been here, coursing through this valley, deepening it, filling its calms with sediment for hundreds of thousands of years, since before human civilisation. And it would be here long after he and everyone he had ever known was gone.

He stood and looked out across the river. Suddenly, a blister appeared on the water's surface. It was moving towards the bank now, trailing a smooth, languid wake. The same head. The crocodile.

Coming straight towards him. The old engineer took a step back, stumbled over a stone, checked his balance. It was still coming. Then something broke the surface, pale against the green water, just near the head. An arm. It hung there for an instant, suspended above the water, and then arced back down without a splash. And then again, its mirror twin, rising and falling, in smooth regular strokes now, a duet, the thing's head turning, first one way, then the other, breathing.

The old man slumped to the ground and sat on the sand, clutching his knees, the fear draining from him as through an opened valve. 'Jesus fucking Christ,' he muttered.

The young man reached the shore and emerged dripping from the water. He stood for a moment there, shin-deep in the current, naked, the morning sun bathing his wet skin. He was tall and lean, with broad, muscled shoulders and a torso of ropy basalt, forearms veined like turgid leaves, not a mark on him. He waded to the bank and waved, his cock and balls swinging heavy beneath a nest of dewy black wire. He flashed a wide smile and combed a hand through his hair.

'What the fuck do you think you're doing?' the old engineer barked.

The kid stopped and looked at him, shrugged his shoulders in a what-are-you-talking-about way.

The old engineer pointed to the river. 'We have a job to do.'

The kid smiled, another shrug rippling through him. 'Good swimming here, old man. You should try. No crocodiles here.' He pointed downriver. 'There, yes.'

The old engineer scowled, turned away and walked back to his tent. One of his own sons would have been about the same age as this kid now. He tried to picture him at nineteen, emerging sunlit from a river, perhaps, but after a few steps, his imagination died and nothing came, those pathways too long repressed.

By nine o'clock it was already hot. The old engineer wiped the sweat from his brow with a corner of his T-shirt and adjusted his cap. Even after a couple of hours of paddling, yesterday's soreness had returned, deep behind the clavicle and into the rotator cuff, the calcifying joint tearing at the tendons. He let the boat drift in the current. He raised his binoculars and scanned the cliffs, studying the structure of the rock, the orientation of folds and faults, the sheets of olivine basalt, the pink blush of the metamorphics. He rolled open the topographic map and laid it on the flat-folded mattress he had arranged across the gunwales as a tabletop. He traced his finger along the line of the shore.

The young man drew his boat alongside. 'Old man,' he said.

The old engineer picked up his binoculars and pretended not to hear.

'Are you seeing it?'

The old engineer jerked his head around and glared at the kid. 'Seeing what?'

'The colours in the rocks, the designs, the shadows. Can you see it?'

The old man shook his head, went back to his binoculars, kept scanning the folds, the points of stress, the splays of brittle fracture.

'This ending will not be good, old man.'

The old engineer looked up from his map and stared into the kid's eyes. 'Endings usually aren't,' he said.

In mid-afternoon, with the sun waning overhead, they pulled the boats up on to an ellipse of sand on the Namibian side and sat on the grass under the fractured shade of an old leadwood. The young man produced a salami, tomatoes, South African Camembert and a loaf of dark bread. They ate in silence. Afterwards, the old engineer set out his camp mattress, lay down, pulled his cap over his eyes and listened to the birdsong and the water flowing over the rocks.

He awoke to the sound of voices.

The young man was standing by the boats talking to two Himba women. They laughed, flashing strong white teeth, naked bodies quivering under the ochre mud that covered every part of them. The old engineer pushed himself up, smoothed back his hair and walked, stiff-jointed, down to the boats.

As he approached, the young man turned and faced him. 'These young girls are from the village past this hill,' he said with a quick smile. 'They are coming to collect water and plants for medicine, to pray to the river spirits.' He put his hand behind the taller one's back, but did not touch her. 'This is Ogandou. She will be married next month. You can see this by the way she has her hair. She is seventeen years. Old to be married. The other is Mokanou. She learns to be a healer. She is sixteen.'

The old engineer stepped forwards, trying not to stare, muttered hello. A thick musk – earth and sap, sweat and something more powerful that he could not place – pulsed from the women's bodies, filling his senses. Their breasts were large and firm, one pair round like cassava ends, the other longer, gourd-shaped. Mudded braids caressed fat nipples. He had hardened. The realisation surprised him. A memory came unbidden: Helena by the sea the first day of their honeymoon, so long ago now, but still so clear that he had to push it away until it was gone.

He shifted his stance and looked up at the women's faces. They smiled at him and laughed at something the young man said. The old engineer felt his cheeks flush and he looked away.

The young man spoke with the women for a long time, sometimes breaking into a long, animated passage, a story perhaps, the language a glottal melody, then listening as the women chattered excitedly back, eyes dancing. They gave their laughter freely, without hiding their mouths as women in some cultures were taught to do. Occasionally, they would glance over at the old engineer, but always their eyes would dart back to focus on the young man.

After a while, the young man collected some food from his canoe. A bag of meal, tins of tuna, sugar, a joint of meat. He put them in a plastic shopping bag and handed it to the women. Evening was approaching.

'Kuhepa,' they said in unison, smiling broadly.

'Kare nawa,' said the young man as the women started up the rocky hillside.

The old engineer watched them disappear into the bush, soles flashing pale. He turned towards the young man, who had started to unload one of the boats. 'What is that stuff they rub over their bodies?'

'It is the oil from *mukange* bark, the perfume tree, and red mud.'

'Beautiful.' He said it without thinking.

The young man razored sweat from his brow with the edge of a mopane leaf. 'These are the people you will destroy, old man.'

The old engineer squared his shoulders and stood to his full height. 'Spare me your righteous bullshit, boy. If you are so concerned, why are *you* here?'

The young man stood looking down at his feet in silence, the boat's bow line hanging from his hand. That had shut him up.

'Yeah, that's what I thought,' said the old engineer, pulling his tent bag from the boat. 'Now, how about we just stay out of each other's way?' He dropped the bag to the ground. 'I presume we are camping here tonight.'

The young man looked up at the sky, the black silhouette of the mountains, the bruise-yellow cumulus that troubled the darkening sky. 'This is the best camp before the big rapids,' he said. 'It is too late to go on.'

They unloaded the boats and set up camp. The old engineer pitched his tent on a sand ledge near an old baobab and used the last of the day's light to update his field notes. After a while, he looked up, having made little progress. The young man was sitting on a folding canvas stool on a patch of grass by the water's edge, looking out across the river, dabbing with a slender brush at a piece of card propped on a wooden easel. He gazed out over the river for a moment, then turned to the easel, dipped the brush into a tin on the ground and touched bristles to paper in a series of slow arcs.

The old engineer looked in the direction of the young man's study but could see only the smooth meandering curls of the river, the far shore already in shadow. Then he followed the young man's gaze. Just beyond the shallows, a black-and-white bird was perched atop a branch that protruded from the water. Unremarkable, no larger than a fist, it had a long, bladed beak too big for its body and a small black crest. He went back to his notes.

Night came on, cool and cloudless, a blanket of stars. The Milky Way carved a frosty equatorial arc above them. The old engineer sat by the fire. Steaks sizzled on a steel grill. The young man reached into the icebox and pulled out two cans of Windhoek lager and passed him one. They drank in silence, watching the flames.

After a while, the young man passed him another beer, and opened his second.

'Don't you own a camera?' asked the old engineer.

'Too easy,' the young man said, wiping his lips with the back of his hand. 'Tourists all day clicking cameras, trying to capture everything, take it home, own it. And then all night at the fire with blue faces, delete, download, edit, not looking up at the stars or the bats swooping their heads. They are in their own country already, making Facebook of themselves.'

'You know,' said the old engineer, swirling the beer around in the can, smiling to himself, 'that's the first thing you've said that makes sense.'

The young man smiled, lifted the can to his lips and drank.

'I've taken thousands of photographs over the years,' said the old engineer. 'And you know, I've only ever kept four.' He thought of the faded picture in the little silver frame on his desk in the cramped room he used as an office. Helena, the day they were married, so long ago now, an eternity – her hair flying in the sea breeze, face freckled by the sun, that impossible aching smile, a swathe of Gulf of Guinea blue in the background, the only testament now that it had ever happened. And how stupid he'd been to think that he might recapture even a fraction of what he'd had with her by remarrying. You only ever get one chance at something so rare. If you're lucky. He looked into the night. 'I don't know why I even keep them.'

The young man reached into his pocket and pulled out a Ziploc bag. Inside was a blue fabric wallet. He slid out a small square of paper and offered it to the old engineer. 'I have only one.'

A tall blond man in military field uniform stood on a faded dirt road. Next to him was a small boy, naked but for a loincloth.

'My father,' said the young man. 'The war killed him.'

That explained something. The old engineer said nothing, handed back the photograph.

That night, he hauled his mattress out of the tent and threw it down on the sand, as the young man had done, and lay watching the constellations turn overhead until sleep took him. He woke as first light crept into the sky. He pulled on his shorts and walked barefoot down to the fire.

The young man was standing naked in the shallow water next to one of the boats. He looked over his shoulder, smiled and slid into the water. After a few strokes, he turned and waved. 'No worries, old man,' he called. 'Crocodiles are far.' Then he dived, flicked his feet in a powerful kick and disappeared.

The old engineer stood at the water's edge and let the river lap his feet. After three days on the river he felt fitter than he had in years, and without the tyranny of a mirror, he allowed himself to imagine that he was as he had been all those years before, not the overweight, greying, pallid office creature he had become. He waded out across the muddy bottom until he was waist deep, scrotum shrivelling. The boy was almost mid-river now, head down, slicing across the glassy surface. Fuck it, he thought. He closed his eyes and dived, kicked out three long strokes and surfaced, blinking in the sun that had broken over the hills. The water was cool, invigorating.

At first, the grating hinge of his stroke was awkward and he fought for breath, trying to follow the young man. He could feel the current pulling him downstream. About halfway to the other side he slowed and opened up into a choppy breaststroke. The young man was walking on the far bank now, leaving a trail of dark dimples on a shoal of brilliant white sand. He looked up and waved. The old engineer lifted a hand and made a clumsy sweeping motion, a wave of sorts.

When he finally gained the far shore, he had been carried far downstream. Here, the bank was thick with tall reeds and he floated on his back in an eddy, breathing hard. The sky above was clear and blue, the bank alive with song. Birds flitted and wheeled across the water and between the dense weave of green stalks. And there, just above him, perched on the tip of a reed, were two little black-and-white birds, like the one the boy had been painting. They looked down at him for a moment, twittering in a high-pitched trill, and then darted out over the water. He watched them climb high above the river and then stop and hover at treetop height, wings flaring, bodies up, heads bent, peering down into the water, holding position with minute corrections of pitch and yaw, their delicate tail feathers twitching in the breeze. They were like toys, models of themselves. He could not look away.

Suddenly, one of the birds folded back its wings and fell. It plummeted like a dart towards the smooth silvery surface. His muscles tightened. Could something so small survive the impact? Inches above the water the bird wrenched out of the dive and skimmed the surface before climbing to rejoin its mate.

He had been in the water a long time. He was shivering. He wrapped his arms around his body, treading water, and looked back across the river. Where was the kid? The water was dark and murky. Looking down, he couldn't see his own legs, and suddenly he felt horribly exposed, limbs flailing just below the surface like pale lures. He should go back. But the birds were still there, hovering above him, watching him, tracking upriver now, swooping in small arcs as he followed. How honourable they seemed, these tiny creatures. How noble. Was it the cold, playing tricks? He swam on, following the birds. They were moving slowly enough for him to keep up, a game. Each time he got close, fighting the current, they swooped a bit further upriver.

He had just reached the white shoal when one of the birds flared, stalled and flipped into a vertical dive. This time he knew there would be no reprieve. The bird hit the water like a bullet and was gone. There was barely a sound. He was surprised by the delicacy of the impact. If he had blinked, he would have missed it. And then the bird was climbing again, wings trailing little diamonds of water, a tiny silver fish in its beak. The old engineer watched it disappear out over the reeds.

By the time he reached camp, he was exhausted and cold, strangely elated. He could feel his muscles rippling, twitching as he waded up the bank. It was a long time since he had felt this way.

The young man was by the fire, squatting on his haunches, watching him, a wide grin dawning on his face.

'What have you got to smile about?' said the old engineer with a scowl, covering his nakedness with a hand.

'The river, *oud* man. It makes you alive.'

The old engineer coughed. 'Let's get going,' he said. 'I have work to do.'

Soon they were on the river again, moving steadily with the current. Another hot, cloudless day spread over them. The old engineer unfolded the map across his knees. The big rapids were still about ten kilometres away. Letting his boat drift in the current, he scanned both sides of the riverbank through his binoculars. Ahead, a zebra pelt of dark, mafic dykes striped the salt-and pepper granite bluffs on either shore. He noted the feature on the map in pencil, then folded and stowed it. He was about to turn his boat towards the Namibian shore when the young man pulled alongside.

'Over there,' said the old engineer, indicating with his chin a place where the bluffs had been worn flat by the river, a horizontal slice of the underlying rock laid bare. 'I need to take some measurements.'

'Before you do, have a look,' whispered the young man, pointing to a sandbar on the Angolan side. The old engineer squinted across the water.

'Do you see? At the waterline.'

The old engineer raised his binoculars and brought the bank into focus, tracked upriver. A crocodile lay motionless in the sun, head to water. The pale skin of its midsection was stretched tight to bursting.

'As big as your canoe,' said the young man.

The old engineer's stomach knotted. He let the binoculars fall on to their strap and picked up his paddle. 'I'm not here to sightsee,' he said, altering course towards the opposite bank.

The old engineer landed his boat in a small patch of black gravel on the bank, stepped over the side and drew the canoe up on to the shoal. The bedrock here was sculpted smooth by the water, hot through the soles of his sandals. He set off towards the dykes. By now, the young man had drawn up his boat and was bounding after him. The old engineer crouched next to the first dyke and took out his compass and notebook. The rock was heavily fractured.

'What do you measure?' said the young man, peering over his shoulder.

The old engineer stood, snapped his compass shut and pushed the notebook into his pocket. He looked at the young man. Gone was the face he'd first seen, first judged. This was the face of a small boy, a boy without a father. And, ever since Helena had died, so long ago now, he'd been a father without a child. She'd had every right to leave him, of course, the way he'd treated her, the things he'd done. And in his guilt, he'd compounded error with error, hadn't done the things he should have, hadn't been there for her, worked to put it back together. And then the crash. He remembered hearing about it in the news. He was away, working in Egypt. And then when the man from the embassy had come to tell him the news, it was like a hand reaching inside him and grabbing his heart and tearing it out of his chest. What she'd been doing there that day, in a rented car with a man more than ten years her junior, he'd only ever been able to guess. And so, as penance, to punish himself for all his failures, and for the boy's own protection, he'd banished the only person he had left. He looked down at the rock, swallowed hard. 'Fracture orientation,' he said. 'Number, character, spacing.'

The young man nodded. 'This is important?'

The old engineer closed his eyes, watched photons swim red across his eyelids. Opening them again, he said: 'What?'

'These fractures, they are important?' the young man said.

The old engineer blinked once, twice. 'Fractures create permeability and instability. Neither is good.' It was becoming pretty clear to him now, based on all the data he had collected, that the thing wasn't going to work. The geology just wasn't right. And if they went ahead and built it, as it appeared they were determined to do, large-scale failure was inevitable. It would only be a matter of time.

The old engineer stood and started towards the next set of fractures. The young man followed close behind.

'Do you want to know the name of that little bird, old man?'

The old engineer stopped and turned around. 'What?'

'The little black-and-white fishing bird. I saw you watching him, this morning in the river.'

The old engineer sighed and took off his cap and ran his fingers through the bristles of his hair. 'Why do you insist on thinking that I give a shit?' He turned away and kept walking. He could hear the young man's naked soles soft on the rock behind him. He pushed on. The young man followed. He gave it fifty more metres and then stopped and spun around and stared the young man in the face. 'Goddamn it, kid, just let me be, please. I can look after myself. Go back to the boats.'

'I am a professional,' said the young man, standing hands on hips. 'If something happens to you, the responsibility is with me.'

The old engineer laughed. 'Professional? You don't even know the meaning of the word.'

'Say what you like, old man. I am glad you did not use the helicopter.' The young man waggled him a sign he'd seen other young people use: the thumb and little finger extended from the fist like the horns of a bull. He had no idea what it meant. 'Meet at the boats. But come soon. The big rapids we must cross before darkness.' And then he was gone, loping like a gemsbok back towards the river.

By the time the old engineer reached the boats, the young man was busy tying down and making fast equipment and supplies, decking over spray skirts from bow deck to stern thwart. It looked like he was preparing for a rough ride. The old engineer removed his sandals, tied them to the safety line that ran the length of the starboard gunwale and, without looking up, said: 'Let's get this over with.'

'No worries, old man. The water is not as angry as it looks. Follow the line I make. Stay close. You wanted to see the river; this way is best.'

As they approached the bend in the river, the old engineer could see why the project team had chosen this site. The profile of the banks had steepened. Massive granite outcrops framed each side of the constriction, ideal for anchoring buttresses. Any number of spillway and penstock options presented themselves. Approaches for equipment looked good. He scanned the walls with his binoculars.

They moved into a deep, sunlit canyon, drifting with the accelerating current. The sound of the rapids filled his ears, echoing from the cliffs that towered above them on both sides now. The rock was heavily fractured here, the water's edge a litter of splaystone from the cliffs above. Mist and spray shrouded the water ahead, rainbows dancing in and out of existence like phantoms.

He watched the young man manoeuvre his boat to the middle of the river, flicking the paddle with quick movements of his forearms. The water surged into smooth, standing waves, scalloped surfaces of translucent green hemmed with a lacework of froth. The boat flexed beneath him. He plunged the paddle blade deep and pulled until his muscles burned, following the kid's line down the heart of the river.

And then he was around the bend, careening towards the rapids, white churning foam as far as he could see. Spray fell in sheets and soon he was soaked to the skin, but he was holding his boat straight, still following the line. The young man looked back and flashed a broad smile. The old engineer grinned and followed the kid into another set of steep-sided waves, the bow pitching skyward and then tumbling down to bury itself, before emerging again, over and under, until finally he was through.

The young man was waiting for him in an eddy of calm on the Namibian side. The old engineer drew alongside.

'Good, *ja?*' said the young man, water beading on his face, eyes shining.

'Good,' said the old engineer. Good.

The next rapid was slightly longer, the waves taller. The old engineer followed the young man down into the core of it, working the blade of his paddle instinctively, those years spent on the Capilano and the Fraser with his father there still, memories drilled into his muscles. Out the other side, into calm water, they drifted side by side, saying nothing, the diamond spray drifting over them, atomising the sunlight. The old engineer breathed deep of it, as if this vapour were youth itself, quickening his heart, healing the damage of years. As they drifted downstream, the sound of the next rapids built, funnelled along the valley.

'The next one is rougher,' said the young man. 'Stay low in the boat and paddle strong. Follow me.' As the curve opened up, the rapids came into view. It was as if the river simply ended, the green lassitude of the flat water ruptured white, a war of churning waves and flying spray, beyond which nothing existed.

The kid pointed downriver. 'This big rock is the danger. Can you see it?'

The old engineer nodded. It wasn't a rock; it was an island – a single monolith spearing the soul of the tumult.

'Keep to the right side of the river,' the kid shouted above the din. 'Right side. After, we can rest in the flat water.'

The old engineer gave the thumbs up. His heart raced. He could feel the adrenaline pounding through every living part of him as they were pulled towards the turbulence.

This time the surge was stronger. The first trough pulled the boat down hard, pitching the bow deep and sending a sheet of green water crashing over him. The force of the water knocked him back into the stern deck and carried away his cap, but he recovered quickly, spluttering out a mouthful of water, paddling hard as the boat sprang free, and lurched up the next wave. At the crest, he caught a glimpse of the young man, just ahead, immersed to his shoulders, and the black dragon's-tooth rock ahead. And then down again, steeper this time, so that he was looking into the maw of the vortex, the water like oil, viscous and spinning, the sky collapsing away behind him. The old engineer whooped as the boat sprang from the trough and hung for a moment on the next crest. He was right on track, the young man no more than a few metres ahead, awash in churning white foam.

The young man glanced back, pointing with the blade of his paddle. 'Right side,' he shouted above the roar.

The fear was gone now, and the old engineer was back on the Capilano river, one drizzling September day on his fifteenth birthday, skittering down between the rocks in his new kayak, following his father in the old banged-up two-man with the yellow stripe. And then the rock was there, much bigger than it had looked from upriver, steep-sided rhyolite glistening wet in the sun. The young man was almost abreast it now, nearly at the calmer water beyond. The old engineer dug his paddle deep and pulled with all his strength. He was drifting too close to the rock, the current pulling him towards the black wall. The young man was waving his arms frantically over his head. 'Too close,' came his voice over the churning of the river.

I know I'm too close, goddamn it. I know.

He was sliding beam-on towards the rock. He paddled till his shoulders screamed, trying to turn the boat away from the rock and back towards the line, clawing back the lost water. He dug the paddle deep and pulled. He was making progress, regaining the line. Another hit of adrenaline surged through him. Then something whipped the boat into a violent turn and he was facing upriver, the rock behind him now, drawing him in, magnetic. He dug the paddle in deep to port and the boat started to yaw left, twisting against the flow. But it was not enough.

The boat hit the rock at speed, full amidships. The fibreglass flexed as the boat tried to wrap itself around the rock. For a moment, it was stuck fast, pinned to the anvil, water rushing over the port beam, filling the space around him. He could hear the fibreglass scraping across the rock, straining against the force of the water, the hollow groan as the gunwales began to splinter, the weave of the fibreglass starting to come apart. He was glad he was on the far side of the rock, glad the young man could not see him, could not witness this wrecking.

And then something gave way; some balance in the forces that had held him there tipped and he was tumbling, free of the boat now, twisting in a deep vortex, limbs flailing, the sound of rushing water filling his ears. Somehow, he had managed to fill his lungs before going under. He fought for the surface but was pushed deeper. His hip collided with something hard, a sickening dull cartilage thud. A spear-point of pain drove through him. He spun away again, the oxygen in his body burning up in panic, a cold ache spreading into his legs, daylight laughing down at him through a thousand warping lenses. When his head hit the rock, it registered only as the briefest flash of white surprise.

M

Thirst. It was the first thing. A burning desperation, deep and wide. He reached for the cup and held it to his mouth, gulping down the cool, pure liquid, not letting go of the wrist to which it was attached until every drop was gone. And then the pain came, flooding his senses until there was nothing else.

After a while, he opened his eyes. He was lying under a blanket. A fire burned nearby. It was dark. He forced a thin rasp across his vocal chords. He tried to sit up, but was driven back by a crushing wave of agony in his lower back. His legs felt numb. He closed his eyes and drifted away on a river of pain.

'Old man.'

The old engineer opened his eyes. The young man's face peered down at him. Behind, a trillion stars. And then it all came flooding back. 'I was thrown,' he gasped.

'It's OK,' whispered the young man. His voice was gentle, like a mother's. 'Don't talk. You need rest.'

'What happened?'

'You were knocked unconscious. Please, rest.'

'How long have I been out?'

'Two days.'

Jesus. The old engineer sank back on the camp cot and stared up at the night sky. 'I was caught in a whirlpool. I couldn't get to the surface.'

The young man reached over, poured more water into the cup and raised it to the old engineer's lips. 'You must stay still.'

'I can't feel my legs.'

'You have bones broken. There is bleeding inside.'

'Helicopter after all, then.' The old engineer tried a smile.

'Sorry, *oud* man, the sat phone is gone, and the equipment in your boat.'

'Shit.'

'It is my fault,' said the young man, head bowed.

'No.' The old engineer reached up and touched the bandage around his head. 'The boat?'

'Gone.' The young man tossed another piece of wood on the fire. 'Tomorrow I will walk to the village. Mokanou will come to care for you. She is a good healer. Then I will bring the helicopter.'

'How long?'

The young man looked up at the stars. 'Two days. Maybe less.'

Too long. He could feel the life leaving him even now. The old engineer looked up at the young man. 'You pulled me from the water.'

'Yes.'

'You could have left me.'

'You are a stupid old man.'

Truer words never spoken. 'That boy in the photo. It was you, wasn't it?'

The young man nodded. 'I was three years old. It was the last time I saw him. After he was killed, his friend from the army came to the village and took me away to Natal. I went to school like an Afrikaner boy.'

The old engineer thought of his own son, sent away to boarding school, married now and living somewhere in London. 'And these are your people,' he said.

The young man leaned over and placed two tablets in the old engineer's mouth. 'Drink,' he said, helping him with the cup.

The old engineer drank, spluttered back some of the water. 'Your people?' he said.

The young man closed his eyes, held them shut for a few seconds, opened them again. 'They are my people, but we are not theirs.'

'We?'

'My wife and son.'

'You live here? With them?'

The young man nodded, poured more water into the cup.

'And those girls,' said the old engineer. 'The ones you gave food to.'

'My sisters.'

'Well, that says something.' The old engineer closed his eyes and breathed deep, fought to keep back the pain. 'They don't need to live like this, you know.'

'Live like what, old man?'

'Like this. Barefoot, naked, healing with herbs and river spirits. The dam will bring electricity, jobs, prosperity.'

'The Himba people have chosen this life. It is not a misfortune. Not something that needs to be fixed. If the land is destroyed, if the graves of the ancestors drown, it will be the end of the world. Everything you have seen will disappear. The Himba will fight to stop it, die if they have to.'

The old engineer tried to shift on the cot, but the pain pinned him. 'This thing is coming, whether you like it or not,' he grunted through clenched teeth.

The young man stood and looked down at him. 'Then you are lucky, *vader*. You have a choice. We do not.'

The next morning the old engineer woke to a grey, overcast sky. The fire had burned down to ash. The young man's boat was gone.

Propped on a camp chair next to him was a litre bottle of water and some food, a package of painkillers. A piece of thick bond paper the size of a postcard was propped against the water bottle: on it, a little black-and-white bird perched on a twig, head turned side on against a blue watercolour background, the pencilled outline washed in delicate, feathered brush strokes. Beneath, in a neat lead-pencil hand was written: 'Pied Kingfisher♂, Kunene River. October 2012.'

March 21st. Calgary

It's warm here. Not much snow in the mountains. The new normal.

The moment I finished that last story, I decided to quit London. I packed up the few things that mattered to me: my camera, a couple of books, some essentials; binned most of the rest. I gave notice on my flat, left my Ducati with a friend, bought a one-way ticket and came here, back to where I was born.

All the way here, all I thought about was that last story, the one about Namibia and the river trip. It's hard to believe that anyone could be that hard, that stubborn, that completely fucked up. All those years, pushing me away every time I tried to get close, rejecting my every attempt at reconciliation, until finally, one day, I just gave up. Penance, he called it. Punishment. Protection. But for who, Dad? You, or me?

I walk along St Stephen's Avenue towards Fourth Street SW to meet with Dad's solicitor. The sky is blue with wisps of high-blown Chinook cloud coming off the Rockies. My feet move across the pavement, but they don't feel like my feet. The lawyer contacted me earlier about selling the house and tidying up the last aspects of Dad's will. He insisted that I meet with him in person.

Before leaving London, I ended it with Constantina. I went to her place and sat there on her sofa and just told her that I was going away, for a long time probably, that it was something I had to do. She cried, said I didn't love her. There was nothing I could say to that, so I didn't say anything. I know I hurt her, but I couldn't lie to her or myself anymore. It was one of the hardest things I've ever had to do.

I arrive at the lawyer's office. The receptionist tells me that he's running fifteen minutes late. I sit in the waiting room, pull the manuscript out of my bag. On the flight over here, I resisted reading the final story. It was the very last one he wrote, one of the three that somehow were added to the manuscript after he died. I wanted to read it here, where all of this started, where it's going to end.

I turn to the last story and start reading.

I've almost finished reading the first sentence – When the old engineer had been a young man, just starting his life, when all of what was to come still lay hidden – *when the receptionist calls my name. I am deep in thought and it registers as if part of a dream, a distant voice from across the mountains. I shake it off, grab the manuscript and follow the receptionist through to the office.*

My father's lawyer is an old guy, stained and grey. He sits behind an old desk, flanked by shelves of old books. The place smells of mould and cigar and dust. There isn't a computer monitor to be seen, not a hint of technology anywhere. He looks up at me over his half-frame reading glasses.

'I knew your father well,' he says. 'We were friends for a long time. I am glad we could finally meet. Please,' he says, indicating a worn leather armchair.

I nod, sit.

'You sold the house,' he said.

'Yes.'

'Good.'

'And the bank account?'

'Transferred.'

'So, we're good?'

'There are only two final items of business.'

I say nothing, wait.

'I see you found it,' he said, glancing down at the manuscript in my hand.

'Yes.'

'And have you read it?'

'All but the last story.'

'Good. He was hoping you would.'

I think about it a moment, decide not to ask.

The lawyer opens a file, reads, looks back up at me. 'First,' he says, 'there is a small property on the coast of British Columbia, near a place called Tuwanek. Ten acres on the water, a small log cabin, off the grid, quite rustic. It belonged to your grandmother, then, for a while, your father.'

'I've been there,' I said. 'A long time ago.'

'Yes. So have I. It's beautiful.' He passes me a dossier. 'It's yours.'

I am sure he can see the shock on my face. Inside, title deeds, a map, keys. 'I had no idea,' I say.

He nods. 'There is one other matter,' he says. 'Of a trust account, bequeathed to you, under condition.'

'Condition?'

'The trust account presently contains just over two hundred and eighty-five thousand Canadian dollars. If you have read the manuscript, I am authorised to transfer half of that amount to you, and half to the charity of your choosing.'

I do the math, swallow. 'And if I haven't read it?'

'I am to give it all to a charity he specified.' The lawyer glances down at the manuscript again. 'It certainly looks as if you have read it.'

'Like I said.'

All the Good Places

When the old engineer had been a young man, just starting his life, when all of what was to come still lay hidden and when everything was still possible, he had decided that he would be a writer.

He had read Tolstoy and Sholokhov and some of the other great Russian writers, and for a time, had been enamoured of Hardy and then Balzac and the war poets, Graves and Sassoon and Remarque. There was so much to read, and all that men and women had ever felt or dreamed or wondered seemed to be there for his consideration and reflection. Later, he had discovered Hemingway and Joyce and Lawrence and Conrad and Dos Passos and Huxley and Orwell, and at nineteen, he knew he wanted to be a writer.

Of the reasons for this, it would take him many more decades to understand, to break apart, finally, into their constituent elements and see the forces between them and the gravity that controlled his own thoughts and the deeper forces that were beyond thought. But at twenty, with his life still unbounded and nothing but the horizon to guide him, he came to the resolution that he would be a writer. That fall, he did not register for his second year of engineering studies at the university, but took the money he had earned over the summer working on the rigs in Texas and rented a room in a crumbling turn-of-the-century house in the old part of Calgary, armed himself with notebooks and pencils and an old typewriter and he became a writer.

Every morning he got up and he wrote. He filled notebooks with ideas, and pages with prose. He could write the words, string together sentences and paragraphs, and sometimes what he had written seemed well formed, and even, occasionally, worthwhile. But he found, after a time, that his writing was empty, without substance.

He had nothing to offer. He didn't know anything. He hadn't lived. Even when he tried to write about his childhood, about his brother and the things he had seen on his travels with his parents, he found that the events themselves were not enough. It was as if everything he wrote was shell, and there was nothing inside.

Mark Twain said, 'Write what you know'. Later, Hemingway, who was a great disciple of Twain's, added to this, asking himself, 'What did I know about and truly care for the most?' Much later, Martin Amis perfected the thought: 'Write what you know so you don't have to write what others already have.' The young man he was knew nothing. He did not know what he truly cared for the most. And everything he wrote was a copy of what others had done – and done better.

He knew it wasn't a matter of trying. Of putting in the time. Some were able to write as if they had been formed with the knowledge and memories and wisdom of many lifetimes already stored within. Rimbaud completed his entire oeuvre before his twentieth birthday. But at this same point in his life, the young man came to know that before he could write, he needed to live. He also began to fear that perhaps he did not have the talent, and that he was deluding himself.

And so, he decided to live. He decided to find what he truly cared for.

Much later, when the knowledge and timing of his end and the reasons for it were made clear to him, he came to understand that for him it had always been a battle between what he knew and his ability to write it. In his engineer's way, he pictured it as a graph with time as the abscissa – birth on the left, death on the right. One curve started quite flat and turned sharply into a steep climb at adolescence, peaking and falling away just before death. This was *what he knew*. The other curve stayed dead flat until sometime in his twenties, and then it slowly started climbing. This curve was *his ability to write it*. The question was, would his writing ability catch up to his knowledge of life, and leave enough time to produce something?

He knew now that the answer was no. He had written a few

stories, worked hard on them over many years, between work and trying to raise a family. He had never shown them to anyone. There were many flaws, he knew. Perhaps, with another lifetime he would have been able to make something good, something worthwhile. But that was not how it was going to be. And it filled him with a great sadness for all the good places he had been lucky enough to see, and for all the things he now knew he would never be able to share. For what he had learned was that the truly good places, the places he cared about, were being destroyed. He felt a great sadness for the forests of his youth that had been cleared, for the reefs and coastlines he had known that had been reduced and dredged and concreted over and for the emptiness that he now knew dwelled in men's souls. And though he had devoted all of his life since meeting Helena to trying in some way to protect these places and the people who had for a long time lived peaceably among them, in balance with nature and the laws of physics, he now knew that his efforts had been of no consequence. That the forces of greed were inestimably more powerful than the endeavours of any one person. And he reflected that in the calculus of life, while at the beginning the variable tends towards infinity, at the end, it tends towards zero.

When he was young, and for a long time, he had taken comfort in the permanence of these places. The long sweep of the beach at Karpasia with the rocky point and the dunes coming down to the sea and the steep wooded ridge, and beyond, the patchwork fields and ancient olive groves of the peninsula. The mossy trail up between the big, charred pines and the ancient cedars, so wide at the base that three people could link arms around the trunk, to the top of the island and the view out across the sound to the harbour and the city. The clearing suddenly filling with a herd of buffalo, hundreds of them, and then, emerging from the far trees, a family of elephants, babies following their mothers across the river and disappearing again into the trees. But now he knew that none of these good and perfect places was safe from the cutting and the mining and the plunder and the unceasing warming, and that in the world he would no longer inhabit, all would belong to the economy and so might be sacrificed to it. It was a good thing Helena was not still here to come to this same realisation. And the only parts of him that would live on, some element within his one surviving son and his one granddaughter, would have to find ways to come to terms with this new reality.

So, he had lived. Not well, perhaps. Imperfectly. He had made many errors. Regrets, too, haunted him. But he had lived. He'd fought. He had tried his best. He had tried hard not to be a cynic, to be honest and good. He had loved many good things and places. The mountains, the last big forests, the desert, too, especially on foot, alone or with Helena, sweating up a high pass or fording a deep, cool stream. Swimming in the sea, across a dark lake. Once, he swam the Nile, in the middle of Cairo, just for a laugh. He'd been caught in the current, swept far downstream, come to ground on a papyrus island. He'd hired a felucca to get back to the shore, missed his meeting. The water was so polluted he was sick for a week afterwards. He hadn't known about the crocodiles. He was happy he'd done it. It would have been easy not to. This was part of how not to be a cynic. You also had to learn what to reject, what to fight against. But most importantly, you had to love. He'd always loved running, riding his bike, sport of all kinds. He loved rocks, reading outside in the sun, fighting, getting drunk, sleeping under canvas and the sound of rain on the roof at night. But everything you love, eventually, you lose. This was the truly hard thing.

He had failed Helena. The only woman he had ever truly loved, he had failed. It was worse than dying. Dying was easy, and he was no longer afraid. He did not care about dying. He could have died in that café in Sana'a. They had actually taken a table right at the front, but moved to the back only because it was too hot. He should have died on that river in Namibia. Either would have been a good death, not like this, just waiting. But failing her, this was the hardest thing of all.

Two months before he was told of his imminent death, the old man had joined a protest against the clearing of an area of protected woodland for the construction of a new highway. The protesters had been fighting the development for years, and for a time, it appeared that they had won. The Environment Agency has ruled that the development would cause unacceptable damage, and the project was killed. But a new government came to power, with a new agenda, and the decision was reversed. Now the work was going ahead. Suddenly, what was irreplaceable had become inconsequential. A few young men and several women chained themselves to bulldozers, took to the trees. The day the old man was arrested, the protesters had confronted police and broken through the fence that surrounded the work area. They'd managed to stop work for four hours before the government ordered the area cleared. Mounted police formed a cordon, the big horses advancing flank-to-flank into the crowd, pushing them back. The cops who led the old man away in handcuffs told him they were only doing their job. Three weeks later, he received a court summons. He wouldn't make it to court, this time. He'd be dead by then.

And now he knew that he should have applied himself to his dreams sooner, long before his body started to rebel and began consuming itself. And now that it was too late, he wondered what might have happened if he had, and if things might perhaps have been different, and if he might have somehow found a way to say he was sorry to his son, and if perhaps he might have been graced with a few more years with Helena.

Helena. Helena.

Helena.

March 30th. Heart Mountain, Alberta

Last night, I received a call on my mobile from a young woman. She told me that she had got my number from the hospital records. Turns out she knew my old man. She's a palliative-care nurse at the hospital, and was looking after him when he died. She said my old man had left her a key to the house and very precise instructions: the day he died she was to go to the house, find the manuscript, insert two stories on the top, and the other, the one called 'All the Good Places', right at the end. Like 'First Snow' and 'Collapsing Infinity', it was handwritten, on the back of his hospital report. There is even the graph, two curves, one black, one red, that cross at a point he has labelled 'death'. At the bottom of the page he'd scrawled: 'Calgary, February 2030'.

She asked me if I had read it. I told her I'd read it on the flight over. Good, she said. He was hoping you would.

I sat there a moment, not quite sure what I'd just heard.

I have it with me now, the whole manuscript. I'm pretty sure I came up here intending to bury it, but now I don't know. I can't decide what my old man would have wanted. I know now that it was some sort of test, but part of me thinks that he'd approve. Not that it matters. Not that anything that made him the man he was is left. Just some ashes that I threw into the river from that bridge where he and Mum first talked, and this. His thoughts, the stories of things he did and saw and tried to do.

Now here I am, sitting on the top of a mountain, scrawling this. It took me all morning to get up here. Started before dawn, watched the sun come up over the valley. From the parking lot, you can see how the mountain got its name, the two big mirror-image ridges that fold over and meet at a point in the valley. The view from up here is amazing. The air is so clear that I can see for miles, as far as there is, all the way to the farthest peaks. It's been a warm winter here, but there are still a few patches of snow about, strewn in places the sunlight can't get to. The cliffs shine bright grey in the sun, and even though they are far away they look very close and I can see every detail, all the cracks and the folds and the places where the rock has fallen away.

Being up here, I'm pretty sure my old man and my mum brought me and Adam here once. They took us everywhere. I can remember parts of the trail, this bit of ridge. It must have been that summer we came back to Canada, the summer Adam died. He was four. Four. That was all he had. Four years. I mean, Jesus wept, I can't imagine it. I loved him so much. It hurts to think about him. I loved them all. I know that. Her, even him.

The old man's house was worth a lot more than I'd thought. He bought it for nothing. The place wasn't much but it was on three lots. They'll probably just knock it down and build three infills, take out all those trees Mum and Dad planted.

Still, between that and the trust fund, I reckon I'm above water for the first time in years, just. I've decided that I'm going to buy a second-hand bike and ride out to the coast, find my grandmother's cabin. I'll buy some tools, maybe get some work as a carpenter. Do something useful for a change, rather than the shit I've wasted all these years on. I'll explore the coast, fish some of the places my dad and grandfather used to take me. And then I'm going to work hard to make it up to my daughter. Maybe one day take her on a trip. Africa, maybe, when she's a bit older, see the elephants before they're all gone. Go to Cyprus. Show her where I grew up.

There is no plot. I know that now, can see it clearly. Sure, you make plans, and one thing may seem to lead to another, but life, if you think about it, is just a series of moments, of things that you do. Some are connected, but most aren't, not in the way you'd like to believe, as if there were some kind of destiny, some plan God has for you. There's just living. Doing the best you can. Navigating this turbulent wake we all leave. Working for things that matter, as my mother said that day on the bridge. She taught my old man that, and it stayed with him right until the end. I'm glad about that.

Acknowledgements

If you've made it this far, dear reader, thanks. I hope you got something good out of the journey. A life. The only thing we have. Like life, writing is a journey. A tough one. The kind where you have moments where you don't think that you're going to be able to finish, where you question why you're even there, on that steep, winding path through the rocks, or in the middle of that dark, windswept sea. It would just be so much easier to turn back and go home to where it's safe and warm. Those are the journeys you can't make on your own. And so thanks go to Karen and West and all at Orenda for encouraging me along this new journey into fiction that is more literary, and helping me when I stumbled. Your willingness to continue to back your authors as they change and grow, and hopefully improve, is amazing and so appreciated. Courage and honour. Two of my favourite nouns. Words that well suit Orenda.